FISH OUT OF WATER

OTHER GUPPY ANTHOLOGIES

Fish Tales
Fish Nets
Fish or Cut Bait

FISH OUT OF WATER

EDITED BY
RAMONA DeFELICE LONG

INTRODUCTION BY JAMES M. JACKSON

WILDSIDE PRESS

Published by Wildside Press LLC.
www.wildsidepress.com

CONTENTS

INTRODUCTION

by James M. Jackson

As president of the Guppy Chapter of Sisters in Crime, Inc., I have the privilege of authoring the introduction to the fourth Guppy anthology. In preparation, I read an advanced copy of the twenty-two stories. Stories from earlier Guppy anthologies have been nominated for Agatha Awards and selected for inclusion in the Best Twenty-Five Mystery Stories of the Year series. As a group, this anthology's stories may be the strongest yet.

The theme requires each story to have a character who in some manner is a fish out of water. With twenty-two fertile imaginations, *Fish Out of Water* readers learn of crime during the Ming Dynasty and of a future where aliens abduct humans for research. Of students using library research and knowledge learned in biology class to solve mysteries. Of adults experiencing the pitfalls of live research and of aging hippies deferring old age. Of trainees, those doing a job for the first time, and entrepreneurs. Of police and politics. Of road trips gone wrong. Of hitmen (and hit women). Of impersonators and look-a-likes. Of families who remain close and those with missing children, cheating spouses, and murdered siblings. Of a mixed-bag inheritance. Of cold crimes and fresh hot cases. Of real hooligans and a mysterious ghost. Of the limits of revenge. Of job sites that include a flying circus, a church bazaar, and working with stock animals (chickens to cows).

And more. Much more.

Judges John M. Floyd, Stephen D. Rogers and Susan Oleksiw had the difficult task of rating all the stories submitted by our 700-member chapter. The Chapter's Steering Committee then selected the top stories for inclusion in this anthology—provided they met the theme. The judges are wonderful mystery writers in their own rights.

John Floyd is the author of more than 1,000 short stories and features in publications like *Strand Magazine*, *Alfred Hitchcock's Mystery Magazine*, *Ellery Queen's Mystery Magazine*, *Woman's World*, *The Saturday Evening Post*, *Mississippi Noir*, and *The Best American Mystery*

Stories 2015. A former Air Force captain and IBM systems engineer, he is also a three-time Derringer Award winner, an Edgar Award finalist, and a three-time Pushcart Prize nominee. John has also had six books published: *Rainbow's End* (2006), *Midnight* (2008), *Clockwork* (2010), *Deception* (2013), *Fifty Mysteries* (2014), and *Dreamland* (2016).

Stephen D. Rogers is a multi-published writer of fiction, non-fiction, and poetry. Over nine hundred of his stories and poems have been selected to appear in more than three hundred publications, earning among other honors two Best of Soft SF winners, two Derringers (with seven additional as a finalist), a Shamus Award nomination, a Rhysling nomination, two Notable Online Stories from storySouth's Million Writers Award, honorable mention in *The Year's Best Fantasy and Horror*, mention in *The Best American Mystery Stories*, and numerous Readers' Choice awards.

Susan Oleksiw writes the Anita Ray series featuring an Indian-American photographer living in South India at her aunt's tourist hotel. She also writes the Mellingham series featuring Chief Joe Silva. The picturesque coastal town of Mellingham is home to a mix of people who are drawn to its sunny beaches and quiet neighborhoods but unable to shake their criminal passions. Susan's short stories have appeared in *Alfred Hitchcock's Mystery Magazine* and numerous anthologies. She was co-founder of Level Best Books, which publishes an annual anthology of the best New England crime fiction. In addition, she published *A Reader's Guide to the Classic British Mystery* (G.K. Hall, 1988), and served as co-editor for *The Oxford Companion to Crime and Mystery Writing* (1999). She co-founded and edited *The Larcom Review* (1998-2003), part of The Larcom Press, which also published several mystery novels.

We are delighted to again have **Ramona DeFelice Long** as editor of this anthology. In addition to her own writing, Ramona works as an independent editor specializing in mystery novels, women's and literary fiction, memoir and creative nonfiction, and short stories. She works with private clients as a developmental editor and through professional organizations such as the Guppy Chapter of Sisters in Crime, Inc. to edit story anthologies. She teaches workshops at conferences, retreats, and online, and visits local writing groups, public libraries, and arts organizations to share thoughts and advice on writing and publishing.

Start to read the stories in the order chosen by Ramona or dive into the middle and pick one based on its title or author. Whatever your choice, I'm sure you'll enjoy!

PLAN A: KILL THE FISH

by Beth Green

Josephina had blood on her fingers.

Thin, oily blood. It stank.

She held her hand out to the side and looked around the cockpit for something to clean herself. The sudden movement of her head made her stomach lurch.

"Breathe, Jo," she said out loud. "Just breathe like Duncan taught you."

Seasickness hadn't been a problem this morning, when Duncan picked her up at the marina. The water had been flat as glass and the sky as empty as her bank account. Since then, big puffy clouds had blown in. They threw azure shadows on the ice-blue waters, and the wind that brought them created a chop and scared up goosebumps on Josephina's bare legs. The ropes hanging down from the mast's cross piece—Did Duncan call it a bang? A boom?—swung back and forth. If Josephina focused on them, she'd throw up.

She stared at the horizon, watching to see if she could glimpse a navy-blue boat, ant-tiny in the distance, zoom toward her from the mainland. Eventually, the urge to vomit passed. She went down the little opening into the inside of the boat. She was careful not to look at the blood pooling on the cockpit floor or to drag her bloody fingers on any of the white-painted wood she passed. More to clean up. She entered the kitchen—no, the galley. This morning, Duncan had tried to teach her all the names of the places on the boat. Grinning, she'd echoed them, just as she'd been asked.

She washed her hands and dried them with some paper napkins she found folded and sticking out of a cubbyhole in the wall. Holding her hand up so the diamonds caught the light, she took extra care to dry the skin around her four gold rings. Afterward, she balled up the damp paper and held it in one fist. With the other hand, she took a long, thin filleting knife out of its wooden block and examined the blade. It needed sharpening, but it would do.

She went back to the cockpit, careful not to stumble and cut herself as she climbed up the short ladder to the outside. The sun had come out from behind the wooly clouds while she was downstairs, and now the bright white deck dazzled her. She wished she hadn't broken her sunglasses this morning.

She went over to the fish on the deck, sidestepping the pool of blood under it and the net bag of coconuts next to it. Duncan had told her what kind of fish they could expect to catch today. Meaningless names she hadn't bothered to remember. Why did fish even need names? This one in question from head to tail measured about the length of Josephina's leg from her knee to her ankle.

It had been a long time since Josephina had learned to gut a fish, but she remembered the basics. Would Mama have been proud? No, probably not. Mama had never admitted to that sentiment in her whole life. Josephina crouched, back braced against one of the seats in the cockpit. She cut off the fish's head, its eyes and skull already broken by repeated whacks from the coconut, and then sawed on the side fins and the tail until they, too, were parted from the flesh. She set these aside. Next, she ran the back of the blade along the skin until the rainbow-hued scales sprinkled down on the deck. Several clung to her hands. Josephina grimaced. She'd do what it took, but she didn't like it.

Gagging from the stench of the blood and the innards, she slipped the thin filleting knife into the fish's abdominal cavity and sliced it open at the belly. Eventually, she had a pile of discarded fish guts and some bony, bloody fillets. They weren't pretty, but they would do.

For a terrifying second, Josephina couldn't remember what came next. Mr. C had spelled it all out to her, so many times. She closed her eyes and concentrated: She'd made the call. She'd prepared the fish ...

Oh, yes.

Josephina carried the fillets over to the barbecue Duncan had prepared before he threw the first of the four fishing lines in. "It's just a given that we'll catch something, Jo," he'd told her. "You're gonna love lunch." She doubted that she'd enjoy it much, but it was certain she'd enjoy it more than he would.

She placed the fillets on the barbecue and looked around for the lighter. Duncan had already put the wood on, and the starting briquettes. She found it in the picnic basket, next to a can of warm beer. She thought about opening it, but didn't feel like her stomach could handle the fizziness. She looked out at the mainland again. Still no sight of the navy-blue boat.

Once the barbecue was lit the fish started cooking. She didn't care much for fish, but it smelled better than the blood, anyway.

She grabbed Duncan's machete out of its holster hanging on the mast. He'd just used it to chop the wood for the barbecue.

We need more wood, Dunc, she thought. She forced herself not to give in to hysterical laughter and focused on the task at hand: chopping.

Part of Mr. C's regimen was for her to do lots of weight training. She liked that better than the mandatory pole dancing classes, but not as much as the Pilates. At any rate, the result of the last six months of work in the gym when she wasn't seeing Duncan was that she was deceptively slim and so strong she surprised herself. The machete made short work of the coconut husk. When she threw it under the barbecue grill, flames leapt up and licked the fish flesh. One more whack on the coconut opened the inner nut. The coconut was old and brown, so there was not much water left inside, but the inside meat was just the right balance of moist and crisp. She re-holstered the machete and wiped down the handle with the towel from her beach bag. She ate some of the coconut meat while she waited for the fish to finish cooking, and then threw the rest of the coconut overboard. The husk on the barbecue was satisfactorily burned away.

Josephina was on a roll now. Would Mr. C be proud? She needed him to be.

While she went back down belowdecks to get two plates, some forks and more napkins, Josephina imagined how Mr. C would react when he saw her later today. She was the youngest one to go through his training program. She hadn't done at all well at first. The other women had told her she wouldn't make it. She was too soft. Too dumb. Too unlike them. But today? She'd done everything he asked.

Oops, well, not quite everything.

Now that she thought back to Mr. C's instructions, in fact, there were a couple of pieces she was still missing. She looked out to the mainland. Still no boat. So she still had time.

She went over to the barbecue and plated the fish. She folded down a wooden table on the side of the cockpit and arranged the two deck chairs beside it. Proud of herself, she even remembered to set the table with the salt and pepper from the picnic bag. She took the bottle of wine from the icebox and poured two glasses.

When she felt ready, she sat at the table, with her back to the rest of the cockpit, and ate half of the fish she'd prepared for herself. It tasted like moldy sand. Scales clung to it and one got caught in her teeth. She gulped down some wine, but forced herself to stop.

Still no navy-blue boat.

Anxiety prickling at her scalp, she decided to go to plan B. Is that what Mr. C would want? They'd covered this in one of the strategy sessions. She had it memorized, right? But why, now, were the details fuzzy?

She stared at the horizon and went over the plan in her head. She tapped once on the table for every point, feeling the slick varnish under her hands. Glancing up, she was sure the sun was just in the right place.

Once she was mentally prepared, she swallowed hard and looked at her hands. They seemed so small. So deceptively weak. She could do this.

Josephina walked to the middle of the cockpit. She had been purposely avoiding Duncan's body, his sticky remains, but now she made herself run her eyes from his bare feet all the way up to his bloody hairline.

She did this. She could do it. She was in. Mr. C would have work for her forever.

"Sorry, Dunc," she said, even though she was sure he was past caring.

Josephina took Duncan's bright blue t-shirt from the bench where she'd thrown it earlier. He'd been so eager to get it off, and she'd been so caught up in the whole scripted rhythm of it all—her performance, she told herself—she'd almost missed her opportunity.

With the shirt protecting her hands, Josephina gathered up the fish guts and took them to the transom. She climbed carefully down to the swim step and threw the guts in the water. Duncan had done some of the work himself—he'd set four lines when they anchored, each of them baited with a nice, fragrant bit of meat. Each line had caught something, and three of them now had fish swimming, tiring, advertising their weakness. She'd already seen one dorsal fin.

One more trip for the rest of the bait, and then, once she was sure she'd seen two dorsal fins flitting just below the surface, Josephina went for the big haul. Duncan hadn't been a tall man. He was wiry and energetic. But Josephina herself was nearly as tall as he was, and had been training in the gym considerably harder. Even so, she was surprised how hard it was to drag him out of the cockpit and down to the swim step. She thought he'd have stiffened up by now, but he was still moveable. His arms flopped everywhere, his neck moved. His legs moved, and under the ripstop fabric of his swim shorts, she could see the outline of his penis shifting positions. The skin on his hands and arms was even warm to the touch—from the afternoon sun, she told herself.

She squinted at the reddening horizon. It must only have been a couple of hours since she sent the message, she thought. That's why Mr. C and his crew weren't here yet. Once Duncan's body was on the swim step, Josephina almost dipped her hands in the water to clean them, then remembered the sharks. There wasn't any blood on her—Duncan's hands were clean and so were hers—but she felt like she needed to cleanse. When she got back to shore, the first thing she'd do after Mr. C paid up was have a really long, hot shower. And then rub herself all over with antibacterial gel or something. Ew.

One more shove, and it was over. The man was gone, her deed was done. She stood on the swim step and watched his body slowly sink under the water, shockingly white below the surface and then obscured like a green veil had drifted over it. She felt a thrill of accomplishment. Take that, Mama, I can too hold down a job. She saw movement under the water—a flash of a white belly, a shovel-shaped nose. She decided not to watch, and cleaned instead. Bleach, brushes and ten minutes later, she'd made the cockpit look clean as ever. The harsh chemicals blocked out the stench of old fish; it even smelled good.

Now, for the rest of Plan B.

Josephina went to her bag and pulled out her cell phone. The evening light was fading by the second, but it was adequate for her to see the bloody thumbprint on her phone case. She must have left it right after starting Plan A. Sighing, she took it off the phone, spritzed some bleach on it, and then tossed the case overboard.

Don't litter, she thought she heard her mother's voice say, crystal clear, better reception than a cell phone. We're trash enough already, honey. And then the breathless, honking laughter. Her mother's bray. She sounded like a donkey—but don't you ever get close enough to her paws and say that out loud.

She knew the sounds were just in her head, but Josephina couldn't help the reflex of looking beside her and behind her to make sure that Mama wasn't there. She counted to ten, just like Mr. C had taught her. Breathe, Jo. Breathe.

Mr. C was going to be so proud of her, she thought, while she called up the number pad on her phone. She touched 9—maybe he'd give her a bonus—1—maybe another gold ring? She loved them so much one of the other women in training called her "Rings" for a nickname—1.

Nothing.

Josephina frowned. She had excellent coverage, usually. She held the phone up to her other ear. If she'd been hearing Mama, maybe she wasn't hearing other things real good. That had happened once before—before Mr. C found her on the beach lifting a gold ring from out of one of his girlfriends' bags and offered her a job.

"You're better than a petty thief," he said. "You got talent."

She'd laughed at him a little then. Who, me? Not worthless? But he'd told her the truth, and now she had somewhere to stay where she didn't have to worry about somebody burning her with cigarettes in the middle of the night. She got a part-time job at a restaurant just to keep stuff looking above-board and so she had some spending money. Mr. C had sent her to night classes for her GED, and after that she'd started training for his real line of work. The other women hadn't liked her much at first—called her stupid—but she managed. And here she was.

Josephina fiddled with the volume control on the phone. Nope, it was up to 100 percent. She switched over to the music app. The rainforest sounds she used to go to sleep at night after a bad day poured out, blended with the lapping sound of the water on the hull. Pretty. Maybe she'd use beach noises next time.

She tried again. 911. Then, she spied the problem: No signal.

Her jaw dropped. She glanced up at the mainland. She could see the city. It was just there. How could she have no signal now, right when she needed it? Did that mean—? Her scalp went cold.

She went to the messages app. A thin red line circled her last message, with a tiny notification: "Message Undeliverable."

Mr. C was not coming in the navy-blue boat because he hadn't known she was ready.

Josephina's breathing went jerky. She couldn't get enough oxygen in her lungs or something. They were going to break out of her chest, she was heaving so hard. She reached for her own throat and stroked her rings against the sensitive skin under her jaw. The diamonds caught the ridge of bone and dug in, causing a sharp, centering pain. It helped her think. Well, sometimes it just made her bleed. But today, damnit, she really needed to think.

Duncan had tried to show her how to use the boat when they were on the way out. But her script said she had to act real dumb, and since it wasn't hard, that's what she did. It had been harder on the last assignment—just a frame-up—when she had to act real smart and classy. Mr. C said she did well, but he'd had a little frown while he said it.

Josephina looked up the mast. Even though she was used to the motion in the cockpit now—the nausea gone along with Duncan—when she looked up to the sky, she could see how much the silhouette of the mast waved back and forth against the darkening sky. Dizzy, she put her head in her hands. It was nearly full dark now.

She needed a plan C, she thought. But Mr. C was fond of saying his girls only needed an A and a B. He was their Plan C, he'd said. And then he'd laugh and laugh, and it scared her a little.

Swallowing back the tight knot that raised in the back of her throat, Josephina tried the phone again. Still no service.

She stared back at the mainland, where tiny sparkles of light popped up as people got home from work. That was where her fifth ring waited for her. Her prize, Mr. C had promised. It would only take twenty or thirty minutes to get back to shore, but it seemed a gazillion shark-filled miles away.

Her phone battery was at ten percent and her eyes filled with tears when she finally heard the deep purr of another boat's motor.

"Josephina? Josephina, you there?" Mr. C's voice echoed across the water. She stood up and waved, then realized he wouldn't be able to see her. She flicked on the flashlight app on her phone.

"Good, good. Hold on, girl. Put the light down. You'll blind us." The boat pulled up to the swim step. After the sudden brightness of the flashlight, Josephina saw it as a matte shape against the glossy water. The engine's purr began a high-pitched whine and a man's voice cursed. "Prop's stuck in the fucking line," a woman's voice said. Josephina heard two sets of feet leap aboard.

"Can I turn the light back on?" she asked.

"You all alone?"

"Yes. Done."

"What happened to Plan A?"

"No signal on the phone."

"What about the radio?"

"Wha—oh, shit." The radio. Now, she remembered. Downstairs, there was supposed to be a black walkie-talkie thing. Duncan hadn't mentioned it on the ride out, and since she'd been using her data to surf the web right up until they anchored …"I couldn't find the radio?" Her voice, already strangled by phlegm from crying, raised up to a higher, questioning pitch. A teenager's voice. "Can I turn on the light now?"

"Not yet." She could tell Mr. C was standing by the barbecue, but she couldn't see his face yet.

"And Plan B was over then, too?"

"Yes. I did everything. Except I couldn't get ahold of anyone."

"Careless, Jo." His voice was just a whisper in the dark. His companion—Jo couldn't think who it might be—was noiseless. Was she coming closer? Moving toward the mast?

"I'm sorry, Jo. You did the job, but you needed me to pull out Plan C."

She heard the *sssnick!* of the machete leaving its holster. Faintly, from somewhere, Mama's laughter echoed.

THE MISSING CONCUBINE

FROM JUDGE LU'S

MING DYNASTY CASE FILES

by P.A. De Voe

Judge Lu sensed his personal guards, Zhang and Ma, hovering at his door. Ignoring them, he continued to bury his head in a pile of case reports requiring his attention. He'd been out of town for a couple of days and needed to catch up. By law, cases were time-limited and had to be solved quickly and efficiently. Eventually, his guards' palpable tension forced him to look up.

As if taking that as a sign to approach, they marched into the office, their faces telegraphing excitement.

"What is it?" Lu asked.

"Sir, we've news about pharmacist Master Ying's second wife's death, the one your coroner determined died from unnatural causes," Ma said.

Lu pulled up the last case on his desk. It was Master Ying's official accusation against his concubine. In the document, Ying alleged his concubine killed his second wife, stole her jewels, and fled. The coroner's report, saying the wife had died of poisoning, was attached.

Glancing up from the document, Lu said, "This looks like a straightforward case of murder and theft. Has the concubine been caught?"

"No Sir, not yet. Regarding this household, you might be interested in knowing that Zhang and I just came from a wine shop near the Ying compound. The gossip is Master Ying's clerk, Cao, was having an affair with Master Ying's first wife," Ma said.

The judge drew his eyebrows together in disapproval.

"Adultery is a crime with a punishment of one hundred strokes with a heavy stick; however, the court won't get involved unless the husband makes a complaint," Lu said. He shook his head at Master Ying's bad fortune.

"People heard Clerk Cao claim that if Ying's wife were free, she'd be his," Ma added. "They think he attempted to murder Ying and killed the second wife by mistake."

"I talked with Old Woman Tan, who shops for the Ying women," Zhang broke in, "She claims the husband was bad tempered and violent. His wives and concubine frequently had unusual bruises."

"Indeed. Well, according to the coroner's report …" Lu again paged through the report. "… except for interviewing Ying, none of the household family or staff were questioned. That was an opportunity lost." While a makeshift inquiry could be set up at the scene of a crime, further inquiries occurred in court, in public. He pressed his lips into a frown. "We need to find out what the staff in the Ying women's quarters know. I don't want to bring the women into court for questioning. It's too embarrassing for Master Ying to have his women paraded before everyone."

"We could hide in the women's quarters and eavesdrop," Zhang volunteered a bit too enthusiastically.

Lu shot him a cold look. "There will be no need." Having a strange male breaching all semblance of propriety, even for an official investigation, would humiliate everyone: the court and the Ying family.

Undeterred, Zhang piped up again. "Right. We're soldiers and shouldn't be there. But you're the magistrate, you could …"

Ma punched him on the shoulder. "How dare you suggest Judge Lu do such a thing! Have you no sense at all? It would ruin him if he was found in the women's quarters. His career would be over!"

Lu nodded. The wheels of justice were already turning, all he had to do was let them move ahead. Once the concubine was arrested and convicted, Master Ying and the law would be satisfied. Case closed. He wouldn't have to look any further and expose Ying's other family problems.

Yet, given his guards' information, that scenario posed at least three problems. First, there would be a miscarriage of justice if the court found an innocent woman guilty of murder and executed her. Second, if the concubine was innocent, a murderer remained on the loose. Third, if the clerk and the first wife were guilty, Master Ying's life remained in danger and his death would be on Lu's hands.

On the other hand, if the concubine was, in fact, guilty, Master Ying would be furious at the loss of face he would suffer if the investigation went forward and displayed his dirty laundry for the world to see: his wife's infidelity, his own uncontrolled violence. Ying would certainly try to make Judge Lu suffer equally.

After a long silence, Lu said, "Bring in Old Woman Tan. I want to talk to her."

****

The fear in the old marketer wasn't hard to see.

"Old Tan," he said using an address reflecting respect for her age, "I understand you are known to the Ying household and do errands for the women of the family."

"Indeed, Sir. I have served the Ying household for more than ten years. I have always been honest and fair in my dealings." She grasped her hands firmly against her stomach as if protecting herself; however, her eyes were bright and direct.

"Of course. I've no doubt." He picked up a paper from his desk. "You've probably heard of Master Ying's second wife's death."

She sucked in a breath. "I know nothing about it. I was not at the house."

Studying her stiff, defensive posture, Lu suspected she was hiding how much she knew. She was, after all, a well-seasoned gossip. She had to be, it was her stock in trade, useful in cementing relationships with the isolated elite women she visited. He decided to take a non-confrontational approach, trusting that it would elicit more information. "No one suggested you were. Master Ying filed an accusation with the court and we need more information, which I hope to get with your assistance."

Old Tan watched his face expectantly, but cautiously.

"I want you to go to the household and talk to the maids working in the women's quarters. Get them to tell you whatever they know or suspect about the death."

The woman readily agreed. "I always spend time with the maid servants, as well as their mistresses. It is not that they gossip. No, no. It's just that they are able to provide useful information for fulfilling the tasks their mistresses give me."

"Just so." He paused. "I would also like you to open the back gate leading onto the street. I will be there, waiting. You will let me inside."

Her eyes opened wide in surprise and she nervously glanced around the room, as if trying to discover if this was a trap. Lu understood her increasing panic. Women in her position were often accused of abetting illegal love affairs. If found out, they could be charged with a crime and severely beaten, which could lead to death.

"I assure you, my request is strictly in the pursuit of justice. Justice for both the murder victim and the accused."

He held her gaze. "It is imperative no one know I am there. Are you willing to help?"

Without hesitating, Old Tan agreed. "I'll go just before lunch to see Mistress Ying. Then, when she has lunch and her maids are waiting on her, I'll go to the servants' room. This would be the best time for me to let you into the compound. Immediately after eating she likes to rest, and her maids have a chance to eat. That's when I'll ask your questions."

Lu, pleased at her quick-wittedness, grinned and began instructing her on his questions. While she kept a neutral demeanor, the gleam in her eyes betrayed her delight. Lu hoped his scheme wasn't discovered and didn't lead to the demise of them all.

* * * *

Before leaving the yamen, Lu changed from his formal robe into a short worker's jacket. He rolled his pant legs up and slipped on a pair of sandals. He told Zhang and Ma to do the same.

"Zhang, bring your Xiangqi game along," Lu said.

Zhang laughed, reached into his shirt and displayed a folded piece of paper and a small sack of pebbles. "It's here, Sir. I never go far without it."

Xiangqi was a popular board game where three armies, representing the Three Kingdoms, battled against each other in order to capture their enemies' generals and take over their army.

Lu nodded, cast a discerning eye over his men, and directed them to follow. They went out through the back of the yamen to avoid inquisitive eyes.

Nearing the rear of the Ying compound, Lu split from his guards. The two walked along the opposite side from the walled mansion and settled down on their haunches across from its gate. To draw attention to themselves, they talked loudly, each baiting the other. Soon, leaving Zhang squatting over the board game spread out on the ground, Ma strode across the street.

"Friend, come play Xiangqi with us. We need a third," he called to the portly fellow guarding the Ying's back gate.

The fellow looked up and shook his head. "Can't. Have a job here. Can't leave."

"You won't be leaving. You'll be right across the street," Ma said. "We've got a bet on this game. You've got to come and help out." He looked up and down the street. "Nothing's happening. You can watch from there."

"Bring the game over and I can play here," the gatekeeper said.

Ma glanced over his shoulder. "He's already got it set up. Come on. What do you think is going to happen? Someone's going to steal the gate?" He laughed raucously.

"Well," the man glanced at the gate and then over at Zhang, "I guess it would be all right."

Ma made sure to sit across from Zhang, forcing the gatekeeper to drop onto his heels with his back to the Ying compound. Lu, standing at the end of the walled area, waited until the game had begun, then slowly made his way down the street. Once at the gate, he stopped and fiddled with his sandal. Soon the door fell ajar and he slipped through.

Old Woman Tan chuckled when she saw his clothing, but remained silent. As soon as he entered and the gate relocked, she moved rapidly through a passageway along the outer wall, then turned into another passage. Lu hurried to keep up. After a couple more turns, she stopped, pointing to a recessed doorway and a nearby paper-covered latticed window.

Lu understood: from here he could hear the conversations between Old Tan and the servants. When he nodded, she scurried down to the end of the building, turned, and vanished.

Lu stared along the now empty passage; he brushed the sweat from his forehead. He inhaled deeply, taking in a lungful of spicy air, which caught in his throat. He fought to avoid coughing. Tears sprang into his eyes.

Cursing himself, he wondered what had gotten into him to try this stunt. Such hooliganism was more like something his impetuous younger brother would do. He stared down at his rumpled worker's clothing. If discovered, he'd be lucky if this was his future attire.

A noise from within made him stiffen: soft, shuffling sounds mixed with low, indistinct female voices. He carefully checked the passage, then stepped nearer the window.

"Ah, Auntie, you've come to visit," a high-pitched, melodious voice called out. Old Tan was known by "Auntie" to many, since it was at once a familiar and a respectful term.

Instantly, several voices called out greetings. Soon the women settled down near the window for lunch.

"Such sadness in the household," Old Tan said, clucking her tongue.

As if they had been waiting for someone to pour their stories out to, the women readily opened up to her.

"She was poisoned," one said.

"The Master said the poison was meant for him, but I don't think so," another said.

"Although there would be reason enough," came another.

An uneasy silence followed this remark.

"Some people are saying Ying's concubine did it," Tan said.

"What proof do they have?"

"People say she stole jewels and ran away. That's proof enough," Tan said.

"Jasmine, tell her what you saw," a high-pitched voice ordered.

Haltingly, a timid voice said, "That day, before we found the young Mistress dead, Master Ying took a bundle into his shop at the front of the compound."

"That bundle was the so-called stolen jewels," the high-pitched voice asserted.

"Lily, I understand you all might have bad feelings toward Master Ying, considering how he treated you, but really, why would he take jewels from his own house?" Old Tan asked.

"He poisoned his wife and took her jewels to make his concubine look guilty," one of the women said.

"When his concubine first came here, she was not happy, but not unhappy, either. Within a few months, however, misery had draped itself around her," Lily said.

"Yes, yes. I met her. A charming woman. Too bad she was sold to Master Ying. That's her karma, though, and we all know we can't change fate. It doesn't make Master Ying guilty of falsely accusing her for his wife's murder. Anything could have been in that bundle. Besides, why would he take it to his store? He'd hide it someplace off his own property," Tan said.

Lu couldn't help but smile. Picking Old Tan to help him had been a good move. In spite of being illiterate, she could be an investigator herself. She knew how to follow up.

"Whatever he took was wrapped in a green and white cloth. The Mistress's chrysanthemum-embroidered green and white brocade shawl is missing. Plus, it was raining hard that day. All day. Water stood in the courtyard," Jasmine said.

"He hates being uncomfortable," Lily offered. "He took it to his store because it was convenient. He walked along the veranda from our living area to his shop. There was no need for him to get wet."

"But why? Why blame his concubine for his wife's death? Not to mention, that would mean he knew his wife was poisoned," Old Tan pushed.

Silence again permeated the room.

Lu grinned again at the wily entrepreneur's questions and nodded in approval.

"Are you saying he knew she was poisoned? That he did it?" she asked.

"We can't accuse our Master," Lily responded. "That is up to the judge. We know he's already tired of his concubine. He's constantly complaining about her weeping—which only causes him to beat her more. He often says he's wasted good money buying her, that he'd been better off buying a new sow for his farm."

"'Course, he also tells his second wife she's a stone around his neck, just another mouth to feed," another added.

"If what you say is true, the magistrate needs to know," Old Tan said.

"No one asked us," several women said in unison.

Lu shook his head; he should have been here to investigate the death himself.

"I've also heard the first wife may be involved somehow," Old Tan led.

"Ah. Her unfortunate friendship," Lily said. She sounded more sad than judgmental. Lu was surprised.

"Unfortunate friendship? What does that mean? She never leaves the house. Who could she have such a friendship with?"

"She doesn't have to go out of the compound," Lily said.

Then Old Tan said, as if she just thought of it, "Ah, she's having an affair with someone who's managed to steal into the household. Could it be with Ying's clerk?"

A general murmur of dissent followed her comment.

"She wasn't having an affair. Clerk Cao does manage to have an excuse to come and talk to her at least once a week. But only to talk," Lily said.

"Maybe he'd like to have an affair," another said, "but she wouldn't, never."

"Yet, Master Ying is not easy on her, either," Old Tan said.

"That's true," Lily said. "He's short tempered with all his women, but she struggles to please him. Clerk Cao is seeking water for his thirst, but he'll never get it."

"Do you think he knows Master Ying beats her?" Old Tan asked.

"Everyone knows that," Lily said. "It's not a secret that can be easily hidden in the compound."

Old Woman Tan asked a few more questions, but the responses were unenlightening, and so she left.

Lu stepped back into the doorway's shadow and waited.

"Sir, follow me," a voice whispered.

He wordlessly followed. The household was at rest; nevertheless, again, Tan rapidly walked ahead of him, checking at each break in the buildings. When they reached the rear exterior gate, Tan unlatched the lock and Lu slipped through. He heard the lock fall into place as he paused to glance over at the gatekeeper still embroiled in the Xiangqi game.

As soon as Ma saw Lu, he yawned and stretched broadly. In doing so, he shoved against the paper board with his shoe. The game pieces went skittering in all directions. Zhang and the gatekeeper yelled and cursed at the ruins.

Lu ambled to the corner and waited. What he'd overheard was worth the unconventional means he'd used. Especially since he didn't get caught. Now he had a clear idea of how to proceed.

"Before we return to the yamen," Lu said when his men joined him, "I must stop at Ying's pharmacy and check for the stolen jewels."

"Like that, Sir?" Zhang asked, eyeing his costume.

Lu looked down at his worker's outfit. "Hmm. No. We'll return to the office and you two will come back with an official order to search the shop. Then you will return to court with Clerk Cao."

They moved along at an easy pace and Lu filled them in on what he had overheard. He concluded by remarking that the women all appeared to think the concubine was innocent and Ying had poisoned his own wife and then blamed the concubine.

"If you don't mind my saying, Sir," Ma said, "they're women."

"Point being?" Lu asked.

"They like the concubine. At the same time, they hate their Master because he isn't easy to work for. They're being emotional. Besides, it's just gossip. None of them spoke up when the coroner was at the house."

"Yes," Zhang said, not to be outdone by Ma. "As for the concubine, women often commit suicide to escape misery. Murder is a man's game. I still think Clerk Cao did it. Passion could drive him to murder."

"Cao definitely has motivation," Lu said. "He could have believed he was protecting his love, the first wife, or he could think that once she is widowed, she would be open to marrying him. In that case, instead of murdering the husband, through bad karma, the second wife may have accidently taken the poison, which killed her. For all these reasons, we must search the shop for the jewels and then I must question Clerk Cao at court."

* * * *

Back at the yamen, Lu tried to review more reports; however, he found it impossible to focus. He kept listening for his men's return.

Finally, he heard boots hurrying toward his office. Ma appeared in the doorway carrying a bundle wrapped in a green brocade embroidered with white chrysanthemums. He placed it on Lu's desk. "I also brought the clerk back with me," he said. "Zhang is still at the store finishing our search. As soon as we found this, however, we thought you'd want to see it."

Lu nodded. "Good work." He unrolled the covering until a tangled mass of jewels fell out.

"Where did you find it?" he asked.

"In the store's back room, where Master Ying keeps supplies and mixes medicines. I found it tucked behind a large jar."

"Was Clerk Cao with you?"

"He had just come into the room. He seemed surprised and said he didn't know where it came from."

"Hmm. He would say that." Lu picked up the jewels.

"He could have been plotting with the first wife after all, and they were going to use them to pay for their escape," Ma said.

"On the other hand, one of the maids said she'd seen Master Ying leave with a bundle just like this one on the day of his wife's death." Lu dropped the jewels back onto the cloth. "We shall soon find out."

He slipped on his court robes and black gauze hat with its wings on either side and strode into court. He took his place on the dais and called, "Bring in Clerk Cao for questioning."

A murmur went up from the audience hovering near the public entrance. Even though no announcement had gone out, the town already knew of the inquest. As Lu observed the on-lookers, they split, allowing a middle-aged observer to move to the front. Lu recognized Master Ying.

Clerk Cao trembled uncontrollably when he was deposited in front of the judge.

"What is your relationship with Madam Ying?" Lu demanded.

"I have no relationship with her, Your Honor."

"Liar! Tell me the truth, or I'll have to use more severe methods to force you to tell the truth."

Cao blanched. "It's true, Honorable Sir. I do see her on occasion to discuss business matters."

"Business matters! Since when does the wife of a pharmacist need be consulted on business matters?" Lu glared at him, then turned toward a soldier standing on the side of the court. "Bring the thumb screws."

Although thumb screws were considered the lowest form of customary government torture, its use could result in permanent mutilation.

Cao fell to his knees. "Sir, perhaps I am interested in her, but she never, ever, tried to tempt me in any way and never led me on. She is completely innocent of any wrongdoing." He was almost weeping as he finished his stuttered statement.

"That doesn't mean you wouldn't poison her husband, to remove him from your lustful path."

"If I wanted to kill Master Ying with poison, I would do it when he's having lunch in the store, to be sure he would eat it and die." Then, as if realizing his words could be taken to mean he'd been plotting his employer's death, he immediately added, "Not that I would, Your Honor."

Lu abruptly changed topics. "What of the jewels we found in the shop?" As Lu asked this, he also surreptitiously watched Master Ying.

At the mention of finding the jewels, Ying lost all color. Licking his lips, he looked towards the door.

Clerk Cao beat his head on the floor. "Your Honor, I knew nothing before your guard found the jewels this afternoon."

Leaving the man kneeling on the floor, Lu called out, "Bring Master Ying before the court."

Ying started back, but couldn't move through the tightly packed crowd. A guard grabbed him and dragged him before Lu.

"Master Ying, can you identify this cloth?" Lu asked.

"It belonged to my wife. It's been missing since my concubine stole her jewels."

"This was found in your shop, hidden behind a pot. How do you explain that?"

"My concubine must have hidden it, intending to come back and get it later."

Judge Lu looked at him askance. "You're saying your concubine, who is known to your entire household, hid these in your store when she fled, and she actually intended to come back later to retrieve the package without anyone noticing?"

Ying stared at the floor.

"Answer me," Lu ordered.

"I don't know what she intended, Sir. She was not a very bright woman."

"Yet bright enough to know how to mix the appropriate ingredients together to make a poison to kill you?"

"It was not uncommon for her to assist me in my preparations."

"Clerk Cao, did Master Ying's concubine assist in preparing clients' medicines?" Lu asked.

"No, Sir. She swept the floors and cleaned the shop. She never touched the herbs."

Ying stared ahead, his face unreadable..

"I have a witness who saw you carry this bundle out of your residence and into your shop," Lu said to Ying.

"Impossible. I didn't even know it was in my shop. Someone is lying," Ying said, but his hands were trembling so much he crossed his arms and tucked his hands into his sleeves.

Disgusted with Ying's apparently persistent lying, Lu leaned forward to challenge his words. Before the judge could ask more questions, however, Ma stepped up to him and whispered in his ear. Without a word, Lu left the court.

Zhang was pacing in the office. When he saw the judge, he stopped. "I believe I found Ying's concubine," he said, his face grim. "I examined the large barrels he uses to steep herbs and found a young woman's body in one that was sealed closed. She hasn't been there long. Ying's apprentice identified her as the concubine."

Lu shook his head. The level of cruelty people were capable of never ceased to surprise him.

Back in court, he stared at Ying for a long moment, then: "We've found your concubine's body—in your store. Ying, the court is charging you with the murder of your concubine and your second wife, who you killed to cover up the first death."

Ying slumped, his face a sickly gray as he mumbled, "It wasn't my fault. She wouldn't stop weeping."

SCREWED UP

by Anita DeVito

There's screwing up, and there's screwing up. My fellow detective and academy classmate, Rob Rigby, screwed up when he gave Madam Deputy Mayor a private tutorial on police procedures. Who had their shield longer? Me, Detective Jimmy Gallagher. Who led the department in closing cases? Me, again. Who got overlooked when the promotion list came out? You guessed it. Rigby, the mediocre SOB, couldn't detect his way out of a paper bag but he is the boss.

I had a heart-to-heart with Jose Cuervo, and we unanimously decided that my ladder screwing boss needed to know what I thought of him. My screw up. Now Rigby's settled into a job guaranteed to double the size of his ass in two years, and I'm … well, if police work were a thoroughbred farm, I'd be mucking out the stalls.

Which brings me to my latest case. May and June Fellino. The sisters-in-law visited the police station the way other septuagenarians visited their doctor. Rumor had it May had been widowed with six kids nearly forty years ago. Her sister-in-law June moved in with two of her own. The ladies teamed to raise the extended family and run a successful diner that was now a really successful franchise.

Retired, the ladies lived in a grand house in the oldest part of town. I pressed the doorbell, surveying the yard as I waited. The grounds were immaculate. Stone paths wound through front and side gardens bursting with spring colors. Bees buzzed and dipped into the hearts of flowers identified by metal plant markers with elegant black script like my Aunt Margaret used. I peered through the ornate glass door for a sign that somebody was home. A long-haired white cat sat in a stripe of sunlight, watching me as I watched him. He stood, switched his tail and I read his tiny mind—If I only had thumbs … I still wouldn't let you in. He walked away without looking back. I raised my hand to knock when voices came from around the corner.

Two women rounded the house on quick strides, wearing aprons with small tools poking out of a pouch like joeys. "If I were burying a body, I wouldn't ask you for help. You cut corners," the taller and older June scolded haughtily. "The squirrels would dig him up faster than we could bury him."

"It's the dogs you have to watch out for," I said to get their attention. Walking down the stairs, I offered my credentials. "Detective Jimmy Gallagher. I'm following up on the complaint you filed."

"Which one?" May asked, a child-like sparkle in her eyes. "Mr. Stevens sleeping in his driveway under the influence?"

June shook her head. "It's the Tallmadge boy and his drum set. I don't know what his parents were thinking."

"The complaint about Edward Weiss." I didn't have experience with older ladies but I had plenty of experience with high maintenance women. Managed to escape the big "M" but not without a few scars. I'd have to keep this focused and to the point. "Why don't you tell me what you know?"

"You tell it, June. You're the better storyteller. Sit while I get us some of my famous lemonade." May linked her garden-soiled arm through mine and led me to a cozy corner of the porch. "Take my chair."

June sat in a high-back wicker chair, sizing me up as the cat had. I've worked under cover, chased suspects and been in more bar fights than I could count. Patience was a survival skill, silence a weapon. I sat still under the appraising gaze.

After a long moment, June began. "Edward Weiss runs a grocery store, The Paper Sack. He lives behind us, alone. Lately, May and I noticed vans and trucks parking behind his house—not in the driveway, mind you, but behind his house—and men moving things in."

"What types of things?"

"Big boxes, little boxes, crates."

May returned, sans gardening gloves, carrying a tray of glasses and a plate of cookies. Conversation stopped until the table was set, and May sat on a two-person glider.

I accepted the lemonade served in a highball glass and prompted June to continue. "What do you suspect was in the boxes, ma'am?"

June leaned forward and, with a crook of her finger, invited me to do the same. "Art. Jewelry. Small antiques."

"Do you know this for a fact?" I sipped May's famous lemonade. My gaze snapped to her face. "Is there alcohol in here?"

May nodded and grinned. "Takes the edge off, don't you think?"

The hooch would have taken the edge off a chainsaw. I set the glass down. "Back to Mr. Weiss. What makes you suspect he's moving art into the house?"

"We snooped, James." May's innocent voice could have been announcing that the cookies were done.

"It is our duty," June said in a tone indicating she was not about to accept any criticism, "as Neighborhood Crime Watch co-chairs to investigate suspicious activities."

"You're telling me that you two spied on your neighbor's house?"

"We took pictures." May pulled out a slim stack of photos from the pouch of garden tools.

I flipped through each one. Twice. They were ten very nice photos of flash reflecting off a window.

May pointed to the top picture. "If you look close, you can see the painting against the wall. When we went back two days later, it was gone."

"There are other things." June sounded bitter, maybe jealous. "How does a grocer afford three cars and a boat? He had his house repainted and that new deck put on."

"It completely ruined our view." May whined, pouted her lips and took a healthy swig of lemonade. She hiccupped.

There it was. The root of the case. Suburban lawn wars. While I appreciated the lemonade, I needed to get back to work. My phone rang. I rejected the call but used the excuse. "I am sorry, but I have to go."

"Will you be investigating Mr. Weiss?" June asked.

I skirted the table, high-stepped over May's legs and walked backwards toward the steps. "I have to be honest with you ladies, I'm not hearing anything that sounds like a crime."

May picked up my lemonade and pushed it into my hands. "What about all the loading and moving?"

"Ma'am, there's nothing against the law about loading or even unloading furniture." Returning the glass to May, I added my card. "Call me if anything else happens, and no more snooping in neighbors' windows. That is a crime."

Back in the sanity of my car, I was about to put it in gear when there was a rap on the window, close to my ear. May. I put the window down. "Yes, ma'am?"

"James, before you leave, could you settle an argument? How deep do you have to bury a body?"

The child-like sweetness in her voice invited me to play.

"May, I like you. Don't make me have to arrest you." I winked and put the window back up.

As May walked away, I looked past her to the abutting property. Considering. Wondering. The sisters-in-law were eccentric but had their gears in working order. Nothing forgetful about them. Nothing unkempt about their home, the little I saw. They might add hundred proof to their lemonade, but they didn't live in La-La Land. I liked them. It shouldn't matter, but it did, so I'd give them the time that would otherwise go to Rigby.

* * * *

The home of Edward Weiss was a large colonial, not massive and in good repair. A truck parked in the driveway advertised custom tile and floors. Beyond the truck, the driveway turned, and was hidden by the house. All told, Weiss's home was closer to a castle than a cottage.

The grocery business must be pretty good, which made it the next logical stop.

The Paper Sack anchored a high-end strip mall. Inside, strong, savory scents struck my empty stomach. High end cheeses and wines, fancy crackers and fancier vegetables. I indulged in free samples, checked out the hormone-free, antibiotic-free, cage-free, taste-free chicken selection and considered a bottle of wine that cost an hour's wages.

Beyond the basic food groups stood an equal space for knickknacks and furniture, lamps and footstools. The Paper Sack was the love child of Trader Joe's and Pier One.

I approached swinging doors marked "Employees Only." The doors blasted open and a woman rushed toward me. Her name tag read "Rhonda."

"Boss in?" I asked her.

Her thumb pointed over her shoulder. "His office. He's in a mood."

Sounded like my kind of guy. While Rhonda hurried past, I moseyed through the swinging doors into a narrow hall papered in "goes-with-everything" beige. The hall had three doors before ending in a warehouse. His and Hers locker room doors were on one side with a large white board between. The board showed the schedule for the coming week including deliveries. Both during and after hours. Interesting. Across the hall, through a narrow window on a door marked "Office," a wiry man stared into a computer screen. The screen sat on the desk at enough of an angle that I could see a table of words and numbers but couldn't read specifics. I couldn't see Weiss's face, just his combed back hair and sweat soaked back.

I peeked into the warehouse. I'd need a warrant to get up close and personal with the inventory but free information lay at the front of the warehouse with Rhonda. I picked up a boxed set of crackers, salami and cheese and went through her line. "Boss always like that?"

Rhonda's brows lowered. "He's always bad at the end of the month. I wish he'd pop a Midol and get over it."

"The end of every month?"

"Ev-er-y. Month." She sighed. "$22.50."

I choked. "Prices like that are considered a crime in some states."

Rhonda cut me a smile but not a break. I emptied my wallet.

Back at my desk, Rigby got his report. I typed it in six-point font. Conserve paper ... save the planet.

Detective James Gallagher conducted an interview with Mrs. June Fellino and Mrs. May Fellino at 1:30pm on the twenty eighth day of April, 2016 at their residence of ....

I left for the day but the case followed me home. Trading my pants and tie for shorts and my favorite t-shirt, I ate my fancy-assed Lunchables with an exotic domestic beer while I worked the computer systems. On the surface, everything appeared above board, but appearances can be like icebergs—neat and pretty on top but large and lurking below. Couple of cars, loan free. Same for a boat. My gut waved a yellow flag. Everything was just a little too perfect.

My home phone rang. "'Ello."

"James?" The child-like quality in the voice was instantly identifiable.

WTF? "May? How ... how did you get this number? A cop's home number is private."

"He's doing it, right now. Come quick. June is doing recon."

"Tell June to get in the house. This isn't a game. You can't spy on your neighbors." Holy crap! I just channeled my father.

With a click, May was gone. I needed to talk some sense into the pair before they got in real trouble. I ran out of my apartment and twenty minutes later, parked at the end of their crowded driveway. The house was aglow. I stood in the fractured light of the beveled glass door and rang the doorbell. The cat heard but he still wasn't letting me in. No one else in the house heard over the combo of 1960s music and laughter. I let myself in.

"James! You came!" May floated across the room in a gauzy dress that fell to her ankles. Colors swooned with a life of their own as she moved.

"Jimmy." My nose caught a familiar scent. "May, what am I smelling?"

"June's special blend. She's a wizard in the garden." May put her arm through mine and led me through a house jammed with guests. I'd bet money no one was under sixty-five. All wore costumes like May's, throwbacks to the Sixties. Glasses and platters of munchies littered tables in every room. In the kitchen, grinning partiers crowded a near-empty plate of brownies.

There were parties, and there were kinky-hippie-grandma parties. Shit. That guy in the corner, the one with the blue lenses on? Judge Elijah Brown. The party guests were a Who's Who of the elder statesmen and stateswomen of the area.

"What's going on, May?"

"Edward Weiss is moving the loot."

I pinched the bridge of my nose, my only defense against quasi-parental lectures that pressurized my brain. "Not Weiss, May. The party."

"Oh. We're children of the Sixties, James. You don't think we gave up on drugs, sex and rock-and-roll just because we grew up?"

My brain slammed the door on that mental image. "Where is June?"

"Investigating." May opened a screen door and we stepped onto the rear deck. "This is James," May said to a hot tub with ten bathers and not a bathing suit in sight.

"Pleased to meet you, James. Come on in, the water's fine." A woman old enough to be my grandmother licked her lips as bubbles teased dangerously across her breasts.

I spun away from the cougar. "June! Where are you?"

Two figures emerged from shadows of the tree line. June wore black pants with a long black shirt. A peace symbol hung between her breasts and binoculars bounced against her stomach as she walked. A man paced at her side wearing Army fatigues held together by a thick belt looped under a protruding belly. A handgun hung comfortably at his side.

June spoke in hushed tones. "Keep your voice down, James. Do you want to wake the neighbors? What are you wearing? You can't investigate in that. Your white legs glow in the dark."

I bit my tongue. One … two … three. Four.

I let it loose. "I'm not investigating, I'm saving your ass from being arrested. Is there a license for that gun? Do you have any idea how dangerous snooping is? I do not have white legs." And I do not sound like my father.

"You shouldn't have called him, June. We could have handled it," GI Joe said.

June dismissed him with a wave of her fingers. "May, James needs clothes."

May skittered away with an expression that made me afraid.

"James does not need clothes." I shouted after May but she only ran faster.

"This is serious, James," June said. "Butch and I checked it out. Weiss is definitely moving the goods tonight. A moving truck arrived with muscle."

"Two punks. One of them was packin'," Butch, aka GI Joe, said. "He set the piece down on the barbecue. Musta been pokin' him. Amateurs. Back in my day, we took the time to do things right. That's the problem with youth these days, everyone wants the easy way, the fast way. Don't know something? Google it. Can't do something? Get an app that does."

May returned, interrupting the tirade. "This may be a bit tight, James. I made it for my husband. He wasn't as thick as you."

They weren't going to let it drop until I looked, so I put on May's handmade clothes. A thought couldn't fit between the cloth and my skin. The tunic in swirls of dark greens and blues blended into the night, but the fringe on my arms tickled when I moved. The dark pants were so tight up top I had to swivel my hips to walk. They ended with the bells of St. Mary's ringing around my ankles.

I wedged my phone into the small of my back and left the house with the sole intention of getting May and June to stop peeping. I'd investigate tomorrow properly and legally … and in my own clothes. I dropped to one knee behind a thick hedge on the Fellino side of the property line.

June squatted next to me. "Do you see anything?" Her breath smelled of her "special blend."

"Have you been smoking pot? Don't answer that. I don't want to know." I took the binoculars from her hands and surveyed the Weiss landscape. Two men moved a large number of boxes and crates into a Rent-A-Truck. Combined with Rhonda's comments and the board showing deliveries and the cars and boat, June's tobacco wasn't the only thing wacky.

"You calling in support, James?" Butch sounded authoritative and sober. "Time to clean the house, June."

June sighed. "May is going to be so disappointed. It was such a nice party. Take care of yourself, Butch. I want to see you later. All of you."

June thoroughly kissed him goodbye. With my eyes on the neighbors, I didn't see a thing. My ears weren't as lucky. Butch, on the other hand, he was lucky … or he was going to be when this was over.

Seriously. If people knew about the secret lives of the "elderly" they wouldn't work so hard to stave off aging. The fountain of youth wasn't a pill, it was a party.

"Who are you?" I asked.

"Friends call me Butch."

The scene through the binoculars was unchanged. "Got that. What do your enemies call you?"

"Lieutenant General John Michael Fitzpatrick, US Army, Retired. What do you think?"

I offered Butch the binoculars. "The truck is about half full. There's no way to know how much there is to move. I know where it's going, though. At least, the first stop. It's going to the warehouse at The Paper Bag."

"Never liked that place. Too hoity toity."

I agreed, my dinner of processed Peruvian pork and near-Wisconsin cheese falling into the "hoity toity" category. "I ran a few searches. The theft rates for art and jewelry are high in a three county area."

"Weiss is the middle man, right? Facilitating the sale and transport of the goods."

"And storage. This isn't a one-time operation. We move now and we could lose any chance at the thieves and the buyers. I need warrants."

"Doesn't matter if you win the battle if you lose the war." Butch stilled beside me, the binoculars pressed to his face. "We have company. You should call your friends, James."

When a General made a suggestion, a smart man did it. I acted my IQ and made the call. With backup on the way, I took back the binoculars. A black SUV parked in the driveway, blocking in the truck. Two men with trouble in their eyes stormed across the back yard. With back up in route, I wedged the phone between my spine and the homemade pants and settled in to wait. The angry men had other ideas. Ugly, harsh words zipped into the garden like pissed off hornets.

"That doesn't sound good," Butch said. "Got any ideas?"

"Yeah, but none of them good." Do nothing, sure, it was an option. Just not my style. "You ready to play, General?"

"You know that saying 'I was born ready'? Guess who owns the copyright."

"Follow my lead." I pushed through the hedge, singing at the top of my lungs. "We shall overcome. We shall overcome. We shall overcome someday-ay-ay."

Butch harmonized.

F-bombs fell like rain drops, greeting us as we staggered like drunks through the connecting yards. The movers stayed where they were but the angry guys came to greet us.

Butch produced a joint. "You boys have a light? Use to be everybody had a light. Now, nobody smokes."

"We in the middle of some business, old man." The scowl on the taller one changed to a crooked smile. He pulled out a lighter. "Getchya fire and go."

"Business. Back in my day, a man did business in a bar with a fine glass of brandy on the table and a finer piece of ass on his lap."

The angry ones were sniggering at the old stoned guy, letting Butch get close. Real close. Suddenly, shouting erupted from a blur of arms and legs. When quiet came, the General was standing with two men lying at his feet.

Weiss stepped out of the house, looking between the movers, the angry men, and us. "What the hell is going on?"

I grabbed the smaller moving man, putting a pointed rock in his back. "Stop where you are, now." I walked the guy back to the barbecue, finding a gun where Butch had said. "Police."

They all looked at my clothes. Someone snickered.

"Undercover police. Detective Gallagher. Hands where I can see them."

The bigger moving man put his hands up immediately. Weiss edged slowly toward the corner of his house.

The cavalry sounded nearby.

"There's no running, Weiss. We know the whole story." I lied through my teeth to keep Weiss there. "Your store is locked down, your delivery man intercepted. Don't make this any harder. A man like you won't like harder."

Weiss stopped, looked at the other men, looked at the freedom of his front yard and, yeah, he ran, right into the arms of the first responding unit.

* * * *

I didn't sleep much that night or the next day and night. Caught red handed, all the birds began to sing. Once the finger pointing started, the theft ring fell like a house of cards, leaving me with the paperwork. In all, ten arrests were made: five at Weiss's home, three at the store and two more a state away. I wrote the reports and, feeling generous, used eight-point font for Rigby. I hit send and left my desk for a Sunday lunch invitation from May and June.

The driveway was packed again. I hoped daytime meant less nudity, fewer drugs. I followed music and laughter to the back deck where a barbecue was in full swing. I recognized more than a few. Butch raised a glass in salute.

"James! You made it." May looked as sunny as the month she was named for.

"Jimmy. I go by Jimmy."

She linked her arm through mine. "Don't be silly. Jimmy is a little boy's name. You're a man. You need a man's name." She maneuvered me onto the deck. "April, this is the man I told you about."

May skillfully abandoned me, leaving me to face the woman she had called. There was nowhere to hide as the woman turned. She was near my age with a waterfall of dark hair turned and a face that could stop traffic. Her faint smile grew to a grin, matching her twinkling green eyes. "So you're James."

"Yes, I am." When a beautiful woman called you James, you're James. "How do you know May?"

"She's my grandmother. That's my mother, Summer." April pointed to a woman with May's sunny smile. "And you know my father." She gestured behind her.

"Sir." I snapped to attention as much out of surprise as respect. I did not expect to see the Chief of Police working the grill.

"At ease, Detective. It is a picnic." Chief Raymond Battista looked between me and his daughter. "April, would you get your old man a bottle of water?"

April wrinkled her very cute nose. "Leave some of him intact, Daddy."

Once we were alone, the Chief cleared his throat. "I understand you, uh, attended one of my mother-in-law's parties. They are, uh …." He may have blushed.

"Children of the Sixties. I hope I age that well."

The Chief laughed loud and long. "Don't we all, Gallagher. Heard about you. I understand you aren't thrilled with your current departmental structure."

Without Jose Cuervo's influence, I kept my reply short but honest. "No, sir."

The Chief flipped the back row of burgers. "Concentrate on what's important. Politics change. Don't let them distract you or suck you down to their level. Respect the position, if not the man or woman."

My face burned at the thought of my six-point font report. "Yes, sir."

His gaze drifted over my shoulder. I turned and followed his gaze to April's warm smile. She stepped out of the house with the water, two glasses of famous lemonade and her grandmother.

May crowded her son-in-law. "Raymond, don't you think James would be perfect for the detective opening downtown?"

The Chief barely controlled his smile. "There are procedures, May."

May rolled her eyes and turned her will on me. "April lives downtown. You would be neighbors. You could take her out for coffee or something."

April sipped the lemonade while I drank in the bright eyes shining at me. Coffee. Breakfast. Lunch. Dinner. It all sounded good.

Yeah, I screwed up but that wrong turn got me to the exact right place.

THE ABDUCTION OF DESTINY

by Mo Walsh

According to all x-y models, she was the ideal candidate, but the random nature of the z variable negated the whole. I shall elaborate:

LaRupe-X2 and I were hovering over Kan-sas, an area of level terrain assigned to agricultural use. We had yet to make our quota of extracted humanoid studies, due to overpopulation by artificially-altered specimens at our last assigned location, Calif-ornia.

We selected for our next study a female humanoid of approximately fifteen solars, individuated as "Destiny." She appeared, on preliminary observation, to typify the post-pubescent form of the species still undergoing significant cerebral development, a stage in which we have found specimens to be particularly acquiescent to our studies. The original battery of questions in phase one of the examination can often be reduced to the introductory statement: "We want to know all about you."

During follow-up surveillance, the Destiny scored low on our scales for anxiety, reserve, analytical skills, and other disqualifying traits. Furthermore, the subject appeared to serve no essential purpose in the interaction of her co-habiting humanoids, thus assuring us a sufficient interval before an alert was issued to investigators at the *National Inquirer*.

Having confirmed one of the Destiny's near-daily expeditions to a mercantile megaplex, LaRupe and I entered the TRU (Transmutation and Relocation Unit) to proceed with the extraction. Our Calif-ornia experience had led us to believe that our deviations from typical humanoid appearance would occasion no remark, so we retained our natural shapes. This belief was challenged when we reconfigured near an establishment marked "Kansas Komics."

"OMIGAWDLUKITEM!" The auditory disturbance emanated from three youthful humanoids, of which one aimed its primary digit at LaRupe's four upper extremities, each ending in six multicolored digits. Another touched its own minimal olfactory outlet while staring at my dual-purpose prehensile proboscis. I switched on the translator and prepared to reengage the TRU if further utterances were hostile in nature.

"Dudes, your cosplay is WILD!" shouted the third, and the humanoids smiled with apparent benevolent intent. Responding, as the translator recommended, with elevated opposable digits, we ambulated toward the adjacent "Nuclear Nails Salon" to intercept the Destiny. Our approach was undetected, the Destiny seeming preoccupied with some adjustment to a sparkling pink survival device. (Note: Our initial hypothesis that these devices serve a mere communicative purpose has been superseded by observations of previous specimens, which lapsed into extreme respiratory and cognitive distress when detached from them.)

LaRupe wrapped an invisibility cloak around the Destiny, inadvertently dislodging the survival device. The specimen reacted violently, its struggles inside the cloak invisible to passing humanoids. "Bleep!" LaRupe rocked and jerked in an effort to subdue the Destiny, prompting a youthful humanoid to vocalize, "Cool moves, man." I noted the statement for later translation.

"Vurp!" LaRupe's fluorescent green orbits were fading toward bilious yellow when I retrieved the device from an adjacent container for tropical flora we had not believed native to Kan-sas. When the survival unit was reinserted in the Destiny's clutching digits, the specimen retracted its extremity inside the invisibility cloak and ceased resistance. LaRupe-X2 engaged the TRU and conveyed the specimen back to the ship. I seized an artifact—a publication entitled *Aliens Among Us*—but failed to identify the planet of origin of any of the beings pictured within. We were still unknown to the humanoids. Bazinga!

Back aboard, I found LaRupe refueling at the nutriport. Contrary to protocol, the Destiny was not sealed in the observation pod or tethered to the examination panel. She (the translator had corrected my notes to indicate this as the proper pronoun for a female humanoid) ambulated freely in the command sphere, tapping the pink survival unit. "Don't you space nerds have cell service?" she said. "I can't get even one freakin' bar!"

"We will not harm you," I reassured her, as I always do with new specimens. "We wish only to study how you are made. You will be returned to your home and remember nothing of this experience."

"Not a chance, nerd!" She eluded my grasp, darted over to the nutriport, and—I believe the term is "hugged"—LaRupe. "Selfie time!" The Destiny elevated her extremity in front of their adjoining heads, and the survival unit emitted a flash of light followed by a soft "ka-shik" sound. "Yaaaaasssss, that pic slays!" The Destiny tapped a code on the unit screen with her opposable digits, then glared at LaRupe. "What is this? I can't get Instagram, Snapchat, or even that so-done Facebook—what gives?"

LaRupe spun away, slipped in the biofuel still flowing from the nutriport, and hurtled toward the Waste-Away personal processing receptacles. Just before the collision, LaRupe cried, "Blek!" My imperturbable companion rarely uses such language. The last occasion was prompted by a near-impact with a rogue asteroid. To my relief, the Waste-Away cover maintained its integrity, as designed. "Vurp!" said LaRupe.

"This video will go viral on YouTube!" The Destiny indicated the display screen of the survival unit, where SQIMs (sequential images) recorded LaRupe traversing the command sphere in a purple spray of fuel, green orbits pulsating with fear, and four upper extremities extended with all twenty-four digits splayed to reduce impact. "How do I upload or download or frontload this to the 'net?"

"All SQIMs will be deleted before repatriation," I said. "Confiscate the device, LaRupe."

"Nooooo!" The Destiny's grip could not be broken, even when LaRupe deployed all extremities and digits. "I would DIE without my phone! What kind of monsters are you?"

Immediately, LaRupe disengaged. We are not permitted to jeopardize the existence of the life forms we study.

"You know," said the Destiny, "I should be getting something from you guys in this situation. I mean, YOU kidnapped ME. I could make millions off you in court." She whirled on LaRupe. "We need to make a video that will bring me BILLIONS."

"We want to know all about you." I waited confidently for the usual loquacious response.

"I'll friend you on Facebook," said the Destiny. "The big money is in knowing about *you*."

"Enter the observation pod," I said, "and we will examine you and record your physical, biochemical, and neurological specifications. Then you may return to Earth and disseminate whatever story you wish."

"And get dissed as another Roswell weirdo? Not this girl," said the Destiny. "I want to post, like, 'Ten Things You Didn't Know about Alien Life Forms.' Do you have sex?"

I maintained my scientific dispassion, while the Destiny poked LaRupe with her elbow. "Come on, you little Space Sista," she said. "Do you and the Rocket Man here get it on?"

Interplanetary linguistics is not LaRupe's strength, but the increased pigmentation in my colleague's zygomatic region indicated the Destiny's references did not require translation. I filed "get it on" for inclusion in the glossary of Kan-sas.

"How about music? Do you like this?" The Destiny's survival unit emitted discordant tones, sounds of an abrasive process, and a human utterance: "Chillaxin with my bae. She so on fleek." I started to note the utterance, but looked up at LaRupe's cry of alarm: "Bee-burp! Bee-burp!"

The Destiny had been seized by convulsions and gyrated about the command sphere. Suspecting an electrical malfunction of the pulsing pink survival unit, I donned plasma mitts to break the contact between the unit and her hand. "You wanna dance, Rocket Man, grab the other hand," said the Destiny, tightening her grip on the unit. "Those gel gloves are mad cool!"

Despite the protective mitts, I experienced an unfamiliar reaction on contact with the Destiny: elevated core temperature, accelerated cardiac rhythm, increased pigment and diaphoresis of the integumentary surface. When she faced me, saying, "You got it, Rocket Man!" I realized I had begun to gyrate in the same fashion. Note: Destiny's eyes are the copper brown of sunset on Veerdahl, and her lustrous black hair flows like lava from—

"Bee-burp! Bee-burp! Blek!" LaRupe lunged across the command sphere, colliding with the Destiny and breaking the electrifying—elec-triCAL—contact. Wrapping three upper extremities about my thorax, LaRupe pointed the primary digit of the fourth at Destiny and said, "Grrrr wiglask!" Fluent as I am in all languages and dialects of our planet, I was unfamiliar with this particular expression.

Destiny nodded her head. "Yeesh, Sista, you wanna dance with Rocket Man, go for it!" She extended the sparkling pink unit to record more SQIMs. "C'mon so I can mupload that ish!"

"Your Kan-sas vocabulary includes many unfamiliar terms," I said. "Come recline in the observation pod, and we will make a con-vers-ation." I had been untangling LaRupe's extremities from my torso, but they suddenly tightened up again.

"Szepik gilamit?" my colleague asked.

"No. No tethers." I reassured Destiny, "Our intentions are amiable."

"Tew szepika gilamit!" LaRupe protested.

I thrust away the last extremity and addressed my colleague in a language Destiny would not understand. *We will not restrain her. Destiny has initiated no hostile action. The gyrations are apparently some ritual associated with the emissions from the survival unit. It is my conclusion that Destiny's intentions are also ... amiable.*

"Gler ban phlippt," said LaRupe, which translates loosely as *You are a blockhead.*

"You tell him, Space Sista," said Destiny. "Rocket Man, you are chirped."

"Grrrrr wiglask!" LaRupe repeated. (I resolved to research this term at the earliest opportunity.)

"Smile!" Destiny extended one arm across my deltoids in a "hug," and the survival unit she held in front of us flashed. "Gotcha!" From the tingle in my deltoids, I surmised that the unit had malfunctioned again, also causing my arm to extend across her lumbar region and my hand to contract on gluteal tissue. My oral cavity formed a rictus typically indicative of humanoid gratification.

"Gler ban phlippt JUXO!!"

"LaRupe!" I glanced at Destiny. *Your conduct and comments are most unprofessional. I believe you have exceeded your interplanetary travel tolerance. Retire to quarters while I complete the examination of the specimen.* I ignored LaRupe's protests and waited until my colleague had left the command sphere before I approached Destiny. Her gyrations had ceased, and she grasped the survival unit as if in need of bio-stimulation.

I attempted visualization of the illuminated surface. "Is the unit operational?"

"The battery's DYING and vids are eating the memory! I've got to SAVE it." Destiny's fingers scrabbled at the unit in an attempt at resuscitation, but it ceased to pulse and turned dark. "NOOOOOOOO!" Destiny collapsed to the floor.

"LaRupe! LaRupe!" My summons echoed through the command sphere. No reply. I hastened to the crew quarters and pressed the All Extremities on Deck alarm. "LaRupe! Destiny's survival unit has failed! Report at once!" No reply.

I switched to LaRupe's glottal dialect. *We cannot allow Destiny to perish. It is contrary to our mission parameters. It is your duty to assist me.* No reply, in any language. *Please come! LaRupe, I need you!*

The door slid open and LaRupe emerged from her quarters, clutching the invisibility cloak. "Vler dup Kan-sas."

"No! We must resuscitate the device!"

"Vler dup Kan-sas."

"Now, LaRupe," I said with all the authority of my commission. "You know we cannot send her back until I have completed the examination. We are already deficient in achieving our expected quota."

"Blek!"

Interplanetary travel was clearly having an effect on my companion's mode of expression. I resolved to make a note of it when the current crisis was ended, and adapted my own intercommunicative style. "LaRupe! Back to the command sphere—now!"

I was relieved to discover Destiny still in a conscious state and restored to a vertical position, though without sustenance from the survival unit, she appeared lethargic.

"This blows," she said. "I was killin' it with the vids! Tell me you've got a charger in this space saucer, Rocket Man."

Recalling an image intercepted from Earth television transmissions, I lifted my proboscis and touched the rim of my oral cavity to Destiny's zygomatic arch. To my puzzlement, I experienced a residual tingle, despite the defunct survival unit. I said, "We will not permit you to perish."

"What am I—a quart of milk?" Destiny exhaled forcefully with a sound like "huff." I resolved to make a note. "But you're bitchin' sweet, Rocket Man."

"Blek!"

LaRupe swept me aside with two extremities and with the others wrapped Destiny in the invisibility cloak. Her green eyes glowed, and just before she engaged the TRU and vanished from our ship with Destiny, my steadfast LaRupe said, "Gler ban phlippt, Rrrrawkit Maaan."

* * * *

We monitored the *National Enquirer*, *The Star*, and even *OK!* for any account by Destiny Fairchild of a so-called "alien abduction," but detected nothing. LaRupe scanned all 439 television channels for a mention on news, newsmagazines, and infotainment shows with the same negative result. A scan of Destiny's emails and phone calls revealed that she had, in fact, attempted to recount her experience with video evidence, but without success. The replies she received included such phrases as "passé," "done-to-death," "no election tie-in," and "special effects are so-so."

I was confident that our interaction with Destiny would go unrecognized on Earth and therefore not be subject to report—LaRupe urging a purge of the record to preserve our dignity—until we intercepted the transmission of Destiny's SQIMS to the web site YouTube.

"Take this viral, peeps!" said Destiny at the start of the transmission.

"Bee-burp! Bee-burp!" LaRupe sounded the alarm. Then, to our consternation, the "vids" disappeared, leaving no trace.

Now *I* was alarmed. "What has happened to Destiny?"

"Blek," said LaRupe, then in a gentler tone, "Gler ban phlippt."

After some negotiation, I entered the TRU and reconfigured in Destiny's home, not the compact dwelling previously noted, but a spacious dwelling with a superfluity of glass revealing what I identified as tropical vegetation, white sand beach, and waves of an opalescent hue. Destiny reclined on a surface of white hide, stuffed with the down feathers of exotic birds, before an entertainment screen the size of our command sphere.

"Hey, Rocket Man!" she said. "It's not BILLIONS, but the government's paying enough hush money to keep me in this place for life and with the kickin'est new phones. Give my love to Space Sista."

I returned to the ship and, on reflection, I did.

DOPPELGANGERS

by Susan Alice Bickford

The day Robbie Dawson's father punched out Mr. Wallis in the school bus loading zone, students clustered by the front door let out a cheer. Mr. Wallis taught biology. He was just out of college and not much older than us. And he was cute. But he was a teacher, right?

I had to jump out of the way for Mr. Dawson, who was striding toward Mr. Wallis. Mr. Dawson's head was thrust out. He walked fast and stiff like his legs wouldn't bend.

Mr. Dawson grabbed Mr. Wallis by the arm and said something about chins before he smacked Mr. Wallis square on the jaw. When Mr. Wallis didn't get up, Mr. Dawson stalked back to his car and drove away.

After first period, I went to the principal's office and said I had lost my field trip form. While I waited I happened to overhear what had set off Mr. Dawson. Mission accomplished.

In our biology class the day before, Mr. Wallis had pointed out that some of us had cleft chins. Thanks to the inheritance of a dominant gene, we lucky few had at least one parent with a cleft chin.

I pressed my index finger into the dent in my chin and a light went on in my brain. I turned and looked at Tessa. She stared back at me, the color drained from her face.

Mr. Wallis had handed Tessa and me the last piece of our shared puzzle. Finally, we had the key for figuring out who our real father was and how to prove we were sisters.

I could have sworn Tessa and I were the only students paying attention in biology that day. Big surprise. It turned out Mr. D-minus, Robbie Dawson, was intellectually on deck for a change and he went home to discuss his cleft chin with his smooth-chinned parents.

That was last spring. Mr. Dawson got arrested. Robbie had to repeat biology in summer school. Mr. Wallis quit.

Tessa and I love you, Mr. Wallis, wherever you are.

* * * *

I'll bet you've never heard of Hartwell, New York. It's a small place, far from New York City, midway between Syracuse, Binghamton, and Nowheresburg.

I grew up with my grandparents, Mimi and Gee, in a big house in the nice part of town. Most of the houses are painted white with black or green shutters, but some are brick or made of fieldstone, like ours. For the record, Mimi is school board president, Gee is the town dentist, and I am a junior at Hartwell Central School.

I have my mother's childhood bedroom. She stays in the guest room when she visits. I was six or seven the last time that happened. Twice a year I visit her in California where she lives with my stepfather.

I met Tessa when we started kindergarten. Her last name is Pierce and mine is Pritchett, so year after year I stood in back of her in lines and sat next to her in almost every class.

At first I couldn't figure out why teachers gave me Tessa's graded papers. And Tessa got sent to the principal's office as Cassandra Pritchett a couple of times.

I finally realized how much we looked alike when Robbie nicknamed us the Zombie Twins. That was because our eyes were such a pale blue he claimed they were white. Idiot.

Besides that, our hair was also the same reddish blonde and we had identical widow's peaks. Tessa was bigger than me for a while—she was born in July and I was born in November—but I caught up by second grade.

We were friendly but not close. I knew Tessa lived with her grand-mother in a doublewide down in the flats in between the DeWitt Lumber Yard and the Pink Kitty Castle Bar & Grill. Not the nice part of town by a long shot.

I never saw Tessa's mother until she turned up all of a sudden at Gracie Cameron's eighth birthday party. She ran over, grabbed me in her arms and started to carry me toward her car.

I screamed and kicked like crazy. Gracie's mother rushed over, yell-ing that I wasn't Tessa. Tessa's mother dropped me like she'd picked up a piece of dog poop by mistake. I landed hard on my butt.

I waited on the porch until Mimi came to get me. As I left, Tessa's mom stood in the Camerons' yard stroking Tessa's hair, following me with her eyes.

Later, Gracie explained that Tessa's mom had just been released from prison that afternoon. She was confused because she hadn't seen Tessa for a long time.

I was glad to hear Tessa's mom had moved up to Syracuse several months later.

Even after that, I didn't suspect that we might be sisters. I was still too young to notice the sly glances and whispers that followed Tessa and me around town.

All that changed when Robbie informed me of the facts the winter we were in fifth grade. We were fighting about whether girls could play on the hockey team and I was winning the argument.

He spat at me and missed. "You think you're so tough and smart but you're stupid. You don't even know who your father is."

"I do so." But he was right. Not that I hadn't asked. Lots of times.

"Your mother was raped by Tessa's father. Her mother helped and they went to prison. That's why you look like Tessa."

His words struck home, even though I didn't fully understand. My chest tightened and threatened to burst. I beat up Robbie and stumbled home in tears to ask Mimi about "rake."

Mimi rocked me on her lap like she used to when I was small and explained in a soft voice.

"That's why Mom doesn't love me."

"Your mother loves you very much. She chose to be a mother."

"No, she doesn't. I can tell."

Mimi rubbed my back. "She loves you and she needs your love, too. You'll understand as you get older."

A couple of years later, I realized that Mimi was saying my mother chose not to have an abortion. A sunny, warm spot blossomed in my heart. I had been wanted. My mother had fought for me.

I wondered if I could ever be as brave as my mother.

* * * *

Ninth grade was my Angry Year. Why did my mother dump me in a town where everyone knew my own business better than I did? Why did my grandparents raise me where everyone knew my secret? What did these people think life would be like for me?

I decided that I didn't have to be in the passenger seat of my own life. I announced I wasn't going to California for Christmas. If my mother wanted to see me, she could get over herself and come visit.

I lost that fight.

After my trip to California, Tessa stumbled upon my favorite hiding place in the stacks of the Hartwell Public Library. I was buried in a pile of old high school yearbooks and didn't notice her until she cleared her throat.

"Sorry. Didn't mean to scare you," she said, leaning over my shoulder.

I pointed to the high school prom pictures from seventeen years before. "That's my mother. Prom queen. And the king was her high school sweetheart. Bradley Douglas. After graduation they got engaged."

Tessa eased into the chair beside me. "She looks happy. Glowing."

She selected a yearbook from two years earlier. "My mother." She pointed to the girl with the blank stare and dark mullet.

For the next hour we pawed through the yearbooks, tracing our parents from pimply seventh graders to semi-adulthood. No one looked like a criminal, although Ned Pierce, our mutual father, did seem to glower in his senior picture.

"He doesn't look like you, does he?" I asked.

"Not like you either." Tessa traced his straight black hair and tapped his dark eyes with her fingertips. I couldn't bear to touch his picture.

"Maybe we're adopted," I said.

We both giggled.

"At least only one of your parents is a deviant, drug-addled nut case," Tessa said.

"At least your parents are married."

We left the library and slogged through the half-melted snow to Sal's Sandwich Shack.

After we'd tucked ourselves into a back corner with our cocoas, Tessa asked, "Does your mother ever talk to you about what happened?"

I shook my head. "Yours?"

"It's almost like she believes it never happened. Or that we should just forget and move on. 'I made a mistake. I apologized. I did my time. It's over.' That's her attitude."

"Do you see her much?"

"Once a month my grandmother takes me to visit her. We stop at Attica on the way back to see my father in prison."

"What's he like?"

Tessa leaned in close so she could whisper. "Spooky. He stares at me the whole time but only talks to my grandmother. He shaves his head. He's not very tall but he's got big muscles and lots of tattoos."

I shifted my butt on the hard seat. This was not a father I wanted to meet.

Tessa crossed her arms and rocked herself. "He's going to be out in about a year."

I felt like I'd been punched in the gut. I wondered if my grandparents knew about this.

"That's just wrong. Will they let him come back here?"

"I suppose."

"Does he know about me?"

"Duh."

We stopped talking for a while. I don't know about Tessa but I was thinking about moving someplace else.

"You know, everyone around here knows what happened but they won't say anything," Tessa said. "I'm tired of being protected from the truth. We need to find out for ourselves."

* * * *

Being under eighteen is a significant handicap if you are in the detecting business. Not only were we clueless, we couldn't legally investigate anything.

We relied primarily on reporting in *The Hartwell Gazette*, our weekly paper. The Syracuse and Binghamton newspapers provided more detailed coverage but not regularly. We couldn't find any relevant TV news reports on YouTube.

Our first success came when we identified the date of the crime. It had been reported in the *Gazette*, and we knew the approximate date because I was born nine months later. Actually, seven and a half months.

"Your mother was pregnant when she was arrested. Were you born in prison?" I asked.

"Drug rehab program. I'd probably be taller and smarter if she hadn't done all those drugs for the first five months."

I sucked back a snort. "Well, thank God for that." Tessa was half an inch shorter and my grades were a tiny bit higher.

"Where were you born?" she asked.

"Seattle. She brought me here when I was two and a half. My earliest memory is walking with her up the path to Mimi and Gee's house."

"Why'd she leave you here?"

"Mimi says she had some kind of breakdown. Like PTSD or something."

Tessa squeezed my hand. "She's better now, right?"

I wiped my nose with the other hand. "Kind of."

Tessa and I had envisioned our pregnant mothers sitting in the courtroom, listening to testimonies and verdicts. In real life, I was almost one year old and Tessa was a toddler before the trial began against Ned. Her mother's trial would come later, as would the trial of a second man, Lloyd Harris, who had agreed to testify for the prosecution.

"This sucks," Tessa said, after a grim day tracing the details of Ned's trial.

My mother had started a serious running routine while she was a junior in high school. Whenever she came back from college, she would take a loop from the back of my grandparents' house out a couple of miles into the woods and back.

According to Lloyd's testimony, he and Ned had been drinking heavily and doing a lot of meth for several weeks. They became more and more obsessed with "getting a girl."

How that fantasy moved to reality was murky, but on a warm April afternoon when my mother was home on spring break, she went for her run. Tessa's mother, Donna, emerged from the woods and said her car wouldn't start without someone to turn the key in the ignition while she fiddled with the engine.

They went down a dirt track to the car, where the men jumped my mother and Ned assaulted her in the back seat. I was relieved no explicit details were reported.

My mother's ordeal was not over. Lloyd sprayed carburetor cleaner onto a cloth to keep my mother sedated. That wore off fast, but she had the presence of mind to play possum. Lying in the trunk of the car, she could hear the loud argument about what Lloyd and Ned wanted to do with her as Donna drove through Hartwell. Lloyd suggested they head to Ned's hunting cabin.

When the car stopped at a traffic light, my mother pulled the trunk release and rolled out. She was groggy, but she was young and desperate. She dodged out of traffic, and stumbled to the Hartwell Police Department, a block away.

Knowing about the crime was bad enough, but imagining the aftermath was harder. I lost sleep that spring, but I found a new side of my mother.

What had the police said? What happened at the hospital? What happened when she came home? What did she say to her fiancé? Did she ever visit downtown again? When did she find out she was pregnant? How could I tell her how amazing she was?

By summer, we'd run all our leads to ground. We knew what had happened, and when.

I knew why my mother now hated running and why she struggled to love me. It was time to move on.

* * * *

Tessa and I didn't hang out much during our sophomore year. When she didn't show up at school for a few days in March, I figured she was out sick. I caught up to her in biology lab on her first day back.

My stomach hurt just looking at her. Her eyes were dull and her hair was stringy. "What happened to you?"

"My father came home," Tessa said.

I had to take a deep breath. "You don't have to live with him, right? Your grandmother has custody, right?"

Tessa turned to stare and the life went out of me, sucked into her dead blue eyes.

"You don't understand. They don't care about legal stuff. I'm theirs."

The clinking of lab equipment and the smell of formaldehyde filled the room around us. All I could see was Tessa.

Tessa said, "They're letting me stay until the end of school. Then the three of us are going. I don't think they even know where." She wiped her nose with the back of her hand.

"But . . ."

"Shut up, Cassie. Just shut up." Tessa left to go to the bathroom and didn't return.

* * * *

The end of the school year grew closer. In April, Mr. Wallis conducted his now-infamous class on dominant genetic traits and we realized that we had cleft chins but Ned Pierce did not. And neither did our mothers.

After class Tessa and I raced to the library for the yearbooks to double check.

Tessa put her forehead down onto the table. I put my hand between her shoulder blades and rubbed. I could feel her body shaking.

Tessa looked up. Her face had left wet tracks on the table. "What do you think he will do to me if he finds out?"

My tongue froze. Would she be his next plaything? Or worse?

I flipped to my mother's picture at the senior prom. There was our father. Tall, wavy red-blond hair, widow's peak, pale blue eyes, cleft chin.

"Bradley. It has to be him."

Tessa snatched the yearbook and closed it with a snap. "So much for Prince Charming."

"How could he have hooked up with your mother?"

"Maybe he was still living around here. Or visiting. Maybe they met at a party or a bar."

"We need to know for sure," I said.

"Your mother would know if she was already pregnant. You should ask her."

"She'd never tell me. Your mother must know. Ask her."

"She might kill me. Or Ned might."

Our eyes locked. We needed to find Bradley.

* * * *

My grandfather's dental office was closed for the day, but I had my own key. I let us in the back door. As the only dentist in the area, my grandfather knew more people than the Post Office and the telephone company combined.

Patient files are strictly confidential. I knew that. I also knew where Gee kept the keys for the file cabinets.

We leafed through the files until we found Bradley Douglas, Bradley Douglas Jr., and Evelyn Douglas. Bradley Senior was deceased. Evelyn Douglas lived in Charon Springs, which is why we didn't know her. Bradley Junior hadn't paid a visit for sixteen years and lived in Ohio.

"Ohio." Tessa sank into the receptionist's chair. "How are we going to get to Ohio? We can't even drive."

"Shhh. I'm thinking,"

I bent over the desk and started drawing circles with X's and Y's inside on a note pad.

"Remember that web site on DNA testing? Bradley gave us each an X chromosome, right? And it had to be the same X chromosome because he only had one to give. And he must have gotten that X chromosome from his mother. One of his mother's X chromosomes has to match the one that he gave us."

Tessa grabbed my diagram. "Forget Ohio. We need to find someone who can drive us to Charon Springs."

"And someone over eighteen who can request a DNA test."

* * * *

Mrs. White, Tessa's grandmother, stopped her car in front of a farmhouse outside Charon Springs.

"Someone has looked after this place," she said. "Fresh paint and fancy gardens. Not a working farm but real sweet. Come on."

We mounted the front porch and Mrs. White pounded on the door. I have to say that Mrs. White's eyes totally glazed over when I showed her my diagram of X and Y chromosomes, but once she understood we needed a ride to prove that Bradley was our father rather than Ned Pierce, she jumped into action.

Evelyn Douglas opened her front door. She opened her mouth to say something but instead her eyes widened. Tessa and I stood shoulder to shoulder on her front porch, staring back at a woman who could have been our sister forty or fifty years before.

Mrs. White muscled her way past us into the foyer. "Mrs. Douglas? I'm Marcie White. We need to talk to you about your son, Bradley."

Mrs. Douglas could see there was no denying Tessa and I had the Douglas family look. She even agreed to pay for the DNA test.

When the last day of school arrived I was in a panic because I had to leave for California the next morning. I called Mrs. White on my cell phone and asked about the test.

"Not yet, sweetie," she said.

"Where's Tessa? I can't find her."

Mrs. White didn't answer straight away. "Aw, sweetie. Her parents came last night and took her. Nothing I could do."

"Where are they? Have they left town? Are they in that cabin?"

"Yes, but don't you go messing with them. They're mean people."

I raced home, looking for Mimi. Her car was in the driveway but the house was empty and her cell phone was on the kitchen counter.

The year before, Tessa and I had ridden to the cabin on our bikes to check out where her parents planned to take my mother. It had been a long ride and now time was short.

I eyeballed the car. I wasn't old enough for my learner's permit, but I had practiced on back roads with Gee.

With any luck and no on-coming traffic, I might be okay if I stuck to the back roads. I grabbed the keys and left a note.

A little shy of the cabin, I pulled off the bumpy track and parked behind some brush. I made my way on foot for the rest of the trip.

The day was hot and the black flies were thick. The damp ground smelled dank and nasty like something was rotting beneath the surface. I kept looking over my shoulder and into the woods, expecting to see Ned any second.

I reached the clearing and hid behind a tree to check out the cabin. Tessa's mother was hanging wash from a sagging clothesline. No sign of a car or Ned.

Donna must have caught my movement in the corner of her eye.

"Who's that? Get out of here."

"I'm here to get my sister." Donna scared me almost as much as Ned. I inched into the clearing. My voice quavered but I stared at Donna straight on.

"What are you talking about? Are you crazy?"

I planted my feet wide, crossed my arms, and lied. "We did DNA tests and we have proof. Ned is not our father."

Donna glanced over my shoulder, toward the road.

"Shhh. Shhh."

"Bradley Douglas," I said, good and loud.

"Oh, shut up. You're worse than your mother. So proud and smug. Brad was more than happy to play around. I warned him. I told him he should give up your mother and go off with me. He said no way. But he sure dumped your mother fast enough once I fixed her wagon, pregnant or not."

I swallowed, fighting the urge to throw up. "You chose her. When Ned wanted someone, you chose her." I took a deep breath. "Now you need to save Tessa. You know what he'll do to her."

Donna glanced toward the cabin. "You take her and get out of here. You just remember that I loved her. Everything I did was for her."

She called for Tessa, who peered out from the cabin door.

"Tessa. Get your stuff and go."

"Maybe you should come with us, Mrs. Pierce."

Donna spat. "I don't need shit from the likes of you."

Five minutes later, Tessa hugged her mother goodbye and we left without looking back.

That night, the grandmothers—Mimi, Mrs. White, and Mrs. Douglas—held a long meeting in our kitchen. Gee, Tessa, and I had to cool our heels until they were finished.

* * * *

The beginning of junior year was full of new courses and new teachers. Mr. Wallis was gone.

Gracie's mother drove us home after the first day. She nodded as we passed the deserted doublewide.

"Mrs. White has moved, you know. Her heart was broken after Tessa disappeared with her mother. At least they left Ned behind. And now he's been arrested for robbing that pharmacy delivery van. Good riddance."

I craned my neck to check out the doublewide.

"Too bad you didn't get to know Tessa better, Cassie." Gracie's mother fixed her eyes on me through the rear view mirror. "She was a very nice girl."

"Yes, Mrs. Cameron," I said. "Everyone misses Tessa."

"I hear you had a good time in Quebec this summer with your grandparents. Your French must be much better."

"Definitely. *Je ne pige que dalle*." I had learned one excellent phrase: *I don't understand squat.*

"That's wonderful, dear."

That evening a text came in with a picture attached as I was working on trig homework.

Howdy from Pacific Grove.

The ocean was bright blue and waves sparkled in the background. Tessa was in the middle with her right arm around my mother and her left around my stepfather. Mrs. White leaned in from the right side. Tessa, my stepfather, and Mrs. White were laughing. I zoomed in on the picture. My mother was smiling.

I knew it had been a long summer for them. Mom was less than thrilled when Tessa got off the plane instead of me. But Mimi said it was time for her to do the right thing by us, and Mrs. White helped smooth the waters.

I stared for a long time. My mother's face seemed relaxed. At peace. My stepfather's too. And there I was, right between them. Of course it was Tessa. I understood that. But for the first time, I could see myself with them like this. A family. Soon.

I texted my response.

cu @xmas in ca xoxoxo

THE FAR END OF NOWHERE

by Liz Milliron

The first thing I heard when I got out of the car was banjo music. Seriously. A guy sat on a tall stool, picking out notes on a banjo. It was … prophetic.

I adjusted my Ray-Bans and looked down the deserted street. I'd been driving for hours, on my way from New York City to Chicago at the behest of my editor. "Why can't I fly?" I'd asked. I loved my Audi TT, but there was some pretty godforsaken country between New York and Chicago. I didn't love the leather interior that much.

"It's part of the story," she said. "A journey across the heartland."

"The heartland is the Midwest."

"Details." She waved a manicured hand. "Think. Between the haute cuisine of New York and Chicago are the hidden culinary treasures of America. You top it off with the opening of Chez Reveille in Chicago. We can publish it as a serial. It'll be fabulous."

It was nonsense. Who wanted to read a story in a glossy magazine about some backwater Mom and Pop eatery—no matter how good the apple pie was? I'd opened my mouth to decline the assignment. Then she dangled the ultimate carrot.

"Vicky," she said, arching a contoured eyebrow, "Don Carruthers is retiring. That means the four-star review slot will be up for grabs. Do a good job on this and who knows where you'll end up?"

I shut my mouth. Carruthers was an old sot, but he got all the prime restaurant review gigs. Starred, Michelin-rated dinners all the way. The message was clear. If I wanted to replace him—and boy, did I—I'd drive to Podunk, Louisiana, eat raw crawfish, and like it.

That's how I ended up in Turner's Ferry, West Virginia. My gas tank was empty. So was my stomach. There had to be something edible in this wasteland. And a gas station.

I picked my way across the cracked pavement, cringing as my Manolos squelched in the softened asphalt patchwork. A single yellow light blinked at what I was sure was the only intersection in town. I walked toward the banjo player, trying to scrape away the black tar. *I just bought these.* "Excuse me. Hi," I said. "I'm looking for a gas station. And a restaurant, if there's one open."

The man stopped picking. He squinted at me, then spat into a brass bucket at his feet. "You ain't from around here," he said.

No kidding. Now that I was close I could smell alcohol, tobacco, and pig. His scraggly beard might have been black or dark brown. It was hard to tell because of the dirt. His lank hair was dark and I doubted he'd washed in recent memory. His teeth were yellow. Some were missing. As were several buttons from a flannel shirt that hadn't known laundry detergent in weeks, if not months. His mismatched eyes stared in different directions, the brown one somewhere over my left shoulder and the blue one at my face. He plucked a few notes on the banjo.

In my three-inch heels, silk blouse and Armani skirt, I must have seemed like an alien. I adjusted my Marc Jacobs bag. "I'm from New York. The city. I'm on my way to Chicago."

"New York City, eh?" He looked me over. How did a guy with eyes like his manage a leer that stripped me bare? "Gas station at the end of the street," he said, jerking a thumb behind him. "Patty's Grab 'n Go is the place to get food."

What a name for a restaurant. "Thanks," I said, turning to leave.

"Only place to get a room is the EZ Rest. Cross the street from the gas station." He spat again.

"I'm not spending the night." I didn't turn around. I checked for traffic, but my car was probably the only one to have traveled through this backwater in days.

He cackled, a sound that raised the hair on my neck. "You know what they say," he said. "Man plans, God laughs. At the EZ Rest, tell 'em Gus sent ya."

I faced him. There was no breeze, yet I felt a distinct chill and wished my hair was long again so it'd cover my neck. I was metaphorically naked. Exposed. Gus's brown eye still looked off into wherever, but the blue one was squinty, cold, and glittery. Like he knew something I didn't.

* * * *

"What do you mean, dirt in the line?" I gritted my teeth. First, the hag inside the dingy office looked at my platinum Amex with a high degree of suspicion and disdain before running it. Then my Audi wouldn't start. Now this yokel was telling me the car had a problem?

The man—boy, really—spat through the gap in his front teeth. Did everyone in this town spit? His face was a stipple painting gone bad. "Didn't know you spoke a diff'rent language in New York."

"We don't." I forced the words out. "How long and how much?"

He spat again. "Gotta flush the line. Don't rightly know."

"Do you know how to work on an Audi?"

"Fuel line's a fuel line." He grinned. "Better get yourself a room at the EZ Rest. Just in case."

I looked across the street at the grungy motel, noting the peeling siding and the flickering neon "Occupancy" sign. I opened the Audi's trunk and removed my Vuitton roller bag. "Call me the minute you're done. I don't care what time it is."

One might say my stilettos weren't made for stalking, but I blamed the cracked pavement for marring my righteous stride. Behind me, I heard a snicker. Freaking yokels.

* * * *

If the town was *Deliverance*, the EZ Rest was the Bates Motel, complete with ominous, erratic electric lights. I was sure the carpet had been laid before 1969. The woman behind the desk didn't view my Amex as a foreign object, but as I took in the tacky, run-down surroundings I was sure most of the transactions at the EZ Rest were in cash.

"How long ya staying?" The heavyset woman with unnaturally orange hair wore a name tag on her polyester shirt that read *Flo*. How appropriate.

"Not a minute longer than I have to," I said.

Flo's giggle managed to be girlish and fruity at the same time. "You're too cute. One night or two?"

I stared at her. "One." I'd hitch-hike out if I had to.

She handed me a plastic key tag with a dull bronze "12" on it. "If you insist," she said, her voice a drawl that sent shivers down my arms. "You have a good night, hon."

* * * *

I jerked upright at two-thirty in the morning, not sure what woke me. It wasn't the noise. The motel was silent as a cemetery aside from the odd chirp of a cricket or maybe a cicada. Something was wrong. I knew it like I knew the menu at Bar Americain.

I slid off the lumpy mattress. The air conditioner did little against the stuffy air. I pulled on my robe and slippers, grabbed my key, and crept down the hallway.

Flo's desk was empty, an underpowered bulb glowing in the overhead light. Rows of key tags hung on the peg board. The only empty spot was number twelve. I was the only guest at the EZ Rest.

There was only one room off the lobby: the so-called "parlor." Moonlight glinted off the window, the flimsy, faded drapes pulled back. I'd had a decent club sandwich and a more-than-decent slice of blueberry pie with cream from Patty's Grab 'n Go in there earlier. Aside from an ancient coffee pot, some chipped mugs, and a few scratched tables, the place had been empty.

I reversed my earlier assessment. I was the only *living* guest. Gus, the wall-eyed banjo player, was stretched out on the floor, a rusty splotch on his shirt. A large knife, sticky red goo on the blade, was next to him.

I wasn't an idiot. No way was I going to touch Gus or the knife. But I had to see if he was breathing, didn't I?

A scream rent the air behind me. I twitched and spun. Flo stood there, orange hair done up in plastic curlers. A grotesque imitation Oriental kimono strained at her shoulders. Devoid of the heavy makeup, her doughy face was pale.

She pointed a finger at me. "You killed Gus."

Shock, incredulity, and the absurdity of the situation congealed my thoughts. But indignation came to my rescue, breaking the shell and allowing words to come through. "Don't be ridiculous." I stepped back from the body.

"He's dead. You're here. I ain't got any other guests," Flo said, face reddening.

"Preposterous. I arrived yesterday. I didn't know this guy before then. What's my motive?" Motive was important. I watched TV. "Besides, that's not my knife. And you don't know he's dead. Someone should make sure."

"Don't you touch him! I saw you with Gus." Flo crossed her arms over her ample bosom. "You didn't look all that happy."

"Because I was out of gas, hungry, and don't want to be here," I said. "I want to be in Chicago. Civilization. I repeat: how do you know he's dead if one of us doesn't check?"

"He ain't moving, is he?"

"That's not exactly proof of death." I took a step toward Gus, but Flo's shrieking battered my eardrums and I stood still until she stopped.

A man with tousled hair, wearing baggy, patched WVU sweats shuffled into the room. "Aunt Flo, what's all the ruckus?" He stared at me, then Gus. "What the hell is going on?"

It was the guy from the service station. The one who was supposedly fixing my car. "What are you doing here?" I asked.

"I live in the back," he said. "Flo's my aunt." He shook his head. "Why're you asking? What'd you do?"

"She killed Gus, Teddy," Flo said, sniffing.

"I didn't do nothing," I said. Turner's Ferry was destroying my grammar. "I didn't do anything. I woke up—"

"Why?" Teddy asked.

Why had I? "I have no idea. I came to investigate and found him."

Teddy looked from his aunt to me. "You heard Gus?"

"No, I told you—"

His eyes narrowed. "Then why'd you investigate?"

"I don't know. But I did. I didn't kill anyone, though."

Flo sniffed again, and what I was sure were crocodile tears leaked down her puffy face. I didn't know why I was suspicious. But I was.

Teddy patted her arm, but his words were directed at me. "You said you want to be in Chicago. We can make this all go away."

There was a dead guy on the carpet. I narrowed my eyes.

"Gus ain't got no family," Teddy said, his drawl taking on a wheedling tone. "No one to complain. You give us ten thousand dollars. That ought to be enough for a hole in the ground. You go. We bury Gus and don't say a word."

I sputtered. Blackmail? Over something I didn't do? "No way in hell." I stormed down the hallway to my room.

"Where you going?" Teddy called.

"To do what I should have done in the first place." I reached my door and yanked it open. "Call the cops."

* * * *

Thank goodness for Verizon. Even at the edge of nowhere, I had a signal. I avoided the term "murder" when I called, reporting only a dead body. Then I threw on some sweats—far more stylish and in better shape than Teddy's—and waited.

Within the hour, a West Virginia State Police cruiser pulled up in front of the EZ Rest. The trooper who got out was medium height with a trim build, and close-cut dark blond hair. Good-looking. Even a hick could look good if he put on a nice suit or a uniform. But I'd give this guy a second glance no matter what he wore.

"Morning," he said, touching his hat. "You call in a body?"

I brushed my hair back. "Vicky Radcliffe. You are?"

"Trooper Ned Bascomb." He didn't take my proffered hand. "What happened?"

I told him my story and he jotted down everything I said in a notebook. "I'll show you."

"Lead the way."

We walked to the parlor, Trooper Bascomb trailing. "He's right—" I stopped, causing my shadow to bump into me. "What the hell?"

Gus's body was gone.

"He was there," I said, pulling at my hair. "I swear to God. Right there."

Bascomb pushed past me. He looked under all the tables, but the room wasn't that big. "I don't see a body of any kind, dead or otherwise," he said. Green eyes studied me, the expression unreadable.

A step sounded behind me. "What all's the problem here?" Flo asked. "Why is there a state trooper in my parlor?"

I whirled to face her. "Where's Gus? What did you do with him?"

"Gus?" Flo held a plump hand to her chest. Cheap rings cut into her flesh. "I suppose he's sleeping. Like any normal person would be."

I took a step forward. "He was on your floor. Stabbed. You accused me of killing him."

"Aunt Flo?" Teddy wandered in, wearing the same ratty sweats. "What's the ruckus? Why're the police here?"

"Ask her," Flo said, pointing at me. "She seems to think she found Gus dead. In *my* parlor. Nutty as a fruitcake."

Teddy's face contorted. "Gus? Dead? Here? Are you crazy, lady? Or is this your city-slicker idea of a joke?"

"I saw his body. You two tried to blackmail me to the tune of ten grand to get me to leave town."

"We did no such thing," Flo said, swelling in righteous indignation.

"You lying sack of—" I took another step toward her.

Bascomb intercepted me. "Everyone take a deep breath." He looked at all of us, giving me an especially stern stare. "Clearly, there is no dead body. Maybe you were sleepwalking, Ms. Radcliffe. It was a nightmare. Or an optical illusion."

I glared at him.

"I'm willing to chalk this up to a mistake. Unless you want to make a complaint?" He looked at Flo.

"That won't be necessary," she said, pulling her cheap kimono around her. "I want this woman out of here as soon as possible. Total nutcase."

"Your car will be ready tomorrow morning," Teddy said, wrapping his arm around his aunt. "You can pick it up at ten. Come on, Aunt Flo. I'll get you a cup of tea." He shot me a dirty look and led Flo down the hall.

I turned to Bascomb. "I swear by Almighty God there was a dead man here. Stabbed. With a bloody knife next to him. Those two," I gestured in the direction Teddy and Flo had taken, "accused me of killing him. I am not sleepwalking, or crazy, or pulling a prank."

Bascomb sighed. "There's nothing here but cheap furniture. I suggest you go back to sleep." He handed me a business card. "If something new comes up, give me a call." He nodded and left me standing in the parlor, more pissed than I'd been in a long time.

* * * *

When I woke again, I had a choice. I was free to leave, since there was no evidence against me. But was my car ready? There was also the attempted blackmail. What sealed my decision is what I saw when I stepped out of the EZ Rest. Gus was sitting on his stool, picking on his banjo.

I pulled out Bascomb's card, but hesitated. This was obviously a scam—with me as the target. Was Bascomb in on it? No. He was a state trooper. I doubted Flo and company could co-opt a state cop. I dialed the number. "Trooper? This is Vicky Radcliffe."

"Ms. Radcliffe." The sleepy nature of his voice accentuated his drawl.

"Do you know anything about cars? I need someone I can trust to look at mine."

"I know something about cars. No disrespect, but I did work a night shift last night. And it's ... nine-thirty in the morning." He smothered a yawn.

Nice going, Vicky. The poor man had probably only gone to bed an hour ago. "I'm sorry, I forgot. But ... I need help. I don't know what I'm looking for and you're the only person I know in this ... town." Calling Turner's Ferry a "hole" would not help me.

He sighed and I could imagine the eye roll. "Give me an hour." He hung up.

I had some time. Gus had been laid out in the parlor, bloody knife by his side. I headed over and got on my hands and knees, ignoring the dust on the thin carpet. I found what I was looking for in short order. A hard speck of something dark red. Not blood. More like acrylic.

Flo entered and stopped short. "What are you doing?"

"I dropped my earring back." I stood and held out the back. Which, of course, I'd *dropped* for this exact purpose.

She frowned, lips a tacky bright red. "You leaving?"

"As soon as I check my car," I said in a cheery voice. I waltzed out, leaving her behind me. I couldn't make out her muttered words, but I was sure they weren't nice.

Next step. Sure, I was a food critic but I had a journalism degree. I knew a thing or two. I needed Flo's registration books. If Flo and Teddy had tried this stunt with me, chances were good they'd done it before.

With a glance to make sure I was alone, I slipped into the office. If Flo's records were computerized, I was hosed. My luck held. A stack of ratty books was in the bottom desk drawer. I skimmed the addresses, looking for an out of town, high-end one. They wouldn't scam a local or someone without cash.

I found a likely address in a suburb of Philadelphia from a month ago. I memorized the phone number, replaced the book, and snuck out. I went down the street to make my call. "I'm looking for Jessica Groves. My name is Vicky Radcliffe and I'm calling from Turner's Ferry—"

"For the love of God," the woman said, voice a hiss. "You said you'd leave me alone."

I walked further down the street. "Jessica, I'm not *from* Turner's Ferry. I'm a visitor. I wanted to ask you some questions. Do the names Gus, Flo, and Teddy ring any bells?"

Jessica's cursing was quite colorful. But when she calmed down her story sounded a lot like mine, including the disabled car and alleged dead body. "I paid them," she said. "I didn't do anything, but I didn't want to be stuck in Appalachia. I was getting married."

I thanked her and hung up. Fishing a notebook out of my bag, I scribbled her story. I stopped at Patty's and bought a Danish. When I got back to the EZ Rest, Bascomb was waiting. I held out the bag.

"You didn't have to," he said, taking it.

"I rousted you out of bed. The least I could do is buy breakfast." Over his shoulder, I saw a sleek black Camaro. "Yours?"

"Yep," he said, licking glaze from his fingers. "Where's your car?"

"At Teddy's." If Bascomb owned a new Camaro, he could inspect an Audi. "I'll show you."

"You stay right there," he said. "I'll be back."

"Okay, but first I want to tell you something." I summarized what I'd learned. "Fishy, right?"

"Hmm. Wait here." He walked off.

I didn't want to hang out in front of the motel, so I headed back to Patty's. Was I wrong about Bascomb after all? Maybe, but I had to trust someone. I didn't know enough to check the car myself. I ordered a black coffee and a bagel sandwich. "What do you know about Gus?" I asked her while I waited.

"He's a character," she said, snapping a lid on the coffee. "But once you get to know him, he's okay."

"Must be tough, no family. Of course, the town's small enough I guess everyone is family." I took my change and slipped it into my pocket.

Patty's forehead creased. "What're you talking about? He's Flo's half-brother."

* * * *

I met Bascomb back at the EZ Rest. "Get a load of this." I told him. "Teddy said Gus didn't have family. What about my car?"

Bascomb wiped his hands on a kerchief. "Good news and bad news. Your fuel line is clean. But your starter is missing."

I didn't know a lot about cars, but something called a *starter* had to be important.

"Who put the gas in your car?"

I thought. "Teddy. And he checked the oil."

Bascomb stuffed the kerchief in his pocket. "Let's talk to Gus." He headed off.

I tagged along. Gus was Flo's half-brother, Teddy was her nephew. An idea started to take shape.

"Morning," Bascomb said, stopping a few paces away from Gus. "Gus?"

Gus spat.

"You know this young woman?" Bascomb waved at me.

Gus gave me his wall-eyed stare. "Sorta. Sent her over to the gas station yesterday."

"Mind telling me where you were last night?" Bascomb asked.

"Why?" Gus transferred his gaze to the trooper, both eyes focusing.

Bascomb shrugged. "Just curious."

Gus spat again. "I was home."

"Not at the EZ Rest with your half-sister?" I asked, crossing my arms.

"Nope." The mismatched eyes were baleful.

"Thanks." Bascomb took me by the arm and led me away.

"What are you doing?" I asked once we were out of earshot. "He's lying and you know it."

"More importantly, I can't prove it," he said. "I think it's time for you to hit the road."

"They're scamming people," I said, stamping my foot. "Need I remind you, I'm a reporter. I've got connections."

He raised an eyebrow. "Oh, you do? Look." He stopped. "I agree it's dodgy. I can't do a damn thing without evidence. So let's get your starter and get you on the road. Best thing for everyone." He led me back to Teddy's.

While Bascomb looked for Teddy, I examined my Audi. It looked good, everything in place. Until I opened the trunk. Shining against the black upholstery was a knife. The same knife I'd seen next to Gus's body the night before.

* * * *

I waited for Bascomb to return. I did not touch the knife. But I showed it to him the minute he came back. "That's the same knife I saw last night. I'd swear to it," I said.

He said nothing.

"Quite a routine. Identify rich tourists. Disable the car. Send them to Flo. Stage a murder and bribe the target to keep quiet. Nobody like me wants to stick around here."

Still nothing.

"If you think I'm going to let this go …." I trailed off.

"Stop," Bascomb said. He used his kerchief to pick up the knife. "Teddy is missing, but I found your starter. I'll put it back. But this … it's conjecture. If you can prove it, that's one thing, but if you can't you should leave."

My nascent idea grew. I *couldn't* prove anything. It might not matter. "Can I borrow that?" I pointed at the knife.

His eyes narrowed. "Normally I'd say no. But I looked you up online this morning. Seems you're a real food critic. Don't know what you want with this, though."

I took the knife. It was crusted with a glossy red and in the dark, it would look like blood. "You'll see."

* * * *

Back in my room, I packed and headed for the registration desk. Flo was there, fussing with some papers. "I'm checking out," I said. "Oh, I found this in my trunk." I dropped the knife on the desk. "I think it's yours."

She blanched.

I leaned on the desk. "I know what you, Gus and Teddy are up to. Swindling richer clientele. Shame on you."

"That's a wild guess. You don't have a shred of proof."

Maybe not, but the perspiration on her upper lip told me I wasn't far off the mark. "No, I don't. If I did, you'd be having a different conversation, with a different person." I leaned closer. "But I can put a stop to it."

She took a step backward and bumped into the key rack, setting them jingling. "How do you figure?"

"Power of the press." I examined my nails. "Yeah, my destination is Chicago and a bigger story. But my editor also tasked me with writing about any places I found along the way. That was some mighty fine blueberry pie I had at Patty's. I think the country needs to hear about it, don't you?"

Flo's eyes were riveted on me. "What will that do?"

"I write the story right, you'll have people from all over streaming into Turner's Ferry for a slice of pie. More people than you've ever seen. And yeah, you might be thinking that'll play right into your hands. Like shooting fish in a barrel, as one of you yokels might say. However, more people means also means more eyes watching. Watching you, Teddy, Gus … you see where I'm going here?"

I watched Flo's face as the brain under that god-awful hair processed my words. More people, more witnesses, greater likelihood of getting caught.

"If folks complain, won't you get in trouble?" There was a triumphant, yet beseeching note in her voice.

"I'll have reviewed the food. Not the accommodations. Now. Do we have an understanding?"

There was a long pause while she again processed my words. I knew I had nothing to take to the police. She knew it. But we both knew that trial in the court of public opinion could be a lot worse. Add to that the fact that the trio's chances of success plummeted with an increase in visitors, and anyone—even a middle-aged woman from a backwater town—could do the math.

"I understand." Her puffy face was milk-white as she held out a trembling hand for my key.

I handed her my key. "You have a nice day."

Bascomb was outside the service station, checking the Audi. "You're good," he said, letting the hood fall. "Can't say it's been a total pleasure. If you're right and this happens again—"

"Don't worry, it won't. I handled it." I slid behind the wheel of the Audi. It was time to get out of West-by-God-Virginia.

FOR THE LOVE OF RUBY

by Bern Sy Moss

The funeral was yesterday. John didn't come. I could understand if it was anyone else, but Mom? No, never. He wouldn't be a no-show for Mom. I should have known when he didn't answer my text message. I should have known right then something was wrong.

I left early the day after the funeral. Packed my saddlebags with some camping gear, hopped on my Harley and headed for Southern Illinois to the address my brother wrote on the corner of the envelope, the one that held the birthday card he sent to Mom a month before she died.

It took me six hours from Chicago to a little town outside of the Shawnee National Forest where I finally found the address. It was more or less what I expected, an old building, paint weathered down to the bare wood, weeds popping through the concrete sidewalk breaking it into stepping stones, a few cracked windows here and there saved with duct tape. Just another one of those places for my brother to flop for a few months or a few days.

I knocked on the door and caught the curtains discreetly move. I waited, but no one came to the door. Instead, a voice from behind me asked, "You need some help, mister?"

I turned and looked in the direction the voice came from, a garden to the left of the house. An old woman, shorter than the cornstalks growing there, emerged from it carrying a basket filled with tomatoes, green peppers and corn.

"I'm looking for John Olinski," I said.

"He's been gone for a while, maybe a month." She put the basket down and wiped her wrinkled brow on the arm of her faded shirt.

"Why you lookin' for him?" the old woman asked.

"He's my brother," I answered.

"Yeah, been gone a month or so. Got some of his stuff still here in the shed. Said he'd be back for it, but he must have forgot about it. You can have it if you want. You got a name?"

"John, John O'Leary."

She jerked her head at my response.

"Yeah, well, actually we're half-brothers named after our fathers. And that's all either one of us ever got from them, just their names."

"The stuff's back this way."

She led me to a shed behind the house and pointed to a cardboard box.

I stooped down and looked through the contents. I found a picture, my brother and me, taken the year I fell from a tree and broke my arm. I was five. My mother blamed him because he was older and somehow was supposed to anticipate all the stupid things I did and keep me from doing them.

I guess she needed someone to blame for the broken arm. She beat him and I cried. He was my big brother, my hero. When she was done, we all cried, our arms around each other because it was all we had, just each other.

The picture didn't bring back long forgotten memories. I lived that memory over and over, waking often from my sleep grasping at the air for something, anything to grab to keep from falling. I've fallen countless times from that tree, the fear of heights now imbedded in me forever.

I rummaged through the rest: a few paperbacks, some pictures of people I didn't know, a brochure for an air show, some old check stubs and a few other things not worth keeping.

"Do you know where he went?" I asked.

"He said they were going to put him up at the new job," she said.

"Where?"

"Don't know. Paid up what he owed. Got in that red Chevy of his, Ruby he called it, and took off. That's the last I seen of him. Oh, he did say something about joining the circus. I asked him if he was going to be a clown. He just laughed and drove away."

"I'll take the pictures. You can toss the rest," I said and started to leave. About halfway to my Harley, I stopped and turned. She was heading toward the garbage with the box.

"Could I look in the box again?"

She shrugged and put it on the ground. "Help yourself."

I found the brochure, the one for the air show, Madd Mercury's Flying Circus.

"I'll take this too," I said.

* * * *

I tracked down the flying circus to a small aerodrome. It was nothing more than one hangar with a grassy field for a runway on the edge of the Shawnee National Forest. I drove the Harley up to the office and parked.

Instead of going in, I walked toward the back where I caught a flash of red. It was my brother's red '57 Chevy. No mistaking it, Ruby scrolled in gold letters on the trunk.

A guy in coveralls was heading toward me. "You got business here?"

"I'm looking for the owner of the car," I said.

"Oh, you mean Madd Mercury."

"He owns this car?"

"Yeah."

"How long has he had it?"

"About a month. What's it to you?"

I knew my brother would have given up one of his body parts before he gave up Ruby. He loved this car. John must have been here, but something told me not to start asking questions just yet. I needed a reason to hang around the circus.

"Are they hiring?" I asked. "I always wanted to join the circus."

He laughed. "Go in the office and talk to Mercury."

I came around the corner to find someone checking out my Harley. "This yours?" he asked.

"Made the last payment last month."

He walked around the bike like a prospective buyer checking out every detail. "Nice ride," he said.

"It's not for sale."

"Oh, I'm not interested in buying, but I sure would like to have it."

Over my dead body, I thought, but that thought resonated through me like a premonition I didn't want to address now, not ever.

"Do you know where I can find Mercury?" I asked. "I'm looking for a job."

"You found him," he said, turning his attention to me. "You want a job?" He looked back at my Harley. "Let me think about it. It won't pay much if I take you on. Got a name?"

"John, John O'Leary."

"Got a place to stay?" he asked.

"I was going to camp out in Shawnee."

"You can sleep in the hangar, if you want," he said.

* * * *

The next morning as I watched the planes go up, Mercury approached me with a big grin filled with brownish stained teeth.

He spit out chewing tobacco and said, "Way I see it, we got a new act, John." He pointed to a guy looking my Harley over. "Jerry is going to drive the bike and we're going to make you part of the show. How does that sound?" His smile got even bigger.

"Nobody drives my bike," I said.

"Well, John, that's all I got right now. Think it over."

I knew staying with the circus was the only way I could find out what happened to my brother, so I said, "Sure, what do I have to do? I'm a pretty good mechanic."

Mercury's face broke into that big grin again. "Butterfly's around here somewhere. Try the office. Tell her you're taking John's place. Funny, I got a John to replace a John." He laughed at his private joke and walked toward Ruby. "Got to go to town and get some more tobacco." With that, Mercury sped away, leaving me in Ruby's dust.

* * * *

Flies covered the office screen door. They scattered when I opened it and went in.

"Close the door quick before those damn flies get in here," someone shouted.

From the far side of the room I could see long blonde hair, tight jeans on a slim body, and a cast on the left arm. The right arm, covered with tattoos of flowers, was tacking papers to a bulletin board. She turned and I decided she was maybe in her forties, older than what her backside led me to believe.

"Semper Fidelis" was tattooed across her very exposed chest and I wondered who she was "always faithful" to. Maybe a little too old for me, I thought, but then I was flexible.

"I'm replacing John," I said.

"Ever work with an air show before?" She grabbed the fly swatter and started on the flies that came in with me.

"No, like I told Mercury, I'm a pretty good mechanic. Never worked on planes before, but I learn fast."

"I don't think that's what he had in mind if you're replacing John."

I wanted to say John, my brother, was a great mechanic, but then I would be giving myself away. So, I just waited to see what she had in mind.

"Come on outside and see the show. They're rehearsing now," she said, walking to the door and handing me binoculars. She waved at the flies as she went out and held the door for me. "Damn flies."

Outside of the office, she pointed up. With the binoculars, the view gave me a rush. A formation of ten jumpers dressed in wing suits designed to look like eagles were floating above. After a few minutes, they deployed their parachutes and began landing a few hundred yards from where we were standing.

A biplane with a trapeze below the bottom wing came into view. A woman in a red, yellow and lime green neon colored costume that appeared to mimic a butterfly was hanging by her feet from the trapeze. I watched breathlessly as she completed her other stunts, climbed on the wing of the plane and got into a harness.

"She's my understudy," Butterfly said, pointing at the cast.

The plane began to do its own aerobatic routine turning upside down and finally flying out of view.

Another biplane appeared and performed a series of rolls and dives.

"That's Mercury up there now. Well, what do you think?" Butterfly asked.

"Better them than me up there," I said.

"Mercury explain what you're going to be doing?" she asked.

"He said I was replacing John. I thought he was a mechanic."

"No, John wanted to be up there. Touch the sky, he said. You want to touch the sky?"

"Was he up there today?"

"No, he moved on."

"And left that car?" I said, wondering if I said too much.

"He moved on. Maybe he'll be back for the car," she said in a *don't ask me any more questions* tone. "Come with me, and I'll tell you what you'll need to know."

It wasn't a hot day, not as hot as it can get in Southern Illinois in August, but sweat was forming on my forehead and wetting my back. I couldn't climb an eight-foot ladder without hyperventilating, and they wanted me to go up there and touch the sky.

I couldn't quit now. This was my only chance to find my brother. I told myself that tree has held me hostage for twenty years and I needed to fester up and get over it. I just watched the show. Nobody got hurt. It can't be that dangerous, I thought. But no amount of lying to myself could make me stop sweating.

I followed her to the hangar where she explained what I would be doing.

"It's easy," she said. "The motorcycle will be moving at the same speed as the plane. You'll be on the back. You'll reach up and grab the rope ladder. The plane will be low enough for you to get your foot in the bottom rung. When I see that, I'll let Mercury know and you'll start moving up away from the bike. All you have to do is keep climbing the ladder. When you get to the wing, you climb on, hang on tight and wave to the crowd. That's not so hard, is it?" She laughed.

"Did the other John do it?" I asked.

She stared at me for a while and finally said, "Of course he did, and tomorrow is your day to touch the sky, John." With that said, she walked out and left me standing alone in the hangar soaked in my sweat.

* * * *

After a sleepless night, the next day came too soon or maybe not soon enough. When dawn broke, I headed for the office. Butterfly met me halfway. She had a pile of clothing, striped with red and white, over her cast and a paper shopping bag in the hand of the good arm.

"Here's your outfit. Get dressed. Oh, your wallet and cell phone, bring them up to the office before you go up. You don't want them falling in some corn field, do you?" She must have sensed my fear because she added, "If you look like you're having any problems, I'll tell Mercury to bring you down."

As she headed back to the office, leaving me with a silly looking clown costume, I heard her say, "I know you can do this, John."

My costume on, I was slipping into the big clumsy shoes I found in the paper bag when I heard my Harley reviving up in front of the hangar. "Let's go," Jerry shouted over the rumpling noise of the motorcycle. "Mercury's up there already."

I got on the back of my bike, forgetting to leave my wallet and phone at the office. Jerry headed for the runway. I could see Mercury's plane flying over. Jerry maneuvered the bike and coordinated the speed to match the speed of the plane.

Sweating bullets, I could hear my mother's voice telling my brother, "This is your fault, John. You need to keep your little brother safe. He doesn't know any better."

The bike lined up with the plane. I grabbed the rope ladder and put one oversized shoe in the bottom rung. The ladder was so narrow only one of the huge shoes could fit in the rung. Quicker than I expected, the plane started to rise and lift me in the air. I struggled to get my foot in the next rung. Realizing I couldn't, I froze.

The thought occurred to me now, how were they going to get me off this ladder?

It didn't take long to figure this out. We were no longer over the airfield. Instead, acres of trees were beneath me now. The plane came in low over the trees and my feet hit the tops of the tallest ones. I hung on, closed my eyes, and started hyperventilating.

Now I knew what happened to my brother and I was destined for the same fate. My brother's car, now my Harley, was worth a man's life to Mercury.

The plane took another pass at the forest, coming in lower, my body hitting the tops of the trees this time. I hung on for the first pass and the second, but I realized the third would be different. The plane was gaining altitude. Ahead, I could see tall rock formations that would probably knock me off the ladder and kill me in one swift whack.

I decided to take my chances with the trees. I let go while I was still over them, falling on a thick branch and hitting it so hard I heard a crack. I fell though the branches grasping and catching only air, finally hitting the floor of the forest where Mercury expected me to die.

When I came to, it was dark. The slightest move gave me more pain than I had ever known in my life, letting me know where my body was broken. Somehow, I managed to reach my phone, the one I was supposed to leave at the office, hoping, praying I was near enough to a cell phone tower to get to 911.

* * * *

They found me in the morning when daylight came, a mess of bumps and bruises, broken, but still alive. Sirens blaring, they delivered me to the nearest hospital and patched up a few fractured ribs and broken leg.

The State Police told me when they got to the aerodrome, Mercury and Butterfly were hurriedly packing up the '57 Chevy in an apparent attempt to escape. Mercury told them it was all my idea to go up and do the stunt and he *thought* he had told Jerry to call 911 and report I accidentally fell off the plane.

Mercury claimed he bought the Chevy from a guy passing through and came up with some excuses why he had no proof of ownership. They found the title and registration still in my brother's name in the glove compartment of the Chevy.

Since he expected neither my brother nor I would be found, he was going to forge my brother's name and transfer possession of the car to himself and do the same with my Harley, except that title and registration were in my wallet. Butterfly's black eye was testimony to how mad Madd Mercury was when he found out she didn't get my wallet and cell phone.

When she was told she would be charged as an accessory for attempted murder and my brother's murder, when they found him, Butterfly told them everything they needed to arrest Mercury.

* * * *

It's a month later and I'm living in that old boarding house the old woman runs not far from Shawnee. I can feel fall coming with the coolness in the air, see the changing colors in the trees, smell the mustiness the forest sends on the breeze. I know it won't be long before the snow falls and they haven't found my brother. The State Police tell me Shawnee National Forest covers 300,000 acres and it might be a while before they do find him.

The courts will have to decide who owns the Chevy now, but since I'm John's only living relative, I'm sure I'll get Ruby.

I'm still on crutches and my body keeps reminding me what pain feels like, but by spring, I should be better and Ruby should be mine.

And if they haven't found you by then, John, Ruby and I will.

PING-PONG GIRL

by Rita A. Popp

The rose-brick house had twin front doors, something Amy hadn't expected. One obviously was to the downstairs apartment, so she knocked on the other door and waited, a flutter in her empty stomach.

"No need to knock. Go on up." A cute guy, suddenly at her back, startled her. The casual way he carried a backpack over one shoulder made her feel self-conscious, weighted down like for school by her raspberry and pink pack. She should have asked her dad for a replacement when she started high school, but she clung to her old pack like a kid to a favorite toy.

The cute guy opened the door to a flight of narrow stairs. "My place is on the left up there. Who you looking for?"

"My mom."

"The gal with the baby?"

Amy's stomach lurched, like in her dad's rowboat in choppy water. "You know her? Deb Clausen?"

"Only to say hello."

The stairs were so steep, Amy could see the soles of his hiking boots as she trailed him up to a cramped landing. She waited a couple steps below as he unlocked his door, nodded to the one opposite, and left her alone. There was nothing of interest to see except a short loop of rope dangling from a ceiling panel, nothing to hear except a baby crying. Liam, her half-brother, she guessed. If she wasn't exhausted from the overnight trip, she might have run from the sound, but she steadied her breathing and knocked.

"Hold your horses! I'm coming." The door opened, and there stood her mom with a squirming kid. "Baby Doll! Ohmygod!"

Liam was bigger than Amy had imagined, old enough to hold up his head, and drooling buckets.

"Surprise!" Amy's shout came out weak and jokey.

Deb shifted the baby on her hip, gave Amy a fierce hug, and released her. "Look at that shape on you." She furrowed her forehead. "Your father know you're here?"

The apartment was small enough to take in at a glance. Living room, bedroom, galley kitchen, bathroom, all in one straight shot. No bedroom door, only drapes.

Deb waved Amy into a canvas folding chair and plopped herself and Liam on a ratty couch. The baby had eyes as blue as the surface of Elephant Butte Lake—hours and hours to the south—on a bright day.

"I texted Dad when the bus crossed the Colorado line, sprung it on him I wasn't at a friend's." Amy's light tone failed to get a laugh.

"Ditching school?"

"Nope. Spring Break."

"Buy a round-trip ticket?"

"I thought you'd be glad to see me." Amy said it in a tiny mouse voice. She pressed her fingers against her eyelids but couldn't hold back the tears. Liam joined in crying like a back-up singer.

"Oh, for godsake," Deb said. "Stop it, both of you."

* * * *

The kitchen barely had space for two people, let alone the baby strapped in his seat. Amy slathered toast with peanut butter and pancake syrup, her favorite snack. She could almost hear Deb thinking, *What am I going to do with this girl?* In between bites, Amy grumbled about how her dad wouldn't let her date yet and how, for the whole Spring Break, she was supposed to work in the KOA store while everybody else was at the lake.

"Poor baby," Deb said without an ounce of sympathy.

Amy couldn't tell if the comment was to herself or Liam, who squirmed in his seat and mouthed gibberish.

"Want to hold him, get to know him a little?"

Amy recoiled at the idea. "No thanks."

"Weird to have a baby brother, huh? Ohmygod, Amy, you're not an only child anymore!"

Amy was checking her messages. "Dad texted to see if I got here. He's still mad." She tapped a quick, sweet reply. Liam reached for the phone, and when she didn't give it to him, he made a face and started to grizzle.

"Nap time for Mister Liam," Deb said in a fake cheerful voice with an underlying tone of weariness.

Her lips looked dry and pinched. This was not the same reckless woman who had left with "that blue-eyed drifter," as Amy's dad called him.

There was no crib for Liam; in the door-less bedroom, Deb put him down on a single mattress on the floor.

"Won't he crawl off it?" Amy asked.

"I'm saving up for a crib," Deb said. "He can turn over, but he can't crawl yet."

"Where's Liam's dad?"

"Gone with the wind." Deb's sigh fit her words.

Serves you right. "Mom, what are you going to do?"

Deb didn't answer. Without her usual makeup, she looked about thirteen. Choking up, Amy ran the few steps to the living room and threw herself face-down on the couch.

* * * *

The next thing Amy knew, Deb was shaking her arm. "Baby Doll, wake up. I got to drop Liam off at a friend's and get to work."

Deb had twisted her hair into a topknot and put on false eyelashes, so she looked normal. Leaning over to kiss Amy's cheek, she struggled to keep hold of Liam, a tote bag stuffed with his things, and a huge purse.

"Waitress job?"

"Only a diner, but the tips are good. Don't lock the door if you go out. There's no spare key. Take a shower if you want."

* * * *

The bathroom was crammed with a huge pack of diapers, a diaper pail, baby wipes, baby shampoo, and the like. Amy had a bitter taste in her mouth that brushing her teeth didn't quell. She couldn't find a clean washcloth, so she used her hands like in the locker room shower at school. She found the family hair dryer her mom had walked off with. At the mirror, she watched her hair whip around like a flag in the wind.

Without Deb and Liam, the apartment was too quiet. Amy sat thinking of her dad, drained of talk since all the yelling that went with the Big Blowup. Always a neat freak, he had gotten crazy about housekeeping. Dishes had to be washed after every meal, beds made every morning. On Saturdays, Amy couldn't go have fun with her friends until she dusted every surface and object while he wielded the vacuum like a weapon. She came to loathe the droning that penetrated their double-wide's walls.

Deb's apartment hadn't been cleaned in ages. Clothes cluttered the unmade bed, dishes and baby bottles crowded the kitchen sink. Amy got busy setting things right.

The day wore on. From her backpack, Amy took the latest letter from her mom, the one with a return address. Before that, Deb had announced that "we" are in Fort Collins, "we" have a baby, "we" named him Liam. But in this letter, no "we" was mentioned. "I'm weaning Liam so I can get a job," Deb had written. "I miss you, Baby Doll." That last sentence prompted Amy to buy a bus ticket with the cash she earned doing laundry and baking cookies for RVers with rigs as big as houses. Some tipped so generously, she had taxi money, too. Now it occurred to her that her mom hadn't asked about the long trip. Deb had lost her sense of curiosity like a person who had lost her sight.

Zipping up her flannel hoodie, Amy went outside. On a stone wall, a gray squirrel sat rubbing its front paws together. It was nearly twice the size of the ground squirrels living in the rocky crevices around the lake. The animal ran toward her and gave her a brazen stare. What did it want? Was it rabid?

"I won't feed you. Shoo!" She bared her teeth, stamped her feet. The squirrel turned, its tail rippling, and jumped into a leafless tree next to the house.

Dense clouds filled the sky. Amy shivered but loathed to go back inside the apartment. She set off walking past big houses, most cut up into apartments, judging by the number of mailboxes. On Google Earth, she had seen that her mom's place was near Colorado State University. A strange neighborhood for Deb to choose; she never even completed her GED.

Amy turned a corner and followed a busier street to an IHOP across from a line of university buildings. She took a booth by a window, ordered a hot chocolate, and watched the pedestrians, a lot of them toting backpacks, a few pushing bicycles. Amy asked a waitress why they weren't riding. "No bikes allowed on College Avenue. You've got to dismount."

The middle-aged waitress resembled many of the mothers of Amy's friends. It used to be fun hearing people say how young her own mom looked, how the two of them could have been sisters. Now she wished her mom was more like this woman—heavy and plain. Maybe then Deb wouldn't have had a wild affair.

Like a homeless person, Amy huddled in the booth killing time. A skin formed on the top of her drink while she closed her eyes and pictured her friends on Spring Break. The reservoir was a manmade wonder in the desert. The water was still too cold for swimming, but not for jet skiing in wetsuits and partying on the beaches. Her dad might have taken her fishing if he ever got over his slump.

Amy opened her eyes, then popped them wide. Snowflakes drifted from the gray sky. People passing the IHOP were moving faster than before.

At the cash register, Amy asked if snow in March was normal.

The waitress laughed. "Snow, rain, whatever the Good Lord sends us."

Amy flipped up her hood and headed for Deb's street. The sidewalks were slippery, but a slow jog was possible. Up ahead, an unfamiliar white apartment house sat on a corner. She was going the wrong way! Whimpering, she retraced her steps.

* * * *

As she finally reached the rose-brick house, the cute guy rolled up on his bike, grocery bags dangling from the handlebars.

"Can I help you get those upstairs?" she asked.

"Yeah, that'd be great. I'm Tim, by the way."

"Amy."

He locked the bike in view of three fat squirrels watching from the tree's snow-covered branches.

"Don't those rodents give you the creeps?" Amy said it seriously, but he grinned and handed her one of the bags.

"You don't like squirrels?" he asked.

"Not hardly. Creepy things!"

"Ignore them. They're harmless."

At the top of the steps, he shook the snow off his ski jacket. "You look like a wet kitten in that hoodie. Want to come in for a coffee?"

"I shouldn't," Amy blurted. "Anyway, I just came from the IHOP."

He took the grocery bag out of her hand. "I see."

Of course you do. Amy dropped her gaze to her damp ballet flats.

"It's good to be wary," he said. "You know how to look out for yourself. You a ping-pong kid like I was?"

"A what?"

"You know, a kid who bounces back and forth between their parents. No offense. I did it for years. Both my parents remarried and had other kids."

"Mom wasn't supposed to be able to get pregnant again. Sorry, TMI."

"It's okay." He shifted the grocery bags, unlocked his door. "You have to talk to somebody."

"Did you ever see him?" Amy asked. "Mom's boyfriend, before he left?"

"A few years younger than her?"

"Yeah, and a lot younger than my dad. Taller, too." As soon as she said it, she felt disloyal. "Not that my dad's short."

"Right." Tim said. "Well, thanks for the help with the bag."

In the apartment, an image of her dad's receding hairline jumped to mind. She scrolled through pictures on her phone until she came to family selfies that made her dad, mom, and herself appear deliriously happy. There was only one new message, a text from Sonya, her best friend. Amy replied, lying through her teeth: "with mom & liam. so much fun! hv2go".

She took off her hoodie and attempted to blow-dry it in the bathroom. What else did she have to do with her time?

* * * *

After dark, Deb called to say she needed to pull a double shift because somebody went home sick. There might be some microwave meals in the freezer, she added, sounding so rushed that Amy let her go without a word of protest. But jabbing at a layer of frost to extract a chicken pot pie, Amy felt a ball of anger grow in her stomach. She slammed the freezer door, no longer hungry. The fantasy that had sustained her through the long bus ride was ridiculous: showing up to her mom's warm welcome, shopping together, decorating a new bedroom. But there was no spare room for her here; the baby didn't even have a crib.

Amy pulled an ugly chenille bedspread off Deb's bed. She wrapped up in it on the couch, thinking about her room at home with her laptop, her desert rock collection, the curtains her mom had made. She wondered if Deb, who had fled with only two packed bags, ever longed for her sewing machine or the entire life she had ditched.

The city's night noises were nothing like at the KOA; the street traffic never ceased. Police or ambulance sirens set off the neighborhood dogs. Voices of people out on a Saturday drifted up, along with someone's persistent drumming. Amy dozed off but woke to the thump of footsteps on the stairs. Tim, she assumed, home from a date with a girl who wasn't still in high school.

* * * *

When Amy woke again, Deb still wasn't back. The apartment felt chilly. Amy hadn't thought to bring pajamas or slippers, so she had slept in a T-shirt, her leggings, and socks. She shoved her feet into her flats and hoped she wasn't getting a cold. City noises droned on below, but other sounds—faint ones above her head—caught her attention. Something was in the attic; she was sure of it. Those nasty squirrels had gotten in, easy-peasy from the tree close to the house. At the KOA, it was a constant battle to keep all sorts of critters at bay, from snakes to coyotes. You couldn't put up with wildlife invaders.

Another sound overhead, louder this time, made her double sure she wasn't imagining things. She had to investigate, wouldn't be able to go back to sleep until she did. Would the attic be dark? Of course, but she could handle that; in her backpack she kept a flashlight for emergencies.

Amy eased open the apartment door and gasped. Tim, in his own doorway, almost scared the bejesus out of her. He flipped a switch to light the landing and stairwell.

"You heard it too?" she whispered. "Squirrels?"

"Something, all right." He motioned with his chin to the loop of rope above their heads. "Stand back."

Tim pulled the rope, and a ladder dropped to floor level. Amy handed him the flashlight and was rewarded with a look of admiration. He closed his fingers over the end so only a pencil-width of beam showed. He climbed the few rungs, stuck his head into the attic. "What the …?"

Amy leaped out of the way as Tim crashed down, followed by another guy, his back to the ladder. Tim yelped like a hurt dog as the other guy stepped on him and blasted down the stairs.

"Hey! Stop!" Tim yelled. But the guy was out the door and gone.

Tim groaned and picked himself up from the landing floor.

"Are you okay?" Amy asked.

"I'm fine. You know who that was? I sure do."

"Mom's ex-boyfriend. Liam's got his eyes."

"What was he doing up there? I'm taking a look."

Amy climbed up behind him, but he made her stop with only her head poking into the attic. Tim waved the flashlight around, revealing slanted ceiling beams, rough floorboards, a pair of khaki duffle bags, a backpack.

"Those are my mom's duffle bags," Amy said. "We used them for camping."

She took another step, but Tim told her to stay put. "Amy, what about this backpack?"

"Maybe it's Mom's, I don't know."

Tim unzipped it. "It's full of college books. Math mostly. And here are more backpacks. They've got books in them too."

Near the backpacks were half a dozen men's wallets, some leather, some fabric. "Hold the flashlight. Aim it here," Tim said, handing it to her.

He opened the wallets, one after another. They were all empty, except for one splayed open on the floor with cash and plastic cards inside. "Is your mom's boyfriend's name Dwayne? A CSU student?"

"Ex-boyfriend. No, it's Kyle."

"I'm calling the cops. Your mom home?"

Amy shook her head. "At work."

"Call her, okay?"

* * * *

Deb wasn't pleased to get Amy's call. "It'll be a while. The boss won't like me leaving early."

The last time Amy needed urgent help from her mom came to mind in all its horrible, vivid detail. Amy had felt sick at school and got permission to walk over to the restaurant where Deb was nearing the end of her shift, to get a ride home. As Amy opened the door, she saw Deb pouring coffee for some guy who was stroking her thigh. Amy thought her mom would slug him, but she leaned over and gave him a quick kiss. Amy backed out of the restaurant and threw up in the parking lot. As she wiped her face, the guy came out, gazed right through her, and strolled off. She wandered the streets until it was time to catch the school bus. She never told anyone what she had seen.

* * * *

Amy shut the drapes between the living room and the rest of the apartment. No reason for the cops to see every bit of the pathetic place.

Eventually, two uniformed officers, a stocky man and a young woman, showed up. Tim gave a statement to the male officer, who peered into the attic and said the obviously-stolen items would be taken for evidence. The female officer waited with Amy on the stairs until Deb, with a sleepy Liam in her arms, arrived. Deb shot Amy a sour look and let the officer in. Amy sat with her mom and Liam on the couch. The officer perched on the edge of the camp chair and wrote in a notebook.

"You sure it was Kyle?" Deb asked Amy. She gave Liam a bounce. "Blue eyes like these?"

"Identical, Mom."

"It's clear the man is a thief," the officer said. She shifted uncomfortably in the chair and stood back up.

Deb fooled with a strand of hair that had escaped from her bun. "I thought Kyle was long gone. I had no idea he was stashing stuff up there. He put my luggage in the attic, so he knew about it."

"Staying there too, maybe," Amy said. "There's a sleeping bag on the floor."

The officer determined that Kyle was Liam's father but not Amy's. She asked if all three of them resided in the apartment.

"Amy lives with her dad in New Mexico. She's only here for a visit."

Liam fussed in Deb's arms. "I can take a shot at holding him, Mom," Amy said. She was surprised by the sturdiness of his small body, didn't mind when he grabbed her nose.

Deb told the officer she hadn't seen Kyle in weeks, that he might have gone to live with an older brother, that she didn't have the brother's address.

"We'll find him," the officer said. "I doubt if he'll come back here. But call me if he does." She handed Deb a card.

"Do you need to take my fingerprints?" Amy asked.

"Did you go into the attic or touch anything up there?"

"No. Well, maybe my mom's two bags. In the past, not tonight."

The officer pocketed her notebook. "Then I think we have all we need from you."

* * * *

Watching Deb change Liam's diaper, Amy made a mental note not to have kids until she was thirty. While the baby slept, Deb and Amy ate Cheerios in the kitchen.

Deb put her spoon down and grinned. "You really thought it was squirrels?"

Amy didn't mind her mom's teasing tone. "You never heard that noise?"

"Kyle must have snuck in when he saw my car gone. Lucky I didn't marry him. Never substitute sex for brains, Baby Doll."

"Mom, could you stop calling me that? And why not come home? Dad misses you."

"Nah, that would never work."

Amy knew her mom was right. Her dad never would never forgive Deb for having another man's child.

"Mom, did you know Kyle was a thief?"

Deb's eyes shifted to the side. "I saw him tell a cashier that he gave her a twenty when he knew full well it was a ten. And he light-fingered snacks from convenience stores. But what I couldn't tolerate was that he had no love for little Liam. Your dad adored you from the second you were born."

* * * *

Amy spent the night on the couch, her thoughts churning. She had gotten what she came for: to find out if her mom was free of that loser and if the baby was for real. With Liam, her family no longer fit into a single selfie; it would take a connect-the-dots picture from now on.

Before daylight, while Deb and Liam were dead to the world, Amy checked the bus schedule on her phone, called a taxi, and texted her dad. She made herself a peanut butter sandwich and wrote a note: "C U later, Mom. Luv U both!" She signed it with a capital A encircled by a heart, put all her spare cash on the table, and added, "$$$ 4 a crib." She considered leaving a note on Tim's door but couldn't think of what to say.

The ground outside the house was frosted with snow. Squirrels hidden in the dark tree didn't make a sound or show themselves. By the time the taxi arrived, Amy was as frozen as a popsicle.

Beyond Fort Collins, the bus merged with the southbound highway traffic, and Amy let herself nod off. The next thing she knew, she was back in New Mexico: cotton candy clouds floated in the sky, and the sun was out.

GOOD NEIGHBORS

by Cori Lynn Arnold

The Paulsons walked into my apartment rental office late on a Thursday evening. I was busy half watching *Murphy Brown* and studying for my final exams. Normally, the office was closed by six, but I'd forgotten to turn the sign around and lock the door.

"Pretty unusual," the wife, Lisa, said.

I looked up from their application form. "What is?"

"A woman super."

"Women's lib, you know. It's not all about burning the bras."

Lisa smiled at me, and her husband Kevin looked like he was blushing under his heavily tanned face.

She didn't look like a Lisa to me, maybe a Gina or Tracy. Neither looked like a "Paulson" either. Their application form said they'd moved here, to rural Pennsylvania, from Miami, Florida. With his tan, muscles, and scars, Kevin, I figured, worked a blue-collar job, probably construction. His crooked eyetooth didn't show until he bit his lower lip.

"It'll be tough getting used to the weather up here," I said.

Lisa opened her mouth to make a comment, but Kevin's hand on her lap stopped her on the first syllable.

"I don't see the phone number from your last apartment complex."

"I forgot to write it down," Lisa said with a shrug.

I'd need to look it up, which would cost me in long distance charges. The phone in the office was local only. I pursed my lips together. Ralph left it up to me to do the background checks, and I could be as lazy as I chose.

The apartment next to my suite was vacant. Leaving it empty buffered me from the rest of the tenants, but renting it out would provide a cushion in my budget for other projects.

The walls were thin. I didn't want a tenant with late-night party habits, loud music, or screaming children. This couple was in their fifties, according to the paperwork. The probability was low they'd keep odd hours.

"It's 221," I said. "Up the stairs and second to last on the left. Go check it out. If you like it, the first, last, and security deposit will come to $650." I pointed out the window, as most of the apartment doors could be seen from my office.

He nodded, taking the keys. "Thank you."

I still had aspirations of running a business in the city, so I spent most of my evenings and early mornings studying. But the Paulsons were perfect tenants and neighbors. First, and most importantly, they paid their rent on time, every month. They were quiet, friendly. Lisa tended to a pot of cherry tomatoes on their back deck. She would pick them and hand them over to me across the two-foot divide, and I'd eat them right there. They were warm and tasted like fresh sunshine. Her pot of basil reminded me of the best of my grandmother's marinara sauce, not like the bland jars you get at the grocery store. Kevin worked on his car but didn't leave an oil stain in the parking lot like the muscle head in 114. At Christmas, they sent me a bottle of wine—Italian—and spicy, sugar-powdered cookies.

A year or so after they moved in, Kevin helped me out with a guy beating his wife. I called the police, but after five minutes they hadn't arrived, and I felt compelled to step in. My yelling and threatening had little effect, but Kevin, who hadn't said much, had made an impact with his menacing look. The man turned near white and took off running.

I'm not saying Kevin was a big guy or anything. It was something in his steely-eyed stare that made the man want to move along.

With the sirens wailing down the street, Kevin turned to me. "Leave me out of it," he said. "Okay?"

I nodded. I couldn't blame him. The only reason I'd stuck around was to make sure the guy didn't break anything else, including his wife.

The sheriff's deputy, Bordwin, came again two months later to evict her. I didn't want to do it, but I had a business to maintain. I tried to finagle some money out of old Ralph, the owner, to buy one of those new facsimile machines and a service for better background checks, but he wouldn't go for it. I spent more the last year on parts and maintenance for the fifteen washing machines than if I'd purchased a fleet of new ones, but pointing this out only made Ralph angry.

Several evictions, and a dozen medical emergencies later, I knew most of the deputies by name. But the man that arrived at my office door one summer morning wasn't a sheriff's deputy. His red hair fluttered in the wind, giving way to a losing battle with his hairline. His shirt had distinct yellowed armpit stains.

"Woman super?" he said.

"We've been to outer space. I think I can handle a small apartment building."

He held up his badge. It read: FBI, Field Agent Lee Clayden. I'd never seen an FBI badge, so I couldn't tell if it was real or not, but it had the ring of authority, even if Lee Clayden looked more like a door to door vacuum salesman. "I need to talk to you about a couple of your tenants." His eyes shifted toward the parking lot as though I might blow his cover.

I led him through to the inner office. The agent eased himself into the uncomfortable chair across from my desk. "My back isn't what it used to be," he said.

"Too much sitting?"

"Exactly, which is why I got out from behind the desk to take down a man of such importance."

I did a mental inventory, trying to determine who the man of importance might be, but in the end, I just asked, "Which tenant are we talking about?"

He pulled out a piece of paper from his blazer's inner pocket. "Number seven on America's most wanted list."

I raised my eyebrows, looking at the picture over my bright blue plastic frame glasses. The word "Wanted" filled the upper third of the picture and under that a couple, a man on the left, a woman on the right. The man on the wanted poster didn't look familiar at first glance. Details were lost in transmission.

"It's an older picture," he said. "And a fax copy."

I stared hard at the woman in the picture. Something about her deadpan stare and downturned smile reminded me of Lisa when she'd been angry with one of the maintenance men in her apartment. After looking back at the man, I could see the glint of Kevin's eyes. Even his crooked-tooth smile.

I put the paper on the desk and pushed back my chair. The name, James D'Angelo, aka Jimmy the Dentist, was famous in New York and most of the Eastern Seaboard. The headlines of his disappearance years ago had graced the newspaper headlines even down here in Pennsylvania. He'd been an enforcer for the mob. And he was connected to no less than fifteen deaths in the Fifties. His nickname came from his early hits where he'd knocked the teeth out of three men with his bare hands to send a message, "Talking is deadly." All three men had snitched to police.

I looked out the window and stared at apartment 221. "Are you sure it's him?"

"No," he said flatly. "What do you know about them?"

"Lisa," I said and stopped myself, looking down at the paper. I laughed. Her real name was *Gina*. "She keeps to herself. She gardens. I've never had a problem at all with either of them. They pay the rent on time." I shrugged. "He helped me out a few times with an unruly tenant."

He nodded as though most of the men on the Most Wanted list lived quiet lives, the impression *America's Most Wanted* tried to make every week. "Look, we need you to help us lure him out of the apartment. Safer that way."

"Lure him out?"

"Yes, I have a crew of guys about a quarter mile away. I didn't want to spook them. You haven't seen any guns, have you?"

"Guns?" I searched my mind, but I'd never seen Kevin with any guns. The maintenance work in their apartment was always scheduled enough ahead of time for them to spirit away any contraband, but that was hardly a reason to say they had a fortress up there. "No, I haven't."

"It's not his MO, but we need to be careful. I want to get him out in the open and move on both of them at the same time."

I nodded.

"You mind if I smoke?"

"Yes, actually," I said. "What do you have in mind?"

He looked down at his cigarette as if I were asking him what else he might do with it.

"I mean, to help you lure out Kevin."

"His car," he said. "You'll call up to his apartment and tell him that another tenant backed into his car."

I nodded. The idea seemed feasible. It's not like the FBI asked me to do a citizen's arrest. "Right now?" I put my hand on the phone, but Lee put his hand on top of mine.

"I need you to sit tight for fifteen minutes or so while we get everyone into position."

I looked at my watch. It was a quarter till six. Lisa and Kevin—not Gina or Jimmy "The Dentist"—would be settling down to their meal. I'd heard them most nights eating quietly while the television played *Dallas* or reruns of *M*A*S*H*.

I nodded. He spent a couple of minutes detailing the plan, which was incredibly simple, and then left. All I had to do was call Kevin on the phone to tell him his car had been backed into by one of the other tenants. I'd tell him I was meeting him outside as the tenant didn't want to involve the police, and certainly Kevin wouldn't either.

It all sounded so logical when Lee explained it, but with almost fifteen minutes of practicing my lines, I realized the loophole in the logic.

Under a normal situation, I would probably walk up to his apartment and talk to Kevin, not walk all the way back to my office, and call him down.

Even worse, under the current plan, Kevin would be caught, and the FBI would lead him and Lisa to the jailhouse. It wouldn't take him too long to figure out I was the one that set him up. In this scenario, he'd spend his days seeking revenge against me.

I put my hand up to my perfect teeth. I thought about the hours spent in the orthodontic chair, and the years with my smile hidden behind metal brackets. On the other hand, if the Paulsons got away, the revenge would be swift.

My knees weakened, and I grabbed for the corner of the desk before I hit the floor. I blamed my near fainting spell on the heat, but I'd known deep down I was afraid to get involved. I could easily have said no to Lee Clayden, but it was too far past that point. The first domino had already been pushed. I'd need to follow this through.

Five unmarked black sedans pulled into the parking lot, one at a time. The first two pulled into the front of the building, then one to the side, and another two rounded the corner toward the back.

My hands shook as the seconds counted down to the exact minute Lee told me to call the Paulsons.

Lisa picked up on the first ring. Her sweet voice echoed in my mind across the parking lot. I dared not to look out the window.

"Lisa? This is Wendy."

"Hi, Wendy. What can I do you for?"

I bit my lip. This was the do or die moment. The moment that, if I were lucky, I'd play, and replay in my mind for years. "Another tenant, a new guy, accidentally backed into your car. I was wondering if Kevin could meet me outside. The guy wants to take care of it quietly, not get the police involved."

Without a word, she put her hand over the receiver. The line went quiet. All I could hear was the whooshing sound in my ears. In my mind, the jig was up. Kevin would bunker down, guns blazing. I'd be responsible for the "Whispering Pines Apartment Complex Massacre."

Then just as quickly she was back on the line. "He says he'll meet you out there in five minutes. He's got to get his pants on."

"Okay," I said through my dry mouth. I crouched down to the floor and braced myself for the next six minutes. Every creak and groan of the trees rustling in the wind made me jump anticipating the crack of gunfire.

But the rest went as Field Agent Lee Clayden had surmised. Kevin met not me, but a dressed down agent at his car. After a quick confirmation of his identity, he arrested Kevin on the spot. Meanwhile, Lee knocked on Lisa's door and arrested her. They'd been tucked into separate sedans and led back to Philadelphia.

* * * *

For the next few months, I jumped at every noise and looked over my shoulder through every side alley and shadowy figure on the street. I flunked two of the three classes I'd taken that semester. I contemplated leaving my job and changing my name, but then the letter arrived.

My name, Wendy Underman, was scrawled in handwriting similar to an elementary school child learning to write in cursive for the first time. The return address was Leavenworth Penitentiary care of James D'Angelo. I read through it the first time as quickly as I could. He'd put the pieces together for his arrest, but didn't blame me for getting him caught. The trial, it seems, featured a career snitch that just happened to pull through town and spotted James. "Luck of the draw," he said.

He asked about my classes, and when I'd be getting my degree. He asked after Gina's tomatoes.

I read it through a few more times over the next day. I breathed a little deeper. I slept a lot better. I sat down with the last bottle of wine the Paulsons had given me and wrote my return letter.

Gina's tomatoes and basil were adopted by the couple in 129 with the baby. I told him the last semester was rough, but that I'd be graduating by the following Christmas.

We became pen pals over the course of the next year. He was the first person I told about my new boyfriend, and he told me how proud he was when I graduated from business school and opened the accounting business.

About a week after opening my doors, Gina walked in with a baseball bat. I ran, but she caught me by my flowing blouse. She gave me three quick, painful blows to my legs—thankfully not my teeth.

"We've come a long way, baby," she said as she stood over me. I crawled my way to the phone and called the ambulance. The police asked me what happened, but I said nothing.

In my mailbox that night was a new letter from Kevin. Gina got out for good behavior, he said.

DEAD GIVEAWAY

by Chelle Martin

"If you want anything, just take it," my sister Jen said.

I stroked the softness of the cashmere dress as if it were an Angora kitten. The fabric was heavenly, nicer than anything I'd ever owned. I held my breath as I checked the label. It was my size! I folded it neatly and placed it on the edge of Jen's king-size bed, and continued to rummage through the rest of the pile. A Chanel suit, a Halston skirt, an Yves St. Laurent blouse, a pair of Versace trousers, and two Lily Pulitzer dresses, all like new.

"Where did you get this?" I asked, not bothering to hide my excitement. "Did you win the lottery?"

Jen laughed. "Hardly. I was at an estate sale looking for antiques when a woman approached me and asked if I'd like some clothing." She shrugged her shoulders. "Who was I to say no?"

I looked at her in her customary wardrobe of designer-ripped jeans and boho top. My sister, the fashion-plate. I could see why the woman might take her as being needy.

I folded a few more items for my pile. "Don't you want anything?" I asked her. "These are all our size or close to it. Now we can really be fifty and fab."

"Nah, I thought it was more your thing. You're always thumbing through *Harper's Bazaar* and *Architectural Digest* when we go to Barnes & Noble. I have a Gucci handbag and one pair of Louboutins here, too," she said, reaching for another bag. "Now you can be Cinderella."

"Without the castle," I said. "Unless the woman is throwing in the house?"

Jen laughed. "Don't push it. But you should go see it, Kayla. There's an open house tomorrow. You'll love it."

* * * *

I pulled my Hyundai up to a mailbox with a big 23 on it. Brightly colored balloons danced from a string tied to a sign for Holiday Realty.

I turned into the long winding driveway. Either side was lined with immaculately trimmed hollies. I parked in a circular drive behind a Mercedes, a Bentley, and a BMW convertible.

The sprawling stucco and stone home reminded me of a French chateau. Judging by the brick chimneys gracing the slate roof, the place had at least three fireplaces. My dream home.

I grabbed my purse from the seat, stepped from my car, and straightened the hem on my newly acquired Lily Pulitzer dress, which fit like it was made for me. I teetered up the front steps on my Louboutins, hoping I wouldn't fall off the four-inch shoes, which were a far cry from the comfort of my everyday Skechers. I walked across the flagstone porch to oversized polished oak double doors. I was about to ring the bell when the door opened, revealing two women. The first, whom I presumed to be the realtor, assured the second woman that she could be reached anytime and not to hesitate to call if needed.

"I'll definitely be in touch," the prospective buyer said. "I know Henry will love this house. It's exactly what we've been looking for."

We exchanged smiles as she held the door for me. The moment I stepped inside the foyer, I struggled to keep myself from crying out in awe at the expansive double staircase, the marble columns, Italian tile, and exquisitely hand carved moldings that teased my senses like a fine Bordeaux at a wine tasting.

"I'm Charlotte Rothschild, and I'm very pleased to make your acquaintance," the realtor said. "Welcome to Holly Brook," she added. "Feel free to look around, but I must inform you, I already have several parties interested in this very prestigious home."

I thanked her and made my way through the foyer into a very large and impressive dining room with a Waterford chandelier, one of many I'd see on my self-guided tour. I could have fit the downstairs of my modest Cape Cod into the master bedroom.

"Marvelous, isn't it?"

"Indeed," I said, sounding very British. One too many episodes of Downton Abbey, I presumed. But this woman would never see me again, so why not have some fun? Continuing to sound like a royal, I said, "It reminds me a tad of my cousin's place in the Hamptons. Without the beach," I joked.

Charlotte laughed along with me, until a man and woman appeared at her side.

"Oh, Joan and Rich, now these are Hamptons people if ever there were any!" she said.

Rich extended a hand to me. "You've a place there?"

"My cousin does."

"And who might that be?" his wife asked. "We know practically everyone."

I thought of the most snobbish name I knew. "Elsbeth Smythe," I said. My neighbor's tabby cat. Once I got on a good roll, there was no stopping me.

Joan scrunched her nose up in deep thought. "Yes, I think perhaps I ran into her at our garden club gathering last year."

I looked at my watch and invented an excuse to escape. "Speaking of garden clubs, I nearly forgot about a meeting I have with my landscaper today." Little Tommy, the kid who mows my lawn, liked to get paid the same day. Otherwise, the work started to look a little shoddy.

Charlotte brought the conversation back to business and asked my thoughts on the house.

I tried to sound non-committal. "Oh, it's quite charming, but I have a few others to see."

Joan said, "You actually look familiar. Are you a member of Forsgate?"

She was referring to a very prestigious golf club. I couldn't afford to buy a set of clubs, let alone a membership. "I'm afraid not," I said, "I'm not from the area."

"Oh, what a shame," Joan said. "I know you'd enjoy it."

I indicated the time again as I stepped past the three of them. I made it as far as the front door, when Joan called out. "Wait a minute, dear!"

I froze with my hand on the beautiful brass handle. "If you aren't busy next Saturday, Rich and I are having a little social at the Forsgate. Golf for the men, tea for the ladies. I could introduce you around. If you plan on buying a house in the area, you'll need some new friends."

"Well …."

"You don't have any plans, do you?"

My mind raced for a plausible reason to refuse, but my years of yearning to see the inside of Forsgate won out. "Nnnnoooo."

"Well, it's settled then," she said, and insisted we exchange phone numbers. Once more, I teetered carefully down the steps and hurried to my car. When I beeped the remote, Joan called out to me, "I can give you the number for a better car rental service."

I waved as I got into my coach, which had turned into a pumpkin way before midnight.

When I pulled into my driveway, Tommy was finishing up my lawn. "I'll run inside and get your money," I said. He probably wondered why I didn't just open my purse then and there, but truthfully, it only contained a single credit card, which I'd used to buy gas on my way to Holly Brook.

I left the door ajar while I went to retrieve the money. When I returned, Tommy was waiting on the front porch, looking at an unlit joint, while talking on his cell phone. "Dude, I wish I could help you out, but I have no way to pick up the other stuff. I got about twenty grams of weed left. That's it."

Seriously? When did little Tommy from the neighborhood start peddling pot? The kid's two siblings were honor students, one a star athlete. I sighed, grateful I didn't have children. I paused at the door while he continued talking.

"Yeah, ask around. This could be like ... major money."

Tommy turned abruptly and saw me standing there. He quickly flipped his phone closed without saying goodbye to his little friend.

"So," I said, not bothering to hide the fact I had been eavesdropping, "business a little slow?"

He put both hands in his back pockets, attempting to hide the phone and the joint.

"I don't get as many lawns as I used to," he confessed.

"I was talking about your side business," I said, handing him his lawn money. "If you need money, why not just ask your parents for a raise in your allowance?"

Tommy looked at me like I used to look at adults when I was his age and they said something incredibly stupid.

"My dad got laid off. My mom's sick and can't work." He shrugged. "I mean, pot's like legal in some states, so it's no big deal."

"Well, just be careful," I said. "You're a good kid."

* * * *

I debated on having Jen drop me at Forsgate for Joan and Rich Huffington's soiree, but decided to keep the whole thing, as they say, "under my hat" for now. As I handed the parking attendant the keys for my Hyundai, I tried to pretend it was a Rolls. After all, it's all in the attitude, isn't it?

Waiters were milling about with champagne and hors d'oeuvres, and I gratefully accepted a flute while I went in search of my hosts. I found Joan chatting with a bunch of ladies beneath a large canopy.

My hostess stood and extended her hand. "Kayla, I'm so glad you could make it. I was just telling my friends about you. You never did say where you were from with that lovely accent of yours."

I shook hands all around. "England," I said.

The ladies laughed. "We figured as much, dear, but what part?"

I thought of Hyacinth Bucket on *Keeping Up Appearances*. Which seemed to be particularly fitting for my current situation. Thank goodness I liked Britcoms.

"Yorkshire?" I said.

The ladies laughed again, and one said, "Are you asking us or telling us?"

"It's actually been four decades since I've been there. We came to the States when I was a child."

"It's amazing that you never lost your accent," another said.

I smiled and sipped my champagne. Conversation quickly changed to the topics of politics, the husbands' love of golf, finding good help (I thought that was just in the movies), and favorite vacation spots. I found myself joining in and thoroughly enjoying my charade. After a delicious dinner of lobster tails and filet mignon, I thanked Joan profusely for her generosity. I had finally been to the inner sanctum of Forsgate and now it, along with Joan and her society friends, would all be a fond memory.

While the party was still underway, I handed my ticket to the valet to retrieve my car. As he went to bring it around, Joan found me waiting. "Kayla! I'm glad I caught you. Gillian is having a fundraiser for underprivileged children. I thought maybe you'd like to volunteer. Here is her address," she said, handing me the information. "Next Saturday, if you have no plans. I do hope you can join us. The girls really like you."

I smiled and thanked her again as the valet pulled up with my car. "Oh, dear," Joan said. "I see you have that same vehicle. I thought it was a rental, but I guess you're one of those mileage conscious people?"

That happened to be one of the reasons I'd bought my car. The other was my budget. But I'm sure there were wealthy people who cared about the environment. I could be honest about my car, couldn't I? "A friend loaned it to me after my Jaguar was totaled. She's so sweet, I just couldn't insult her and say no."

"Well, there's a wonderful Mercedes dealer that's local. We've bought all of our cars there. I could introduce you to the owner. You do like Mercedes?"

"Who doesn't?" I said, before slipping inside. The valet closed the door and I was on my way back to reality.

* * * *

I sat on my porch drinking a Budweiser while contemplating the vast difference in Gillian's and Joan's homes and my neighborhood. I couldn't resist Joan's invitation to help with the fundraiser, but I'd sworn it would be the last time I would mingle with the upper crust.

That was three events ago. I had to admit I was hooked on the good life, even if it was just a carrot being dangled in front of me. I was even known as "Kayla, the Brit" in their social circle. I liked the sound of it.

Tommy rode up on his bicycle and deposited it against my garage, which I'd left open in anticipation of his arrival. "Hey, Ms. Rivers," he said.

"Hey, Tommy. How's business?" I asked, shielding my eyes from the sun.

He shrugged. "You know. Could be better." He turned to go and get the lawnmower.

"Tommy," I said, "just out of curiosity, how much more money could you make?"

For a minute, he seemed puzzled by my question, then I saw the light bulb register. "Oh, uh, I dunno. Just … lots."

I had a pad and pen with me. I asked Tommy to sit and tell me what he paid for the pot, what he sold it for, how many customers he had. I added numbers, multiplied, added some more.

"If you could increase business by 75 percent, this is what you could make," I said, showing him my calculations. His eyes bugged out like a Pug's.

"That would be really cool, but like I said, I'd need a ride to get the stuff. He sells in bulk."

I had given this a lot of thought, this potential money-making venture. I was running out of designer outfits, and I barely made the mortgage on my salary as a fitness instructor at the local gym. I needed a steady supply of disposable income, even if just to indulge my high-society fantasy for a while longer.

I made Tommy an offer. I'd drive him to this would-be distributor, and we'd split the proceeds 60/40. The kid tried his best to negotiate for a higher percentage, but without my wheels, he would be stuck mowing lawns right through college, if he was lucky enough to be accepted.

We shook hands on our new deal. Tommy went to mow the lawn, while I went inside and booted up my laptop to the Neiman Marcus website.

* * * *

Several weeks later, Tommy and I were counting our profits at my kitchen table. I hadn't had too much guilt about the pot since, as Tommy pointed out, it was legal in some states. But we'd gone on to expand our inventory a bit with more serious narcotics, and I wasn't thrilled with that idea. Our dealer, Benny the Buzz, had insisted "we expand our horizons" to get the best deals he could offer, so what could we do? There wasn't a lot of room to negotiate with thugs.

We were just done divvying up the loot when my cell phone rang.

"Yeah?" I said, rather distractedly.

"Pardon? I'm looking for Kayla. Do I have a wrong number?"

"Oh, I'm terribly sorry, dear," I said to Joan. Tommy had not met Kayla the Brit, so imagine the look on his face as I continued on.

"Yes, I've missed the ladies, but I've been holed up with a terrible cold," I said, now trying to add a sniffle to my accent. "Are there any new social engagements on the calendar?"

"As a matter of fact, that's why I'm calling," Joan said. "I was hoping I could count on you to be a benefactor for a new hospital wing my husband is proposing in honor of his mother, a breast cancer survivor. The woman just turned 94."

"My aunt is also a breast cancer survivor! We do a pink party every year. Everyone invited dresses in pink, with pink mani-pedis and pink streaks in their hair. We make pink cakes and cookies and serve pink lemonade." It felt so good to share an honest moment with Joan. Cancer didn't discriminate by income.

"Just a small donation, ten or twenty, would do."

"Don't be silly, Joan." I looked at the large stacks of bills sitting on my table. "I can do fifty dollars. It's the least I can do for such good friends as you and Rich."

Joan laughed. "Oh, you Brits have such a droll sense of humor. I'll put you down for fifty then."

I could hear papers rustling, then she was back on the line. "Okay, here we go. Kayla Rivers, fifty thousand dollars. We're lunching at The Mill this Wednesday. If you could drop by with the check, I'd appreciate it."

I hadn't heard anything Joan had said after the word thousand.

"Joan, I'm sorry …." *I thought you meant dollars, not thousands.* A police siren wailed in the distance. For a minute, I imagined him showing up at my door. My head swirled and a knot formed in the pit of my stomach.

"Yes?"

"I'm sorry, but I have to go. Someone's at the door." We exchanged goodbyes and I hung up the phone. I looked at Tommy and wondered how I was going to ask a fifteen year old if I could have a raise in my allowance this week.

* * * *

It hadn't dawned on me until later that night that presenting Joan a check wouldn't work. My address was printed on the checks and she would be alarmed if I told her I was residing in this neighborhood. There was no plausible explanation as to why I'd be living here unless I was going undercover to see how "the other half lived." And even if I could give her a check, I'd have to deposit a very large sum of cash, which would rouse suspicion at the bank. The same went for a money order. People just don't walk up to a teller with wads of money. Was a gift of cash considered tacky?

I wondered how Benny the Buzz dealt with such matters. Did I have to get into money laundering next? With a teenage accomplice? Where was my fairy godmother when I needed her?

The house phone rang and I jumped. It was Jen. "It's so good to hear a friendly voice."

"Why? What's going on? Are you in trouble?"

"No!" I said a bit too strongly. "No, I'm just tired. Lots of lunkheads at Pi-Yo class this week. Want to come over for coffee?"

"At this hour?"

"It's only nine."

"We never have coffee at nine. I know you're in trouble. I'll be right there."

A short while later, my sister sat across from me, and I got her up to speed with my adventures with the high society ladies.

"They really are a nice bunch of women, Jen," I said.

"Kayla, you can't keep this up forever. I'm surprised you haven't run out of outfits."

"Oh, I did, several events ago. But I managed to buy a few more."

I grabbed the brown bag sitting on the floor and dumped the cash on the table. My sister's mouth hung open. It was the first time I've seen her speechless. When she finally collected her thoughts, she said, "Kayla, tell me you've found the secret to selling Tupperware."

"I think you know it goes a little beyond that," I said, and proceeded to tell her about my new sideline with Tommy the lawn kid.

I had expected disbelief on her part, followed by a reprimand for being so foolish. Instead, she said, "You have to get rid of this money. You can't donate it to charity. We need a plan." She got up and went to the cabinet where I kept the booze.

"There isn't any," I said.

"You must have twenty grand here and you can't afford brandy?"

"It's fifty grand."

"Whoa. Maybe I should become a partner."

For a minute I thought she was serious, but then she was right back to business. "Okay, think. Where can we go with this cash?"

"And the merchandise," I added.

"You've got merchandise, too?"

"In the garage. The kid needs to keep inventory on hand."

My sister slapped her forehead. "Come on, let's go," she said. "I need a drink."

* * * *

I had no idea if this was going to work, but Jen and I arrived at The Mill on Wednesday as planned. She wore a nice pair of dress slacks and a silk blouse courtesy of Lord & Taylor, while I wore a disguise. I'd stuffed my blond hair into a red wig and something dressy casual from my own closet. Truthfully, it felt kind of nice. Maybe the novelty of champagne and caviar was finally wearing off.

While we waited for the maître d, a waiter walked buy with a bottle of Cristal. My mouth watered. Okay, maybe it would take a little time to revert back to being Kayla Rivers, Pi-Yo instructor.

"Marianne? Marianne!" It took me a second to realize my sister was addressing me by my undercover name. "Are you ready?" The maître d had returned.

My sister asked for the Huffington party, and we were led to a table out on the veranda. Joan was gracious as always, but surprised at seeing two unexpected guests.

"Mrs. Huffington?" my sister began. "I'm Katherine Mackenzie and this is my friend Marianne. I'm afraid we have some sad news. Kayla Rivers has passed away. She spoke so very highly of you, we wanted to let you know in person. She had been looking forward to this lunch."

Joan invited us to sit, and before we knew it, waiters were arriving with a cornucopia of treats, from soup and salad, to steak and shrimp. It had turned into a six-course meal. Ah, lunch with the elite. I enjoyed it almost as much as the nice things Joan had to say about Kayla, who was going to be sorely missed. Indeed.

Rich arrived a short while later with a newspaper in hand. He kissed his wife on the cheek and pulled up a chair beside her. "How are you, dear?"

The rest of their conversation was lost to me. On the front page of the paper was a photo of Benny the Buzz with the headline "Dealer Gunned Down in Alley." I kicked my sister underneath the table and nodded at the *Gazette*.

"We really hate to eat and run," Jen said. "But we have other friends to visit on Kayla's behalf."

"Oh, I almost forgot. Kayla wanted you to have this," I said, handing her "Kayla's favorite Gucci bag." It was stuffed with cash. All $50,000 of it. Let Mrs. Huffington worry about depositing it. I'm sure her bank would happily oblige without any questions. "She was so excited about your charitable endeavor for breast cancer."

"Wait a minute, dears," she said. "What about the arrangements? The ladies and I would like to pay our respects."

Jen and I exchanged a look. "Oh, she's not having a viewing," I said. "She'd want you to remember her as the woman you knew."

Joan wiped a tear from her eyes and hugged us. "Well, you know, dears, any friends of Kayla's are always welcome in our circle."

Jen glared at me. I knew it was her, *Don't get any ideas* look.

When we were back in the car, I said, "Now I have to break the news to Tommy. Our business is officially over."

"You are so lucky you didn't get caught."

"Well, I know Tommy isn't going to talk. I owe the kid five grand."

BOTTOMS UP

by Su Kopil

I sat in the cab of my old pickup, with the engine spluttering, while swollen raindrops pinged the metal roof. Through the windshield, I eyed the Federal-style manor, its straight lines and Doric columns softened by a film of water. A fairytale house built for rich people, not little girls and boys from the Bottoms. Of course, my brother Diamond didn't agree.

I could still hear him promising, "One day, Gin, I'm going to live at Wingate Manor, you'll see."

When I'd frowned at him, he'd flashed that smile no girl could resist, including me, and said, "Don't worry, you and Mama will come, too."

But Diamond got it wrong. Very wrong. Wingate Manor wasn't where he would live. It's where he died.

The invitation lay on the passenger seat next to me, creased from riding in my pocket since Tuesday. I'd come off a double shift at the Lion to find Mama using it as a coaster.

"That Wingate girl's got some kind of nerve writing here. I done lost one child to that house, I don't aim to lose another."

"You make it sound like the house ate him," I said.

"Swallowed him up, spit him out, and left him there to die in the dust." Mama chugged back her gin, her body rocking to the strains of some lullaby only she could hear.

To hear her tell it now, you'd think getting knocked up by a hit-and-run boyfriend was the best part of her life. I know for a fact Aunt Syl had to talk Mama into keeping us, especially when the doc told her she was having twins. But Mama swears the minute we popped out, she'd done the right thing. Heck, she even named us after her two favorite things in all the world, gin and diamonds.

The names fit, too. Gin—a no-frills, get-er-done-liquor, and Diamond—a sparkly, multi-faceted gem. Despite our differences, there was nothing that could drive a wedge between Diamond and me. That is, until Daisy Wingate up and killed him.

For ten years, I'd been looking for a way to prove my brother didn't accidentally fall to his death. The official report said he'd tried to jump from a window on the second floor to a nearby tree so Daisy's parents wouldn't catch him with her. I knew Diamond would rather face a firing squad of irate fathers than climb out a third story window. My brother might have been God's gift to all women, but he was a coward when it came to heights. Everyone knew it, too, but no one cared about a kid from the Bottoms, especially one that died at a rich man's house.

It's a hard thing to prove when the main players up and leave the country for ten years. Then last week rumors started swirling at the Lion. Daisy Wingate was back in town and had opened up the old manor again. Before I had time to let that info settle, the invite from Daisy arrived asking me to come by the place so we could talk. Talk, she said. With an opportunity like that falling into my pocket, I'd have to be dumber than a shoeless salesman not to grab it, despite Mama's dire warnings.

So here I sat, drumming up the courage to face my brother's killer.

Three other cars—fancy, like you'd expect to find on this side of town—lined the drive. My battered pickup sat like a red caboose at the back end of an express train. The rumor mills must have gotten it wrong. It looked like the entire Wingate clan had returned.

For a moment, I wondered if I should use the back door. Squaring my shoulders, I marched to the front entrance, damp but determined. With an attempt to smooth the frizz from my hair, I rang the bell, and waited.

Daisy herself answered. She was shorter than I remembered, or maybe it was the serviceable shoes replacing the hooker heels of her youth. Her perky features had matured into something more classic, though her expression was guarded, or it could be I wasn't the only one who was nervous.

"Gin, thank you for coming," she said. "I wasn't sure if you would."

"You said you wanted to talk. Well, I have a few things to say myself."

Her perfect, blonde eyebrows rose. I'd thrown her off balance. My confidence inched up, along with her brows.

"Yes, of course. Come in." She stepped back.

I entered Wingate Manor for the first time. It was huge, ridiculously so, but musty smelling like it had been shut tight all these years. You could fit our whole trailer into the foyer, and still have room for the crystal chandelier hanging down from on high.

The foyer ended with a sweeping staircase, the kind I thought only existed in movies. Parallel hallways ran past the staircase on each side, with doors opening up to God knows how many rooms. My eyes wanted to bug out, so I squinted instead.

"I bet Diamond loved sliding down that bannister." Although true, it was a stupid thing to say. Maybe because it was the very thing we would have done together, no matter how old we were. Maybe because I was jealous he'd been in this house without me. Maybe because I was pissed he wasn't here with me now.

"Actually, Diamond never saw this part of the house," she said. "He always came in the back door and up the servants' stairs."

My cheeks burned. I didn't belong here, and neither had Diamond.

Daisy must have sensed my distress.

"Please," she said. "Hear me out."

A burst of women's laughter leaked through a closed door on the right side of the foyer.

I looked at Daisy. "What's going on here? Who's that?"

"Please." Her eyes pleaded with me. She steered me towards an open door on the left.

The room was small—well, what I assumed was small for this place—meaning big enough for a fireplace, two sofas, and two chairs still covered in plastic.

I teetered on the edge of one plastic-draped chair wishing for a shot of Mama's gin.

"I'm going to skip the small talk and get right to the point," Daisy said.

"Of course, it's not like we ever had anything in common besides my brother. We don't have to pretend to like each other now," I said. "So, go on."

"I never said I didn't like you, Gin. We barely knew each other back in high school."

"I didn't fit in with your crowd, being from the wrong side of the tracks and all, and not as pretty as my brother. But I guess even pretty doesn't get you in the front door when you're from the Bottoms."

I expected Daisy to protest, tell some pretty lies about how wrong I was. Instead, she picked up a tiny box from a side table and handed it to me.

"What's this?"

"I've heard that you think Diamond was pushed out of my bedroom window. I know you think I pushed him."

It was my turn to raise my eyebrows. Was she trying to buy my forgiveness? I turned the box over in my fingers.

"People talk," she said. "It's one of the reasons my father made us move. At the time, I was too upset to argue. I've had a lot of time to think since then. I came back because I believe you are right."

My head jerked up.

"Diamond was murdered that night, but not by me. With your help, I can prove it. But I need you to trust me."

"Trust you?" I stood, my hand tightening around the box.

She nodded. Her gaze searched my face. If she was looking for some resemblance to Diamond, she was pissing in the wrong pot. No two twins were less alike.

She must have found something, though, because she looked me straight in the eye, and whispered, "Shadows are for sissies, Gin."

I sat down hard, like I was gut-punched. Those were Diamond's words. Something he'd say whenever I got scared.

"I know you don't believe this," Daisy said. "I made mistakes, but I loved him."

"Is that why he had to hide from your family?" I said. Daisy might have been young and stupid but my brother was dead. I couldn't let it go that easy.

She didn't answer, but it didn't matter. My curiosity was piqued. "You still haven't told me what's in the box."

"You'll see." She pushed her hair behind her ears. "Put it in your pocket for now. There's something we need to do first."

"What?"

She smiled for the first time. "Talk to Diamond."

Mama told me, when I first started working at the Lion, that if I ever came across crazy I should nod my head, wait 'til they looked the other way, then run.

So I nodded my way across that giant foyer, waiting for Daisy to take her eyes off me. Next thing I knew, we were standing in front of the closed door where I'd heard laughter earlier.

"Follow my lead."

Before I could protest, Daisy turned the knob, and pushed open the door.

Lighted candles filled the room with the scent of burning wax. The flickering flames transformed the shadows into something living. Three women, seated at a round table in the center of the room, stopped talking and turned to stare at us.

My mind flashed back to the high school cafeteria when someone had stuck their foot out. I'd tripped and fell into the popular girls' table. Laura Lane, Cat Avery, and Reena Sherbow stared at me now, with the same shock and distaste they wore back then only their faces seemed looser, more lived-in somehow.

My skin started to itch. I was out of my element—stripped of the intervening years, and once again the awkward, poor girl from the Bottoms. I turned to bolt, but Daisy was there, her hand on my back, guiding me to one of two empty seats at the table.

Laura's glance took me in from head to toe. She nodded, causing her second chin to jiggle. Her father owned a bakery franchise. I remember having donuts for breakfast every morning when she and Diamond dated.

"What's she doing here?" Cat spoke through lips that looked like they'd been inflated with a bike pump. She was the governor's daughter, but aside from money, I never knew what Diamond saw in her. Daisy glanced at Reena and gave a slight nod.

"To call upon a spirit," Reena said, "you need the blood of a family member. Gin is Diamond's twin, which makes her blood very potent." On the table in front of Reena rested a leather pouch. She loosened the draw string, and drew out a small knife.

"What?" I backed away from Reena, who sat in the chair to my right. Her eye makeup was so heavy it put raccoons to shame. I didn't really know her. She was a year or two older and Daisy's cousin. Diamond hung out with her a few times, but they never dated. He said she was weird, but he didn't tell me she was talk-to-the-dead kind of weird.

"It's okay, Gin," Daisy said. "It's only a pinprick."

Daisy was to my left. Laura and Cat sat across from me.

"Can we get started?" Cat whined. "Daddy's having dinner with a senator, and he promised to bring him back to the house."

Reena held out her hand for mine, but I wasn't so willing to give up my blood just yet.

"Why are Cat and Laura even here?" I asked.

The women exchanged glances.

"This might be hard to hear, Gin," Daisy spoke. "But, as I explained to the others, I believe the manor is haunted. They came to help."

"Haunted? By Diamond?" I laughed out loud—laughed even harder thinking of what Diamond's reaction would have been.

Daisy ignored my outburst, and continued. "All of us were in the house the night Diamond died. Laura and I were studying for a test. Reena was staying with my family while her parents were away. She and Cat were baking cookies for a party the next day. If Diamond's lingering because of unfinished business, maybe it's because of one of us. Reena knew I wouldn't let this go, so when I told her I was going to contact you, she offered to hold a séance—she's done it before. She was positive that with your help, she could contact Diamond and ask him to move on."

I let that unfinished business nonsense wash right over me. It was the first part of what Daisy said, the part about them all being here that night, that had me sitting up straighter. And for the first time, I wondered if I was wrong about who killed Diamond. This séance business just got a whole lot more interesting.

I stuck out my hand and let Reena prick my finger. She pulled a tissue from her pouch along with a small bundle of dried herbs. She handed me the tissue. I pressed it against the cut, only to have her snatch it back a second later, and set it on a small plate. She held the herb bundle over the flame of a candle. When it caught, she placed it on top of the bloody tissue.

While the offering burned, Reena spoke. "Any spirits we contact will speak directly through me, so don't be frightened. I'm going to ask everyone to hold hands." Reena took back my right hand, while Daisy claimed my left. "Now close your eyes," Reena continued, "and stay still."

A candle on the table sputtered and died.

"Diamond Mackey," Reena intoned. "We have come together in Daisy's house, the place of your death, hoping to receive a sign of your presence. Your sister Gin is with us. You are welcome here. Please, come and join us."

Nothing happened. I snuck a peek out of one eye and watched the shadows flicker across the faces at the table.

Cat sniffed.

Laura whispered, "Are you sure you're doing it right?"

Daisy and Reena both shushed her.

"Diamond Mackey, we ask you—"

A door slammed somewhere in the house. I jumped. Laura and Cat did the same.

"I'm here."

My head whipped towards Reena. Her eyes were closed, her head thrown back so that I could see the pulse beating in her neck.

Daisy squeezed my hand.

"Uh, Diamond?" I felt like an idiot addressing Reena as my dead brother.

"Gin, I'm sorry I had to leave you so soon." The voice was still Reena's, but huskier.

"Yeah, okay." I didn't for one minute believe Diamond's spirit was talking through Daisy's weird cousin. But what the hell? So I asked, "Diamond, what happened the night you died?"

"Ask Daisy. She can tell you." Well, wasn't that convenient, I thought.

"We had a fight and broke up," Daisy said.

"And?" Cat's eyes were open now and she was staring at Daisy. "Tell her what the fight was about," Cat said. "Tell her how he stole my grandmother's ring."

"What?" This was new information to me. "If that's true, why wasn't it in the police report?"

"Because Daisy wanted to cover it up to protect Diamond, even though he was already dead. And even though my ring was never found." Cat's bottom lip was stuck to her teeth; either that, or she was pouting.

"It wasn't found because my brother didn't steal it," I said.

"What Cat says is true." Laura was looking at me now.

Reena expelled a breath across the table, causing the remaining flames to flicker. *"It's true, Gin. My guilt is tying me to this house. I need forgiveness so I can let go."*

"Where's my grandmother's ring, Diamond?" Cat asked.

I had enough of this. The whole thing smelled like a set up to me. Right when I was about to let go of Daisy's hand, she squeezed mine tight.

"Ouch."

"What happened?" Laura's eyes went wide.

I ignored her.

"Diamond, how did you get upstairs?" Daisy asked. "When we heard my parents come home, you were supposed to go out the back door."

"I hid in your room. I needed to talk to you alone."

"Then why did you try to leave before I got up there?"

"Someone was coming. I didn't want to get you in trouble. I need to go. Will you forgive me?"

"Tell us where my ring is, Diamond. Then we'll forgive you," Cat said.

"Hey," I said. "That's my brother you're talking to. He never stole your damn ring. Was it insured? Maybe you lost it and needed someone to blame. A guy from the Bottoms is an easy target, right?"

"Laura saw him take it," Cat shot back.

Everyone looked at Laura, except for Reena, whose eyes were still closed.

"I didn't exactly *see* him do it. Reena told me he took the ring. I believed her. She had no reason to lie."

"Someone must have followed him to Daisy's room because he wouldn't go out that window on his own." I turned to Reena. "Who followed you, Diamond? Who pushed you out that window?"

"No one. I fell. It was my fault."

My eyes stung, and not from candle smoke. Diamond always took the blame whenever we got into trouble. No matter how mad we were at each other, he always protected me. Could Diamond really be talking through Reena or was it wishful thinking on my part? I couldn't believe I was even considering it, but I had to know for sure.

"Your dying," I said, "it's been hard on Mama and, even more, on Daddy. What should I tell him?"

"Tell him I love him." Reena made a spluttering noise, and then her head dropped forward.

I pulled my hands away in disgust. "This has been real entertaining. But I'm pretty sure my brother would tell our Daddy to go to hell, *if* we had ever met him."

Reena opened her eyes and look at us. "What happened? Did we make contact?"

Everyone stared at Reena as if—well, as if they'd seen a ghost.

Laura was the first to speak. "Reena, didn't you tell me you saw Diamond take Cat's ring? Remember, she took it off when we were making cookie dough?"

Cat frowned. "Didn't Reena disappear right after that? Daisy and Diamond were arguing. I remember I saw the headlights of your daddy's car as he pulled into the driveway."

"That's when I told Diamond to leave by the back door," Daisy said, "while you and Laura went out the front to distract my parents. I remember them asking where Regina was and I didn't know."

"Regina?" I asked.

Daisy nodded. "That's her real name. Reena is a nickname."

"Wait a minute." Memories of that night came flooding back—Diamond primping to go out, me standing in the bathroom doorway asking if I could borrow his phone because mine was dead. "My brother had a block on his phone for a Regina. He told me she was some freaky girl who was stalking him."

"Stalking?" Reena shoved away from the table. "Ha! Diamond Mackey from the Bottoms thought he was too good for me. What a laugh. He was a thief and a cheat."

"No, he wasn't." Daisy also stood. "Gin, open the box."

I wasn't sure what was happening here, but I was starting to get a good idea. I pulled the box from my pocket and lifted the lid. Inside rested a delicate gold ring with a large red stone. I held the box out to Cat.

"My grandmother's ring." Cat glared at me. "Diamond did steal it. How else would you have it?"

"I gave it to her," Daisy answered. "It's been in this house the whole time. Isn't that right, Reena?"

"I don't know what you're talking about." Reena fussed with the pouch on the table.

"I think you do," said Daisy. "You stole Cat's ring that night and told Laura you saw Diamond steal it. Instead, you put it in your sweater pocket. You also told me Diamond cheated on me with Cat. Remember the fight we had, Cat?"

"Diamond was fun, not to mention gorgeous," Cat said, "but I only went out with him to get Daddy's attention. And that was before you two got together."

"I figured Reena was just being overprotective. But I was wrong, wasn't I?" Daisy watched Reena. "You wanted us to break up so you could have him to yourself. And since the cheating story didn't work, you thought calling him a thief would. You followed him upstairs that night, didn't you? Maybe to talk him out of waiting for me. Or maybe to console him. But he didn't want any part of you, did he? You were just a crazy stalker girl to him."

"I loved him," Reena shouted, "but he wouldn't even look at me. He said he wanted to marry you, did you know that? *I* was trying to save you, cousin. It's your *money* he wanted. You should be thanking me." Her finger jabbed her chest. "He said he loved you, but he didn't. He was afraid to go out that stupid window. I had to practically push him out so your parents wouldn't find him in your room. He was supposed to grab a tree branch, but something happened. He slipped. I reached for him. My sweater caught on the window, and ripped, and suddenly he was falling."

Her eyes glistened. "I panicked and took off the sweater and threw it in the closet. I was scared. It was an accident, but I knew nobody would believe me, so I ran into the bathroom, and pretended like I was in the shower the whole time. When I heard screaming, I went downstairs toweling off my hair, and acted like I didn't know what was going on."

My fists clenched. I wanted to slam my knuckles into her nose.

Reena was shaking, tears ruining her mascara. In that moment, she could have been any frightened kid from the Bottoms, but she wasn't. For the first time since entering Wingate Manor, I didn't feel like the one who didn't belong here.

Reena ran out of the house but it didn't matter. Daisy had recorded the whole séance. She turned the recording over to the police.

When I told Mama and Aunt Syl the case had been reopened, they both cried. The next day, I told everyone at the Lion and they cheered. Now rumors have started to swirl that Reena's Daddy plans to hire the best lawyers money can buy.

*   *   *   *

Daisy had a small garden planted around the tree where Diamond died. She put in a bench and a birdbath and had a little plaque made, *In memory of Diamond Mackey, a rich man in all the ways that matter.*

Mama and I were invited to come sit whenever we wanted. Every so often, Daisy would sit with us. That's when she told me about finding Cat's ring in the corner of her closet when she first returned, and how that helped her to start putting the pieces together.

Sometimes she'd invite Mama in for tea so I could have a few moments alone. I'd sit real quiet, listening, and every once in a while I could hear Diamond promise, *One day, Gin, I'm going to live at Wingate Manor, you'll see.*

THE WRITER

by Steve Shrott

R obert waited.
He sat at a table in the back of the Cob Web Bar drinking a now-cold cup of coffee. He checked his watch numerous times, hoping the man would show.

A few moments later, a thin figure wearing a leather jacket and high-top sneakers ambled in, a toothpick sticking out of his mouth.

Could this be him? The man who would change his life?

He saw enough in the swarthy face to indicate it was. He waved to him. "Nino, over here."

Nino meandered over to Robert's table, dragged out a chair and took a seat.

"It's great seeing you again. I've really missed you, cousin." Robert put his hand out to shake Nino's.

Nino didn't budge.

Robert awkwardly dropped his hand to his side. "How have you been?"

"Okay."

"I wanted to apologize."

"Oh?"

"The reason I stopped seeing you. I can't tell you how much it hurt me. It was like a piece of me went missing. I thought of us as bros."

"Bros."

"Yeah. The thing is, I've always been under my parents' thumb. They had good intentions, wanted to keep me from going down the wrong path. But it also kept me from trying new things. That's why I looked up to you. You always took risks."

Nino inhaled sharply, stared at Robert with cold eyes. "You know, if you loved me so damn much, you coulda called. Your mommy didn't tear out all the phone lines, did she?"

Robert's body trembled and he itched all over. He felt like his hives were coming back after being cured for sixteen years. Maybe this wasn't such a good idea. He'd heard rumors about Nino's wild mood swings where he'd be nice one minute, enraged the next. But knowing him as a child, Robert couldn't believe Nino was like that.

"I still remember you and me at the beach, Nino. I'd built a fort, then that big kid stomped all over it. He was at least a foot taller than you, but you punched him so hard, blood poured out of his nose. I always felt indebted to you. Do you remember?"

Nino leaned forward, his blue eyes intense. "Look, I'd love to go down memory lane, kid, but I'm kinda on a tight schedule. I figure if someone calls a meet they want something."

Sweat rolled down Robert's forehead. "Uh, right, right. The thing is Nino, I'm a writer. Well, actually, I'm an accountant, but I'm a writer too."

Nino raised his eyebrows. "A writer?"

"Yes." Robert smiled as if he were John Grisham.

"Done anything I mighta heard of?"

Robert figured that Nino was probably not much of a reader. "Well, I've just kinda started. I write about, uh, crime."

"Crime?"

"Uh huh." Robert felt Nino take in his baby-face, moisturized complexion, perfectly-manicured nails, suit, tie.

"Know a lot about crime, do you?"

Robert shook his head. "No, and that's the issue. See, my book is about a family man who gets involved with a criminal organization, and how it changes his life. That's why I thought of you. I know you did that stint in jail for armed robbery."

Nino glared at him, took the toothpick out of his mouth and broke it in half as if snapping someone's arm in two.

Neither spoke for a moment.

Nino leaned back in his chair. "So, you have a wife and kids now?"

Robert studied the bottom of his coffee cup. "No, still single."

"So let me understand this. You're writing a book about a man with a family who gets into crime."

"That's right."

"Only you don't have no family, and don't know nothing about crime."

"Well, uh, yeah, I guess."

"This sounds like a very successful book." Nino laughed, but not a normal laugh. The kind in movies just before one gangster shot another. "I gotta take a piss." He stood up and left for the men's room.

Robert put on his coat and took one last sip of cold coffee figuring Nino was going to blow him off.

A moment later, Nino returned to the table, another toothpick in his mouth.

"Meet me tomorrow night at Tousie's Bakery on Baldwin."

"You're gonna help me?"

"We're bros, ain't we?"

Robert's face formed a wide smile. "Yes, we are. What time?"

"Midnight."

"Midnight? That's a little la—"

"Do you want me to help you?"

"Yeah, yeah. Twelve's fine."

Nino left and Robert drove home. It was past nine, so he went up to his room the back way. He didn't want to wake his parents. He sat at his desk and began writing on his computer.

After an hour, he had completed chapter three. But when he read it over, his lip curled with disgust, and he tore up all the sheets he'd printed. That's why he had gone to see Nino. Nothing he wrote seemed right. But he figured once he and Nino talked, he'd be writing up a storm.

The next night he snuck out of his house at eleven thirty and dashed to his Honda in the driveway. He loved that car—the gold color, leather seat covers, the racing stripes on the side. He saw a tiny spot of mud on the hood and quickly wiped it off. He hopped in.

He still couldn't understand why he had to meet Nino at midnight, but what the heck, it was Saturday. He could stay out late for one night as long as his dad didn't know. Ever since Robert was a kid, his father had told him that the night air would give him pimples.

Robert saw the sign with Tousie's Bakery in big letters, and parked in the lot beside it.

As he headed toward the door of the bakery, Nino exited holding a black bag and a shovel, of all things. Another man, with a grayish complexion, walked beside him. He had small eyes that darted back and forth like the ball in a ping pong game, and a long scar down his cheek. When he whispered something to Nino, his lips hardly moved, like the bottom part of his face was already dead.

"Hey kid, this is Lepki. He's going to come with us. We'll use your car."

Robert wanted to object, but Lepki's crazy-ass eyes bored into him and he changed his mind.

Nino and Lepki climbed into the back seat. Robert drove.

"Take the next left and turn right on Swansea."

Robert did as he was told. "I just wondered, what's the shovel for?"

"Just in case."

"In case of what?"

"In case anyone dies on the way."

A worried expression fell across Robert's face. "Nino, about my book…"

"We'll talk later, kid, I'm a bit busy now. Bullets won't load themselves."

Robert's throat froze and he couldn't get any more words out.

Ten minutes later, Nino instructed Robert to park on a dark side street. He and Lepki left the car. Robert opened the door to get out but Nino banged it shut, almost making him sterile.

"Here's your first lesson, kid. During a job, one man stays in the car. He's the getaway driver. Got it?"

Robert, his eyes wide, looked up at Nino. "No, no, I didn't want to be part of a crime. I just wanted to …"

But in the next instant, the two men were gone.

Robert's body itched all over. He got out of the Honda and raced after them as they headed to the next street. There he saw Nino and Lepki standing in front of the bank door, each holding some kind of metal instrument.

Robert moved toward them but stopped when he saw sparks and heard a loud bang as the door collapsed. The two men hurried inside the bank, the alarm ringing.

Oh my God, oh my God, oh my God, Robert repeated a hundred and ten times to himself.

He didn't know what to do. But he thought it might not be such a good idea to hang around a bank where a robbery was being committed by his cousin and another man who looked like a cadaver.

He dashed back to the car intending to drive away. Far, far away. Just before he reached it, his cell phone rang.

"Dad? What are you doing up? I'm, uh, just withdrawing some money from the, uh, bank … I get that it's late … Yeah, I know, pimples … I'll be home soon … Yes, I am aware there's lots of crooks out there."

Suddenly, gunshots filled the air.

"What's that?"

"Uh, f-f-firecrackers."

"In February?"

"They, uh, celebrate early in this part of town. G-g-gotta go, Dad."

Nino ran toward the car holding a gun, the black bag now stuffed. Lepki followed, walking slower and holding his stomach as blood poured down his shirt.

Oh my God, oh my God, oh my God.

Nino glared at Robert. "I told you to stay in the damn car."

Robert quickly slid into the driver's seat. Lepki struggled to get into the back while Nino sat in front.

"Get us the crap out of here."

Robert started the car and drove. "Where?"

"Newport."

"Newport? There's no hospital there."

"We're not going to the hospital."

Robert looked in the driver's mirror at Lepki. Saw the closed eyes, heavy breathing, blood-stained shirt. "He looks bad."

"He's a known felon. If someone sees us bring him into a hospital, we'll be in trouble. We gotta bury him."

"Bury him? But he's not dead."

"Bullet that deep, he's gonna be soon."

Oh my God, oh my God, oh my God. They were going to arrest him for attempted robbery, getaway car driving, and murder. He'd never be able to go back to work. AAA Accountants got upset if his tie was askew.

Nino looked through the back window and shouted, "Faster. Now!"

Robert sped up. He'd never driven over fifty-nine in a sixty mile zone. His heart was beating so hard, his breathing so heavy, he didn't notice the itching so much.

"Turn left, then make a quick right."

The car screeched as Robert rounded the corners.

"Go behind the trees."

Robert parked his Honda next to the willows, then watched as a police cruiser raced down the main street, sirens blazing. His heart rate slowed down to, what he felt, was somewhere in the mid hundreds.

"Now get us the hell to Newport."

As Robert began driving, Nino moved close to him. "I want to tell you something, kid."

Robert figured it was going to be some compliment about how he kept his cool. He didn't need it, but it was nice that Nino noticed.

"I think someone tipped off the cops."

Robert looked at the gun still in Nino's hand. "W-W-What?"

"Someone told them about the robbery." Nino's unblinking eyes fixed on Robert. "I seem to remember you had your phone out when we came back to the car."

"No, no, I ..."

Nino gripped the gun more tightly in his hand. "I don't like squealers. You ain't a squealer, are you?"

"Noooo, I never squeal. I didn't even tell Aunt Sophie when she asked who ate the last blintz at her birthday party. And I knew it was Uncle Benny. Didn't say a word."

"So how do you explain the phone in your hand?"

"My dad called."

"Your dad? At twelve thirty in the morning?"

"He didn't see my car in the driveway. He was worried."

Nino's eyebrows rose. "You still live with your parents?"

"Uh, yeah."

Nino snickered. "You know, not too many getaway drivers live with mommy and daddy."

As they neared Newport, Robert glanced at Lepki, pleased he was still breathing. Nino had him pull off the road in a wooded area.

"Help me," said Nino, grabbing Lepki's right arm. Robert took his other arm and the two dragged Lepki out of the car.

"He's still alive, Nino. I told you we should have taken him to the hospital."

That's when Nino took out his gun and shot Lepki in the back.

Robert shook all over. "Nino, what …?"

"Put him out of his suffering. Just like a dog when he's sick, you gotta take him out. Lepki woulda understood."

Robert went into the bushes and threw up.

Nino shouted to the bushes. "When you're finished, come over here, we gotta bury the son of a bitch."

Robert stumbled out of the bushes, his face pale.

Nino threw the shovel over to him. "I gotta take a piss."

Robert stuck the shovel into the earth and dug, not thinking about anything else. When Nino returned, he sat on a nearby rock, smoking a cigarette and watched.

"This is gonna be great for your writing. Not too many authors get this kind of experience."

When Robert finished, he and Nino pushed the body into the hole and covered it with dirt.

Nino tapped Robert on the shoulder. "Let's get out of here, bro."

"Now you call me bro?"

"I figure when two guys bury a body together, there's a bond." Nino walked toward the car.

Robert didn't move. "We gotta say something."

"Whadya mean?"

"We knew him, we gotta say a prayer or some good words."

"What do you want me to say? He had a beautiful heart, gave to charity, loved kids?"

"That sounds good."

"He wasn't any of that. He was a killer who whacked people for money. I was trying to take him off that early death route and get him into something more stable like bank robbery."

Robert whispered, "Rest in Peace, Lepki."

The two men walked back to Robert's car.

"Alright, one final thing we gotta do."

"What's that?"

"Roll your car down the hill."

"What?"

"Cops find the Honda with Lepki's blood, gonna find us. There's snow tomorrow. Lots of snow. It'll cover everything up."

"That's my new car. You can't throw it down the hill."

Nino spread his hands. "You wanna go to prison?"

Robert scratched everywhere it was possible to scratch, wiped his eyes. Nino had him take a position at the back fender while Nino took the side. Both men began pushing the Honda. Robert's pant leg got caught on a tree branch and ripped. He barely noticed.

The car rolled down the hill hitting shrubs and weeds, finally crashing into a tree at the bottom.

Nino called for a pal to pick them up. The two men walked out onto the main road and waited.

When they reached Robert's house, Nino turned to him. "I hoped you learned a little tonight for your writing, bro. We should stay in touch." Nino gave him a thousand watt smile.

Robert took a deep breath, and stared at Nino. "Stay in touch? Are you crazy? This has been the worst night of my entire life. I had to push the car I loved down a hill, watch a man get shot, bury him, throw up in the bushes, and have my hives return after I'd gotten rid of them for sixteen years. Worst of all, the person I most looked up to turned out to be a criminal, a creep, a murderer, and was going to shoot me because he thought I was a squealer. I don't want anything to do with you ever again."

Nino shook his head, and muttered under his breath, "You try to help someone …"

Robert got out of the car, his leg feeling cold from the tear in his pants, and walked with as much dignity as he could toward his house.

* * * *

The next day Robert wrote from morning to night. He had so many ideas. It was like a fire had been lit under him. And every day to follow, it was the same.

He finished his book and found an agent and publisher. Months later, his novel, *Crime Town* was on the market.

His agent instructed him to begin his second book immediately. But despite trying to write every day, nothing came to Robert.

He knew what he had to do.

He took out his phone and punched a number. "Hello, Nino. How's it going, bro?"

FROM THE ASHES

by Kate Fellowes

You might think life was dull in a small town like Silver Lake and most of the time it is. Not lately, though.

I'm Madison Campbell and I've lived here my whole life. Okay, I'm only seventeen, but that's still a long time.

Since the start of the school year, I've been working at the public library as a page. That sounds like something from King Arthur's court, but it means I shelve materials for minimum wage. Mostly it's kind of dull, but I like it. So tidy and organized. Who knew it would turn out to be exciting?

See, not long after I started, Miss Everly, the ancient librarian, was all worked up one day, in a good way. She doesn't smile much, but that day, at the end of the staff meeting, she did.

"I'm pleased to announce we'll have a marvelous display here next month," she said.

I looked around at the others. The Library Director, Mr. Kinnic, seemed mildly interested, but I'm pretty sure he was faking it.

Candy Clark, the children's librarian, set down her the scissors and tuned in. She was pretty, about thirty, with a purple streak in her hair and full of energy and fun. She'd been snipping out name tags for story hour all through the meeting while the rest of us sat and ate donuts.

The two clerks, Linda and Bev, looked bored. Whatever Miss Everly had to say wouldn't make any difference to them.

"Mary Ramsey, the granddaughter of Judge Ramsey, will be loaning us a priceless collection of books from the judge's library!" Miss Everly crowed.

Other than an enthusiastic "Oh!" from Candy, the group was silent.

I wanted to ask, who's Judge Ramsey? What kind of books? Are they old and valuable? But since no one else broke the silence, I didn't either.

In our second grade school play, I portrayed Miss Mouse. All the characters were animals, but it was still type casting, I'm afraid. It's not that I'm shy. Or maybe it is, I don't know. I've never wanted to draw attention to myself. Lots of times my brain buzzes with unspoken thoughts, but I've found if I wait, someone else will voice them.

"There will be twelve books," Miss Everly went on. "We'll put them in the display cabinet, by the Community Room." Her smile drooped. "It's a shame we have to house these treasures in that decrepit old cabinet. Why we have a twenty-first century computer lab and still use that display case from the Eisenhower administration ..." She went on, warming to her theme.

"Tell us more about the books, please," Mr. Kinnic broke in.

With a sigh, the librarian said, "The books will be representative of the judge's family collection. The Ramsey family founded our town over one hundred years ago, so this will be historical. I've designed a flyer to promote it."

She pushed lime green flyers around the table at each of us. Miss Everly doesn't have Candy's flair for graphic design. The flyer was just words, centered on the page and in varying fonts, colors, and sizes. We read it over in silence.

A Dozen Delights: books from the collection of Judge Ramsey, it said at the top and then listed the dates of the exhibition, October to December, and the library's hours.

If I were making the flyer, I'd add drawings of books and use one old-fashioned but legible kind of lettering. For starters.

"I could jazz this up for you, if you'd like. Maybe Madison can add an illustration."

My thoughts came out of Candy's mouth, as if she'd read my mind.

"Good idea," Mr. Kinnic said.

Miss Everly narrowed her eyes at him as the meeting came to a close.

* * * *

I forgot about the exhibition until it was due to arrive one weekend. Miss Everly handed me a bottle of window cleaner and a cloth, with orders to clean every inch of the display case.

"I'd like you to make that your first job of the day when you're here," she said. "No fingerprints!" She'd wagged her finger at me and walked away.

Pushed up against the outside of the Community Room, the case was about six feet high. There's glass on all four sides for most of it, with two wooden doors at the bottom. It took a while, but when I was done, all three shelves sparkled and every wall, even that back one which was hard to reach, was spotless.

Miss Everly nodded her approval when I returned the key to her.

Mary Ramsey showed up with the books when I was alphabetizing and shelving a cart in the children's department. She was nearly as old as the librarian, but that was all they had in common. She ran a real estate business in town, dressed sharp and looked like she lived in this century, whereas Miss Everly was definitely stuck in the twentieth.

I was really close to the display case as Ms. Ramsey handed each book to Miss Everly, who read the title out loud and placed it on a shelf.

They took about an hour arranging the books. It was to be a two-sided display, since the case was up against a glass wall. Patrons could see the books from the main area of the library or from inside the Community Room. I wondered if that meant I'd have to clean fingerprints off that glass, too. Probably. Eventually, the key was spun on the lock and the judge's granddaughter flipped the switch to turn on the light inside.

The books did look impressive. Old, clothbound histories and references, they weren't anything someone would read for fun, like the mysteries I read on weekends. I wondered, had anyone ever read these?

For the next few weeks, the library had extra foot traffic, thanks to the display. The newspaper ran a picture of Miss Everly and the library director standing beside the cabinet like proud parents. The grade-schoolers made trips to the cabinet as part of their weekly visits and left fingerprints everywhere. The Mayor and a couple Alderpersons took a peek after their council meeting in the Community Room.

But people forgot about the old book display as they began gearing up for the holidays.

And that's when it happened.

Fire! At the library!

It was a Sunday afternoon and I was at the high school with nearly the whole town for the "Home for the Holidays" event. After the Mayor's speech, a magician put on a show. Then the choir sang some secular tunes. Little kids stood in line to see Santa and every civic group in town had a booth selling something.

I was at the student newspaper booth, sitting behind a stack of our latest issue, doing Sudoku puzzles.

Fire engines roared out of the station across the street and within five minutes the news had spread.

Candy rushed toward my table.

"C'mon, Madison!" she said, sounding frantic. She'd been doing face painting in the library's booth and sported stars on both her cheeks.

I hurried to keep pace as we raced to her car. I wasn't sure what she thought we could do—toss books from person to person, maybe?

Two fire trucks sat out front, their red lights bouncing off the windows, but no acrid smoke filled the air and no flames were shooting out of the library windows. Several firemen stood on the lawn, the big fire hoses trailing through the open front door.

We headed for the staff entrance.

I recognized the police officer blocking the way. He was my dad's high school buddy, Ken Merrill. Usually I saw him with his feet up in our family room, watching ESPN with Dad. Now, though, he held up his hand.

"No admittance," he said.

"Is the fire out?" Candy asked. "We don't see any flames."

"Fire's out," he confirmed. "But the firefighters are still in there, making sure. You'll have to wait for the all clear."

Candy groaned. "Do you know where it was? The computer lab? The archives?" She cringed. "If the sprinkler went on in there—"

"Seems the fire was pretty localized," Officer Merrill said. "We'll know more soon."

Candy sat down on the concrete step.

"We'll wait here," she said, "until we can check."

Officer Merrill's radio crackled just then.

"10-4," he said, then addressed us. "Do not attempt to enter this building, Miss, Madison."

I plopped down beside Candy as he went in the staff door. We sat there for ages. At first, Candy kept fidgeting and talking about the irreplaceable archives, but then, as time dragged on, we talked about school and college majors and our favorite bands. Finally, the door opened again.

Officer Merrill said, "The department has cordoned off the public area, but will allow entrance to the staff workrooms."

"Great!" Candy said.

I knew she was thinking of the staff hallway that ran behind the computer lab and the archives.

"I can just peek in," she whispered, and I nodded.

Inside the building, the doorway leading from the staff space to the public one was blocked off by yellow tape. We stood just inside it, looking at the scene from a distance.

No fire hoses were trailing around and only a few firefighters remained. Yellow tape was stretched across the main entrance, too, but the really shocking thing was all the tape set up around the old display case.

"Look!" I pointed. Amid puddles of water, broken glass and ashes, just outside the Community Room, the ancient display case was in ruins. The contents—a dozen delights from the judge's library—had been reduced to lumps and mush.

"Oh, no!" Candy gasped then gasped again.

Miss Everly was shoving up behind us, elbowing us aside. Her face was pale and she looked as if she was about to keel over.

"I'd better go check those archives," Candy said, heading down the hall. I stepped away, too, but didn't go far. How had a fire started in the cabinet? Did someone forget to turn off the lights inside at closing time Saturday? I felt a pang of guilt even though a) that was not my job; and b) I hadn't even worked the day before.

I heard Miss Everly moan as she spied the cabinet. Then Mr. Kinnic barged through the staff door. Taking in the situation at a glance, he looked relieved—until he joined Miss Everly and saw the cabinet. Then his lips pressed into one flat line. The fire chief approached Mr. Kinnic and they exchanged a few terse words.

"A short in the wiring, do you think?" Mr. Kinnic asked, but the chief couldn't say.

Candy returned, joining the others.

"Archives and computers are fine," she announced. "Miss Everly, you need to sit down."

She and Mr. Kinnic led the old lady away toward the lounge.

No one was near the cabinet when I glanced at it, and I realized I could take a peek at it without crossing any yellow tape. I walked quickly down the staff hallway to the door leading to the Community Room. My heart pounded, even though, technically, I wasn't violating any orders.

Hurrying across the room to where the cabinet stood on the other side of the glass wall, I peeked inside.

All the glass from the front had broken, from the fire or from the firefighters. Inside, the carefully arranged books were now cinders. That old paper had burned easily. A few solid pieces remained—a blue square here, a gold fleck there. I looked closer, trying to make out the lettering barely visible on one fragment.

"O-U-S," I read aloud.

"Madison!"

I jumped, hearing my name barked.

Officer Merrill approached me at a clip.

"You were to stay in the staff area," he said, using his policeman's voice.

"I'm sorry," I said. "I just thought—"

"Weren't you at the high school?" he interrupted, steering me back across the room. "Do you have a ride back there?"

"I'll just walk home now," I told him, making a hasty escape.

Outside, it was brisk, but not cold. As I walked, for a brain teaser, I tried to remember the titles of all the books. Since I'd been dusting them four days a week for ages now, I was pretty familiar with them.

"Bet I can," I said aloud and started ticking them off on my fingers.

The first few came easily. The next few, not so much. I closed my eyes, trying to see them as Miss Everly had said their titles and placed them in the cabinet. But it was useless. I'd have to try again, in my room where it was quiet. I'd sketch the shelves and fill in the blanks.

Later, when I held my drawing of the cabinet, each title had been written in because, of course, I remembered them all. And I remembered something else, too.

None of the books had gilt on their covers, or their page edges. So, why were there bits of gilt among the ashes? None of the titles had the letters o-u-s in them, in that order, either. So, where had that bit of book cover come from? It was a real mystery!

I wanted to tell Mom about it, but she was coming off a double shift at the hospital. Dad would listen—or seem to—and then dismiss it.

The next day was Sunday. Officer Merrill and Dad were going to watch a football game in the family room. Even though I figured he'd blow me off, I knew I had to tell him.

"Well, that's mighty interesting, Madison," he said, pouring his beer from the can to a glass.

"Do you think—" I began then broke off. Who was I to tell him, a veteran of the force, how to investigate a mystery? But I went on, anyway. "Do you think you could tell the fire chief?"

"Sure. Seems it might have been an electrical thing, though. Short in the wiring or some such. Investigation's not over yet."

"Wouldn't surprise me," Dad put in, turning from the fridge. "Wasn't that trophy case there when we were kids?"

And they were off to the family room.

The next time I went to shelve kids' books, only a big empty space and some clean floor tiles marked the spot where the cabinet had been. I rolled my cart past them as I headed over to the beginning of the alphabet.

Just how much money were the judge's old books worth? I wondered. The library had gotten all that publicity about the collection. If thieves had read about them, could they have broken into the library and stolen the books? But then why start a fire?

My brain leapt from one idea to another, as I started with A and slipped books into their proper places. I thought and thought and by the time I got to the Z's I'd had a thought too crazy to say out loud.

* * * *

After school the next week, I set up online accounts with some second-hand book sites, using the name I'd given my Barbie doll years ago, Samantha Kettering, and added each of the "dozen delights" titles to my Wish List.

Then, I just waited.

Christmas vacation came and went with no hits on my list. Other stuff cropped up to distract me—namely college prep work and practicing for my driver's test. The cabinet was replaced with a new one twice as big, donated by Mary Ramsey.

One day in March, when I checked my alias email account, I got a surprise.

Some of the books on my Wish List had appeared for sale, complete with photos of books I recognized. My suspicions were confirmed when I looked to see where the seller was located. Sure enough, my own home town.

I wanted to run down the hall to the family room, where Officer Merrill and Dad were encamped for March Madness. Instead, I tucked my tablet under my arm and poked my nose into their territory.

"Can I get you guys anything? More soda? Chips?"

"Thanks, honey. We're good," Dad assured me without looking over.

"Want to join us?" Officer Merrill kidded, expecting me to turn and run.

"Thanks!" I surprised him by plopping down on the sectional.

"What do you have there?" he asked, pointed at the tablet. "Homework?"

I swallowed. No one else was going to say what I wanted to say now. It was all up to me. He had to believe me.

I told him about looking for the book titles online, and how now, there they were, for sale in the very city where they had supposedly gone up in smoke months earlier.

"Weird, huh?" I asked.

"Could be different copies, Maddie," Dad said. "They print a lot of books, you know."

I turned to the police officer for a better answer.

He hedged. "What are you thinking?"

"I thought Dad and I could put in an offer. Arrange to buy the books. Then, see who answers the door when we go to pick them up."

"What?" Dad asked, looking away from the screen.

Officer Merrill shifted so he could look me in the eye. From the expression on his face—curious, serious—I felt like he was treating me like a grown up. "Who do you suspect?"

My stomach quivered. Of course I had my ideas. Maybe I'd had them all along since the day of the fire, but now I had to actually say them out loud.

I took a deep breath.

"It was an inside job," I said.

Dad gave a hoot. "You've been watching too many detective shows."

Officer Merrill asked, "The one with the purple hair?"

"No!" I was indignant. "Candy would never do something like that!"

"Who, then?" he asked.

So, I told him.

"We should go there right away," I finished, "before someone else buys all the books!"

"That hardly seems likely," Officer Merrill said. "And if you're right, it could be dangerous, dealing with a criminal. You'd better let me check it out."

"Who's paying for these books if you're wrong?" Dad kidded me.

"I will," I stated. "I'll use the money I was saving for the class trip." It was easy to promise because a) I knew I was right; and b) if I wasn't, Dad would never make me pay.

Officer Merrill took the info I gave him and set off. Dad turned back to the television. I tapped my toe, thinking.

"Can you take me out driving, Dad?" I asked, oh-so-casually. "It would take my mind off this and my test is in a couple weeks."

"Yeah, sure. Just let me watch the end of this quarter."

He didn't get up off the sofa, but I ran for the keys, anyway. It was nearly half an hour before we actually hit the road.

Obeying all the traffic rules and going the speed limit, I drove while Dad looked out the window.

"Where are we going?" he asked when we'd gone about a mile.

Keeping my eyes on the road, I squeezed my hands on the wheel then turned on the left blinker.

"To that address I gave Officer Merrill," I said, risking a quick glance sideways. "Don't be mad, but waiting at home would be torture!"

By then we were in the parking lot of the Winter Garden Courts apartments. I pulled in to a parking space a few spots over from the car I recognized as Officer Merrill's.

"Kenny said it could be dangerous, honey," Dad said patiently. He looked around at the peaceful, empty courtyard, well-tended lawn and tidy patios. "Although it doesn't look like it now."

"Can we stay for five minutes?" I wheedled, but Dad was firm.

"Nope. Let's go get some ice cream. He'll tell us all about it later."

But just then a squad car rolled to a stop practically right next to us and a uniformed officer got out fast, moving quickly toward Number Eight.

"Is that the apartment where—" Dad began.

"Yeah," I jumped in.

We watched as he reached the door and it opened to reveal Officer Merrill.

In seconds we saw Miss Everly appear and she did not look happy.

"You were right, Maddie," Dad said, sounding amazed. He gave me a pat on the arm.

"But, look, Dad!" I said. "There's Mary Ramsey, too!"

I never expected to see her there, but, sure enough, the two women were heading toward the squad car, escorted by the police.

Miss Everly was looking around, probably hoping none of her neighbors were watching, and that's when she saw me, sitting in Dad's car, about twenty feet away.

"I should have known," she said, stopping dead and glaring over. "Why couldn't you just mind your own business and shut up?" she shouted at me.

I slipped down in my seat, then looked over at Dad. He looked at me. I knew we were both thinking the same thing. This was the only time in the history of the world that I, Madison Campbell—aka Miss Mouse—had ever been told to shut up.

Officer Merrill gave us the stink eye when he saw us and I knew there'd be trouble later. I hoped he wouldn't blame Dad. He didn't, but I sure got a lecture when he came by the house that night. I said I was sorry and promised I'd never, ever do it again. And I meant it.

Then, he gave us the details.

The two old friends cooked up the scheme together. It had been Mary Ramsey's idea to display some of the judge's books and then have them go up in flames for the insurance money, which they'd split. But Miss Everly had sweetened the pot. By replacing the valuable books with leftovers from the library's annual book sale, they could collect the insurance money and still sell the books online, profiting twice.

"She admitted making a short in the wiring of that old cabinet," Officer Merrill said. "Mary Ramsey told me they burned the books first, right there in that fire pit on the patio, so they could be sure they were really incinerated." He chuckled. "Miss Everly was really steamed when I told her it was the gilt in the ashes that provided the big clue. And as soon as she saw you, she knew you were the one who figured it out," he concluded.

"Guess you should have worn a disguise," Dad teased.

I thought about the priceless books, safe and sound back in the judge's library. They might have been up for sale, but Miss Everly and Mary Ramsey would be the ones paying the price now. Would they share a cell in prison, I wondered, picturing them sitting side by side, catching up on their reading. That would be a suitable ending, I thought.

GOSSIP

by Susan Daly

The Reverend Kelly Keith paused in the doorway of the Fellowship Room, and the conversation came to dead halt. Why did everyone seem to think ministers should be protected from the seedier side of life?

"Sounds like a lively discussion." She looked around at the four women working on various projects for the Spring Bazaar.

Ginny Harlow gave close attention to her crocheted toilet roll cozy, in the form of a pastel poodle.

"Oh, just some long ago happenings." Eileen Pronovost barely glanced up from the orange and lime green knitted concoction in her lap.

"If it's juicy gossip," Kelly said, "I'm happy to listen."

The women glanced at each other. Margaret Gates, altar guild president and church secretary, straightened her shoulders. "It's not gossip, Reverend. It's true."

"Even better." Kelly claimed the empty armchair. She'd brought her knitting today, with a plan to join the women and help them relax with her a bit. Even after nearly a year at St. Mary's, she still found some parishioners uncomfortable around a woman minister. She settled in to work on her scarf.

Ginny was the first to heed the call. "Seems Amy Hartmann is back in Carpathia." *And up to no good*, her voice implied.

"An old parishioner?" Kelly focused on her knitting.

A chorus of sniffs and half laughs was the response.

"Not *her*," Eileen said. "Though her father was a longstanding member." Her tone suggested more to come. "Till he died of a stroke."

"She didn't even come home for his funeral." Margaret gave what would have been a snort, had she been anything less than a lady. "Hardly surprising."

Kelly was only human, ready to find out what had the Bazaar Ladies so exercised they'd now shed their reticence about gossiping with the minister.

"Really?"

"Well …" Margaret concentrated on counting her stitches for what looked like warm and practical slippers, popular items at every church bazaar in Kelly's career. "Thirty-three, thirty-four … I don't like to talk about old sins—"

"She was a wild one—" Ginny began.

"She was an ungrateful little tramp," Margaret snapped. "Mind you, I'm not saying Clive Hartmann was an easy man to live with, but he was her father and he did right by her, bringing her up Christian and putting food on her plate and clothes on her back."

This was punctuated by various nods and affirmative noises from the others.

"She should have been taking care of him after her mother died, not wasting all her time with all her lah-di-dah 'art.'"

"To say nothing of her carrying-ons."

"Carrying-ons?" Kelly murmured, marveling at the effectiveness of echoing the last word or two.

"Anything in pants," Margaret said. "No man was safe from her once she turned sixteen. Starting with that teacher."

It sounded bad, but Kelly had learned a lot about truth and gossip in her ten years as a minister.

"When did she leave Carpathia?"

"Right after high school. You'd think she'd realize it was time to stop messing around with her paints and clay and wires, and settle down, but—"

"She ran off with Louise Mathieson's husband." Sharon Carter, silent until now, had just appropriated the best bit.

Margaret sniffed and sent Sharon a Look. Kelly attempted to ward off bloodshed by turning pointedly to Margaret.

"I thought Louise's husband was dead." Surely Louise had mentioned him once or twice with a hint of *the dear departed*.

"He might as well be." Margaret appeared mollified by this appeal to her superior position. "No one's heard from either of them since the day they left town together."

"Well, we've heard about *her*," Eileen said. "That magazine article somebody brought to the altar guild meeting."

The Bazaar Ladies were now eager to supply the details.

"She's a sculptress. People actually pay money for her figures."

"Married to some bigshot millionaire out in B.C."

"Clearly she dumped Brad years ago, once he'd served his purpose as her ticket out of town."

"Of course Louise never speaks ill of him."

"No one else does, either. Out of respect, you know."

"Louise is a good woman," Margaret said. "She works hard. Runs the farm and supports herself without any help from anyone. Well, they neither of them had any family left anyway."

"Runs it a far sight better than Brad ever did," Eileen added.

"If you ask me," Sharon spoke in low, confidential tones, "she's better off without him."

There was a moment of silence, then more murmurs of agreement.

Kelly noted that while the Bazaar Ladies had delivered the scandalous history of Amy Hartmann in normal voices, clearly the idea that a woman could be better off without her husband, however unsatisfactory, had to be imparted in hushed, half-ashamed tones.

* * * *

Amy Hartmann parked on the main street near the Co-op and lit a cigarette and waited. How stupid was it to come back? What could she achieve? Although no one had said anything to her face, she knew half the town—the half over forty—remembered her as the girl who stole Louise Mathieson's husband.

She'd felt like a fish out of water in this hole since the moment she was born. Too smart, too ambitious, too full of ideas. Eighteen years ago, she'd vowed never to return. Carpathia wasn't Vancouver. Hell, it wasn't even Vernon. It was the dreariest dump in Canada, and she'd seen a lot of dreary dumps in her hungry years.

Damn the luck anyway, running into Leon Briggs last month. If only she'd looked through him, instead of letting herself wonder where she knew him from. Leon, in no way memorable except for how he would hang around outside the high school, eyeing the girls. They'd all made fun of him. Creepy old Leon.

Though no creepier than a lot of the men in the town. Her father included.

Leon had remembered her, all right. Along with the unknown history she'd left behind. That had been the shocker.

There she was. Louise Mathieson hadn't changed in all these years, except to look even more dowdy and plain. Jesus, was that the same coat she'd worn eighteen years ago? Amy stubbed out her cigarette and got out of the car.

Louise knew her immediately. She didn't appear surprised. Just angry.

"I heard you were back." She seemed oblivious to anyone who might be within earshot. "Well, you wasted a trip because I have nothing to say to you."

She turned towards her own car, but Amy shifted herself to block her getaway.

"But I have something to say to you. Why did you make up that story about Brad and me?"

"Story? Everyone knew you two ran off together. After you chased him for months."

"They knew *nothing*, except that your husband couldn't keep his pants zipped."

Louise's eyes narrowed, but otherwise her expression didn't change. "Okay, so he fooled around a bit, but if you hadn't led him on, if you hadn't seduced him, he would still be here with me in Carpathia where he belongs."

"Louise, I never went after him. I never slept with him. I never ran off with him."

Louise wasn't buying it.

"Look, I don't understand why you've come back to stir up old trouble. It's all in the past and I don't want everyone talking about it again."

Before Amy could find an answer, Louise's hard face softened the faintest bit.

"If it means anything, I forgave him—and you—a long time ago."

Amy hadn't come here for forgiveness.

"Louise, listen to me. I left Carpathia that night—alone—and never gave the town or anyone in it another thought. Except for—"

"We had a deal," Louise snapped, slipping between Amy and her car door. She got in and started the engine. "You welched on it. *That's* the part I can't forgive."

She slammed the car door and pulled away.

Well, that went well.

Amy was shaking so hard she didn't trust herself to get back into her car. But even as she stood watching Louise drive off, she became aware of someone nearby. She turned to see a woman who looked like she was offering to be her only friend in the world. Or at least in this town.

* * * *

Kelly poured her guest a coffee and set it before her on the rectory kitchen table.

"I admit I did a search on you," Kelly said, "after the church ladies mentioned they'd seen your work in some magazine."

Amy shook her head with a half-smile. "I'll bet that's not all they mentioned about me."

"You're right. They're all friends of Louise's."

"Of course. Why wouldn't they believe what's apparently been common knowledge for eighteen years?" She added copious cream and sugar to her coffee.

"But they don't understand why you came back to Carpathia after all this time. It's actually none of my business, of course, unless you'd like me to talk to Louise."

"I don't suppose she's interested in finding out what really happened."

"Well, try it on me." Kelly sat down with her own coffee.

"No doubt those women would have you believe I gave it away to every guy in town."

"Something like that."

"Thing is, I didn't have any boyfriends. I was more interested in art, especially sculpture. This one teacher—Mr. Wills—was really supportive. I think he was thrilled to find one student who actually cared about style and form and creation, instead of makeup and clothes.

"But right after graduation, Mr. Wills left for greener pastures. Of course. I got a job at the Co-op and tried to figure out how long it would take to save up and leave town and go to art school. About a million years."

"And Brad Mathieson?"

"He talked to me one day at the store, said he'd heard from his buddy the art teacher about my work, and acted all interested. Honest to god, it went to my head that this grown-up was interested in sculpture too."

"He was a farmer, right?"

"Sure, but farmers—anyone—can at least be interested. And he seemed pretty cool, for an old guy of forty, I mean. Louise was always, well, frumpy. I admit I wondered what he saw in her."

Kelly nodded.

"I was just happy someone in this town thought I had talent. We met for a coffee a few times and talked about my 'career.' Shit, where are our brains when we're seventeen?" She shook her head with a cynical laugh and Kelly appreciated she didn't apologize for her language.

"But—big surprise—soon he started in with the old 'my wife doesn't understand me' routine. He suggested maybe he could help me if I was thinking about art school."

"How could he do that?"

"I know, it's crazy, because like most farmers in the area, they were barely managing." Amy took a long drink from her mug. "But let's face it, I couldn't see any way of getting out of this town. My father wouldn't have given me a penny. We didn't exactly get along. All he saw in me was someone to keep on doing all his housework. If I went to Toronto alone and broke, I'd probably end up on the street, one way or another. So for about a minute and a half, I actually imagined what Brad could do for me."

"Did Louise find out?"

"Hey, by then it was all over town I was sleeping with him. Funny what a few art discussions with a guy can turn into. Then I found out he made a habit of messing around with teenage girls."

Amy ran her finger around the rim of her coffee mug a couple of times. "Anyway, next thing I knew, Louise came to me with an envelope full of cash. Five hundred and sixty dollars. She'd been saving it up for years, kept it hidden from Brad. It was mine if I left town. Alone."

"She bought you off?" People actually did that?

"Can you believe it? Like some old movie. Full of conditions. Leave, never come back. Never contact Brad again. And never tell anyone—not my father, not anyone—about this transaction."

"So it just fell into your lap."

"The answer to a prayer. If I'd been praying." Amy sighed. "It was cruel to take her money, I know, but I didn't wait to be asked twice. I was on the bus to Toronto that night. And I never looked back."

"Five hundred and sixty dollars wouldn't go far," Kelly said, and sipped her own coffee. "How did you manage?"

"Shitty rooming houses, shitty jobs. But I worked hard and took night courses. I just kept moving west and finally went to art college in Vancouver. And somehow, I've managed to make a living and a name for myself as an artist."

"But now you came back."

Amy took a drink of her coffee. "I ran into someone from Carpathia last month. He took great pleasure in filling me in on the reputation I'd left behind. I was stunned."

"So that's when you realized all these years Louise thought you took her money *and* her husband."

"Sucks, eh? I was surprised how much that bothered me. So I came back east and confronted her—I guess you saw part of that—and she wouldn't listen."

"She's believed it so long, I guess she can't begin to believe anything else," Kelly said. "Would you like me to try and talk with her?"

Amy shrugged. "Okay …. For all the good it'll do."

* * * *

Kelly looked at the uncompromising woman sitting across from her in the vestry, arms folded across her chest.

"I suppose she told you her pack of lies," Louise said.

"She says she didn't leave with your husband." Kelly kept her voice low, aware that Margaret, as church secretary, was working in the outer office. "She wasn't even interested in him."

Louise gave her a look of amused contempt. "And you fell for it. Because she's pretty and sophisticated, while I'm just an old farm woman who couldn't possibly understand about independent women."

"You seem pretty independent yourself, Louise."

"I've had to be, Reverend, but let me tell you, women like Amy Hartmann will always find a man to lean on. Even if he's someone else's man."

"Apparently she didn't have to, since you gave her money to leave town and never come back."

For a moment Louise's face lost its assured arrogance. But she recovered.

"Oh. She told you that, eh?"

"Didn't you?" Kelly winced inwardly at all these prescribed responses, but they kept Louise talking.

"Oh, that part's true enough." She paused, as though deciding how much more to reveal. "I guess you think I was pretty desperate."

"You did what you felt you had to."

"When your marriage—your whole life—is on the line, you throw pride out the door. That was my money, saved from years of selling eggs, selling my needlework. Money Brad never even knew about."

Louise's belligerence was seeping away.

"Of course I didn't want anyone to hear about *that*. How pathetic I was, paying her to leave my husband alone. And if they knew she took the money *and* my husband, they'd know I was an even bigger fool."

Were those tears forming in her eyes? "Your friends seem very sympathetic about what happened."

"I suppose so. But I bet they also hinted I'm better off without him."

"Uh, it came up." Brutal, perhaps, but true.

"Well, maybe I am, but—I *loved* him." Now the tears began to flow. "No one seems to understand that. Yes, he cheated on me—sometimes—and yes, he drank a bit too much, and maybe he was sort of shiftless. But he loved me, and never a day goes by when I don't miss him like crazy." She began to shake with incipient sobs. "Is that so wrong?"

"Of course not." Kelly pushed the ever-handy tissue box in her direction and forced out another platitude. "When we really love someone, we don't stop because they're not perfect."

"Perfect!" The word seemed a trigger point, and Kelly watched helplessly as Louise disintegrated into a puddle of misery.

Kelly gave up trying to persuade Louise that Amy was blameless. She summoned Margaret from the next room to take her friend home.

* * * *

"How did everyone in town know Brad and Amy left together?"

Kelly had crashed the Bazaar Ladies' meeting again.

"Well, it was obvious," Ginny said. "Amy just packed up and left in the night. Left a note for her father saying she was off for Toronto. For good."

"*He* didn't care," Eileen added. "Willa Fenster moved in with him before a week was out."

"And the next morning, turned out Brad was gone too. Said he was going into Peterborough to look at a new second-hand truck."

"Oh? Was that a sudden decision?"

"He'd been talking about it for ages," Sharon said. "Bert said he was always going on about it at the Co-op."

"Even though Louise said they couldn't afford it," Margaret muttered.

"So no one thought anything of it," Eileen said, "because Louise said he'd left early Friday morning. Got a ride into Peterborough with a produce driver who'd stopped by the farm."

"She thought he might spend the night in Peterborough." Margaret gave a cynical sniff. "Well, we all knew what *that* meant."

Again the murmurs of agreement made the rounds.

"But on top of that," Margaret's eyes were angry, "he took her egg money."

"I'd forgotten that," Ginny said. "Nearly $600! She'd been saving it for years. It was hidden in her, uh, sanitary things, but he found it."

"The *shit*," Sharon said. "Oops! Sorry, Reverend."

"Don't be," Kelly said, her mind churning. Six hundred dollars? Again? How many times was this famous egg money going to pop up?

And who had *really* left town with it?

"So, when *did* Louise decide they'd gone off together?"

The four women looked at each other.

"Two weeks later," Margaret finally answered. "When she got his letter."

* * * *

"Amy, did you know Brad wrote to Louise telling her he'd gone off with you?"

Kelly heard a few moments of silence on the phone, then Amy burst out laughing. "That conniving bastard. I suppose he wanted to throw Louise off his trail."

"Did you also know that, according to legend, he stole $600 from Louise before he left? All her egg money."

Amy received that news more seriously. "Are you saying I've been lying?"

"I'm saying a lot of things don't add up." Kelly told her everything the Bazaar Ladies had said about Brad's sudden departure, supposedly for Peterborough, to look at a used truck.

Amy listened quietly, then said, "Kelly, whatever Louise says, I only know she gave me the money, and once I'd packed, I caught a ride to Lindsay to catch the night bus for Toronto …." Her words trailed off.

"Who'd you get a ride with?" Did someone else know she'd caught the bus?

"Uh, some guy. Look, Kelly, I'm sorry, I've got to run. Thanks for all the information."

She disconnected.

* * * *

Louise was preparing mash for the chickens when she saw Amy Hartmann's fancy rental car pull into the yard.

Now what? When is this going to end?

And how?

Amy got out and headed straight towards her, looking grim.

"You again?" A firm front was best. "I told you—"

"You arranged for me to get a lift to Lindsay that night," Amy said. "Remember? Some farm produce trucker, passing through. I'd forgotten all about that until today."

"So what if I did?" Louise made a point of keeping her eyes on Amy. *Don't look over at the orchard.*

"So you *always* knew I didn't leave with Brad. Yet you spread that story, embellished with tales of him pretending to go to Peterborough to buy a truck, and stealing your egg money. And the letter you got weeks later, confirming it all? Did you ever show anyone else that letter?"

"I burned it." Simple was best.

"Of course you did. The last letter you ever received from the man you claimed you loved so much, even after the way he treated you."

Louise couldn't speak, as she felt her carefully rebuilt life crumble around her.

"I kept wondering why you didn't ask me about him, where he was now, or even if he was still alive. I'd have thought you'd be just a little curious."

Yes, she should have thought of that. But Amy's return had been so sudden. Just like the night she'd left.

"And you know, I've been hearing some of the gossip around town, and the one thing everyone agrees on is that him leaving was the best thing that ever happened to you."

Okay. Louise decided she'd heard enough.

"What about you?" she asked. "Aren't you better off too?"

"Me? Yeah, but—"

"You got away. I never did."

Amy nodded, saying nothing.

"I had ambitions like you once. I felt just as out of place as you did. I was going to take on the world, get myself out of this crap town and make something of myself."

"But you stayed and married Brad."

"I got pregnant and married Brad. The baby died, and there was never another. But I still had Brad, and his drinking and cheating and spending and letting the farm go all to hell.

"Then when he actually threatened to leave this time, to make a new life with you, my first thought was, *Fine. She can have him. And good riddance.* But my second thought was, *Why should he get to destroy another life, like he did mine?* That's when I decided to let you have the chance I never had."

"You did it to save me from Brad ...." Amy murmured. "Not to save Brad from me."

Louise nodded. "Call me a fool. I'd been saving up for years, thinking maybe I could run away myself. But I knew it would never happen."

This was the first time she'd ever talked about it. It felt good, though the consequences were unthinkable.

"That's why you insisted I leave right away, before he found out?"

"When he heard you were gone, I threw it in his face what I'd done. Stupid. Lord, he was mad. I'd never seen him in a worse temper. I thought he was going to kill me for sure, this time."

"This time?" Amy's complexion turned gray.

"But he didn't."

Louise could still feel the power the cast iron frying pan had given her.

They both started at the arrival of another car. The minister's. Kelly Keith and Margaret got out.

Louise yanked herself back to the present. "Seems I'm popular today."

Kelly looked uncertain and Margaret said, "The Reverend thought Amy was heading out here, and she decided to come too. I was in the office, so I came along."

"So I see." Louise felt a weariness in her bones and in her heart. Weariness from the years married to Brad, the years keeping her secrets. She was ready for it to be over. "Well, it's just as well you're both here, I guess."

"Wait a minute, Louise." Amy's voice held a warning. "Kelly, I have something to tell you. Brad and I *did* go off together. I took the bus, and the next morning he went to Peterborough, put a down payment on a used truck and drove to Toronto to join me."

"What?" Kelly looked blown away. "Then why did you—?"

"It sounds stupid, but now that I'm in the public eye as an artist, I felt uneasy that my unsavory past might come to light."

"You're right," Kelly said. "It sounds stupid. In fact, I don't believe it."

"I believe it," Margaret stated. "Though I guess no one cares about that any more. At least, not outside of this town."

Louise noticed her friend didn't look at her. How much had she guessed over the years?

"Well, Amy," Louise said, "since you've admitted it, tell me, where is Brad now? Is he even still alive? I've always wondered."

Amy looked unapologetic.

"I'm sorry, Louise. I have no idea. Six months later he met someone else and moved on. Later, I heard he'd got into some serious trouble and changed his name." She looked around at the others. "That's the last I knew of him."

"So that's that," Margaret said. "I don't suppose we'll ever hear from him again."

Louise took a deep breath and let it out. "No, I don't suppose we ever will."

ON LIKE DONKEY KONG

by Rhonda Lane

From her hidey hole under the oak trees on the hillside above the Blanchard County High School parking lot, Tammy Jo Armistead spotted her soon-to-be ex-husband Kenny's new red crew cab heavy-duty pickup truck roll up for the annual charity donkey basketball game. Which, according to the public address announcements she could hear through the gymnasium walls, was about to begin.

She swung binoculars up to her face. Kenny's ride gleamed under the parking lot lights. What if that S.O.B. parked under an overhead light? Or, worse, what if he sprawled across three spaces? He'd done that, at first, with all their new "pre-owned" trucks.

Shoot. She should've factored in his habitual parking lot behavior.

Sweat broke out on her palms inside the black leather gloves. Maybe this wasn't a good time? Maybe she should chalk this one up as a re-hearsal, suss out what else she'd forgotten, and hone her plan.

He eased the big truck in her direction. Good thing she was high above his sight line. One of the overhead lights illuminated two faces inside the cab. One, of course, was his. On the passenger side was fluffy red hair over sparkles.

Tammy Jo's blood pressure spiked. Her heart juddered around inside her ribs.

Tammy Jo, this is what you wanted. Them alone together in the truck and not hauling horses.

Kenny pulled into a space on the other side of the school, near the Donkey Sports Fundraisers rig. The driver's door opened and he hopped out.

Had he lost weight? His shoulders narrowed in to a V going into crisp new Wranglers. Maybe he was sick? Dying? A girl could dream.

He swaggered around the rear gate to open the passenger side door. He held out a hand, like one of Cinderella's coachmen.

Tammy Jo swung the binoculars to the left with a sharp masochistic thirst.

Dainty cowboy-booted feet with slim legs clad in dark denim emerged and floated toward the asphalt. Slender arms slid up his wide-again shoulders. She tilted her cloud of red curls and leaned in for a lipstick-smearing kiss.

Tammy Jo froze. Watching them kiss was as bad as driving past a pile-up on the interstate. All her fears and nightmares. All the gossip in town. All come to life, swirling in a vortex of red hair and sliding arms.

Back in the day, Homewrecker had been one of Kenny's beginner riders. Later, she showed their older horses in the Riders Eighteen-and-Under classes. Back then, when she was little Ashley Corcoran, long before she became Homewrecker, she drank iced tea and ate the homemade oatmeal cookies Tammy Jo served for the kids and the teetotalers at the horse show tailgate parties. She and Kenny treated all clients well, even the high-maintenance complainers, but the child riders, especially those who moved through the horse show divisions under their training, were the children they'd never had.

The trouble started a few years after Ashley aged out of the juvenile rider division. She went to work selling real estate and bought show horses of her own. Of course, she sent them to her old barn—Kenny's and Tammy Jo's. That was when Tammy Jo's life started hitting the skids. She could not abide their insolent betrayal always gnawing at her gut.

She tore her mind from the past to the present, where Kenny and the girl who'd done the unthinkable unwound from their embrace. He shoved the truck door shut and clicked the key fob for the chirp. They clasped hands together before heading off toward the gym.

Not so long ago, before it happened to her, Tammy Jo would've enjoyed being a fly on the wall in the gym to watch heads turn and tongues wag. All those lookie-loos. Who needed a halftime show?

But she'd just as soon not be where she could be seen. She'd had enough of the sidelong pitying glances. The view from the moral high ground wasn't as satisfying as she'd been sold in Sunday School.

Man, they were taking forever on that walk through the parking lot. Finally, they went inside the high school gym. Showtime.

All Tammy Jo's doubts vaporized. It was on like Donkey Kong.

* * * *

Tammy Jo glanced around to see if anyone was watching. She shoved the binoculars inside the big black tote bag she'd paid cash for at WalMart, not the local store but one up in northern Kentucky, a ways away from her usual haunts and in the dead of winter so she could be wrapped up and unidentifiable.

She snatched up the bag by its handles to run down the hill. If anyone saw her, she'd be a moving shadow, all dressed in black like a ninja. Instead, she stumbled and baby-stepped down the steep grade of slick grass.

Fretting brought on second thoughts. Maybe she should've worked her way through sympathetic friends of friends for some hard case needing fast cash. Or maybe she should've figured out that Dark Web she kept hearing about on TV to hire herself a hit man.

She knew two things for sure. Number One: some things you just have to do yourself to get right. Number Two: two people can keep a secret only if one of them is dead.

When her black sneakers passed from grass to asphalt, a PA announcement from the gym snuck through her focus. A missing child, a little girl separated from her mother. Everyone was to keep a lookout for a little blond girl about four years old. Answered to Kaylee.

Lindsay Harper had a baby girl named Kaylee. Poor li'l angel. Poor momma. Perfect diversion.

Tammy Jo could wrap this up *tout de suite* while everyone else was looking for the lost child. With any luck, they'd find that girl curled up in a corner next to the snack bar with a KitKat.

Tammy Jo hurried across the parking lot with her bag of tricks clanking against her leg. She didn't want to be a shadow casting a shadow, so she headed out away from the overhead lights. Thank goodness for those years sweating to cardio workout videos. They may not have helped her keep Kenny interested, but they sure got her across the high school parking lot while lugging a bag o' doom.

Ahead, Kenny's truck glowed like a beckoning treasure.

She was about fifteen feet away when she heard the wheezing start of a donkey's heehaw. Then, another. And another, only this one louder than his pals, so loud it like to split her eardrums. The off-key chorus built into a cacophonous chain reaction.

Her heart leaped to make a run for it out her throat. Her feet danced in place, hot-potato-style.

Gawd Almighty, please shut them up.

She'd be seen for sure if she didn't get under that truck ASAP.

The passenger side was closer so she ran up to the truck and dropped the bag on the ground next to the running board. From the bag, she yanked out a mechanic's creeper, painted black and matte with wheels greased like a skillet for silence. She lay face up on the creeper, grabbed the bag in her left hand, and shoved off with her left foot.

She careened under Kenny's truck like a piglet outrunning the vet, almost fast enough to shoot out the other side by the rear wheel. She halted her exit by catching a foot on the rear tire. She'd done too good a job greasing those creeper wheels. With her gloved fingertips and her sneakered feet as brakes, she tugged on the dark undercarriage and eased back up under the driver's side.

Good thing the donkeys had gone off when they did, but their racket was fading fast. She stared up at the dark undercarriage to wait out any donkey attendant coming to check on the commotion.

The rollers on the creeper had been taller than she'd anticipated. Dark shapes and shadows of the truck's underbelly loomed mere inches from her nose. The thick musk of motor oil snaked down into her nervous stomach. Gosh, she'd better make this quick.

She braced her feet harder to still the creeper while pawing inside her open tote bag. She grabbed the mini flashlight and placed it between her lips like an unlit cigar. Yuck. Car lube tasted nasty. No telling what her gloves had picked up when she dragged herself along. Good thing the truck was too new to carry much horse manure.

With her flashlight's focused beam, she scanned along the shadowy nooks and crannies under the truck to find the brake line, as illustrated on the diagram she'd found on the Internet.

Just a little snip for a slow leak of brake fluid. Just enough so they could get out of the parking lot and away from the other spectators, their lifelong friends and neighbors who may have been church-goers but still took their horses to Kenny because *he* won them trophies. Just time enough for the truck to make it out to the old county roads where he liked to speed and show off, winding through hills and pastures flanked by stone walls and tree trunks and fence posts. Oh, my.

She patted inside the tote, pushed the binoculars aside to find the wire nippers. She dragged them out and re-adjusted her grip. Her flashlight beam hit the spot. Good thing. Drool ran down her chin.

Slobbers? Nausea? Lying under a truck? What had she come to?

Her hand gripping the cutting tool trembled. The smell of motor oil may not have been the only thing messing with her stomach. Maybe she should just shove off and slip away into the night?

Except Tammy Jo always prided herself on seeing things through, unlike *some* folks she knew.

Those two wanted to be together? They could be together in Hell.

"Hi, donkeys." A chirping child's voice chilled Tammy Jo's blood. "Good donkeys." The little girl voice cooed. "Cute donkeys."

Tammy Jo froze with her wire nipper a hair away from notching the brake line. She held her breath and jammed her feet into the pavement to hold the silence.

"Ooh. That tickles." A girlish giggle. "You're friendly."

Where children went, so went adults. *Damn it.*

"We could be best friends. My name's Kaylee."

Aw, shoot. Kaylee Harper. The missing child.

Tammy Jo removed the soggy flashlight from her mouth, held it pointed up to avoid moving the beam, and clicked it off. Drool dried on her face. She lowered her quivering arms.

It was only a matter of time before someone came out and found Kaylee. As long as Tammy Jo didn't move a muscle, no one would see her. As long as she was silent. Didn't attract attention.

"I wish I had carrots for you."

Good Lord, where were the adults? They had to know that corral of donkeys was kid bait. Irresistible. Candy, cookies and critters—catnip for children.

From the bag at her side, she slid out her burner cell. Good thing she'd bought one at the last minute. Still. Risky. She typed in an old friend's personal cell number and texted, "kid out w donkeys." Now she had to be absolutely quiet and wait this thing out.

"Sweet donkeys. Krogers has lots of carrots. I'll go get some."

What? Tammy Jo turned her head to see small pink cowgirl boots stride by, on her way out of the parking lot.

Kaylee was *leaving*? How would adults find her?

Damn it. She had to stop that child before she left the high school grounds or got hit by a car or got picked up by a pervert. My gosh, the disasters facing that girl were endless and frightening.

Tammy Jo had to make sure that child stayed put. She pushed off with her foot and launched herself on the creeper out the other side of the truck. She hopped to her feet.

"Hi, Kaylee." She glimpsed herself in Kenny's side mirror. Yikes! All black. Dark stuff smeared on her face. Black knit cap with brown hair sticking out from under the bottom. She'd make a pervert look decent. She stayed behind the cab of the truck. "I'm—"

Well, who? She looked like walking stranger-danger. "I'm Tammy Jo Armistead. You came to our barn party and went for a ride on Scooter, our pony. You remember? A little spotted pony? Fat as the dickens?"

Silence. Too much silence. Had she left? *Oh, please, no.*

The girlish voice lilted with hope in the night. "Is Scooter here?"

Tammy Jo heaved a sigh of relief. "No, honey. He's home." She had to think fast. "He's got to get up early tomorrow morning." She had to get out of there. She gathered her gear.

"Why?" Kaylee's voice pulsed in genuine curiosity. "Why isn't Scooter here?"

"He likes to get in an early workout." Tammy Jo cringed at the fib. Scooter was a good little kid's pony because he was slow and lazy.

"I can't see you. Where *are* you?"

"Oh, honey, I don't want you to see me because," this would have to be good, "I fell down and got dirty. I'm a mess." Her blood pressure spiked so hard she saw sparklies behind her eyes. She needed to leave. "I have to—"

"Do you have any carrots? The donkeys need carrots."

A legitimate out. Finally. Hooray. "You stay there, and I'll go get some."

"Why?"

Tammy Jo was on the verge of snapping, *because I have money and you don't and I gotta go*, when she heard a male voice.

"Well, hello, girls. You just stay right where you are."

Tammy Jo's blood chilled her to the bone, even though he sounded cordial. She'd known that voice for decades, all the way from kindergarten to his job in the courthouse, ever since his days as a high school linebacker so good his nickname followed him into adulthood and his professional life.

Blanchard County Sheriff Dozer McClure's voice came closer. "Kaylee, honey, the donkeys get carrots for dessert, like you do, after their work and supper. The hay will do just fine and keep them light on their feet for the game." He paused.

Maybe he hadn't seen her.

"Evening, Tammy Jo."

Tammy Jo cringed as his voice closed in behind her. Her cheeks burned hot enough to boil tears filling behind her eyes.

"Evening, Do— Sheriff." She caught herself before calling him by his nickname. Not such familiarity in front of the child, let alone while she was up to no good, especially to his viewpoint.

This was it. She was caught. Arrest. Jail. But not before disgrace, even though she'd stopped, changed her mind, and was ready to leave.

No more would she face those sympathetic, pitying whispers she thought she hated. In the scheme of things, a homewrecker was still a better person than a "murderer," even an "attempted murderer." Oops. Make that a "double murderer."

For the foreseeable future, the punch line for every bad ex-wife joke would be "Tammy Jo Armistead." Maybe it wouldn't follow her into *prison*.

No more freedom. No more horses.

His voice lilted into a child-friendly tone, "Miss Kaylee, your momma would love to see you."

"I want to show her the donkeys. They're so happy."

"Tell you what, sugar. You go wait with your donkey friends, and I'll radio one of my deputies to bring your momma out." He sounded so cheerful, as if they were making plans to go out for ice cream. A pause, then, in a solid voice, but not so intimidating as to upset Kaylee, "Tammy Jo, put down the bag. Walk away from it about ten steps and stay put." Less cheerful. "We need to talk."

He radioed in and stayed with Kaylee until he heard the deputy had sent Lindsay on her way. While he waited he asked Tammy Jo, "Are you still with me?" She answered with a, "Yes, sir," and wouldn't dare ask if she could be on her way. She suspected those days of coming and going as she pleased were over.

From her view obstructed by the donkey ball truck, she spotted Lindsay Harper, barely old enough to have a baby herself, hurry through the parking lot. "Kaylee! Honey! I missed you so much." She ran up to her child with open arms.

Tammy Jo couldn't see much of the reunion, although her heart ached to see some happiness before she officially was branded a criminal. After mother and daughter thanked the sheriff and walked away, Tammy Jo heard slow footsteps on the pavement behind her. She braced herself. How could she even face him?

"That was you calling on my personal line?"

"Yes, sir." Only answer the questions, nothing more.

"Why didn't you use your personal cell?"

"Left it somewhere." She stopped short of adding she'd gotten this one at a quickie mart.

"Really." He sounded as if he were a parent trying to keep his cool. "What are you doing out here anyway?"

She'd have to remember the lies she told. "It's quieter out here than in the gym."

The Sheriff heaved a resigned sigh. "How long have we known each other, Tammy Jo?"

"Long enough doing the math makes it sound a mite depressing."

He placed both hands on his duty belt. "There's no fool like an old fool. Am I right?"

Her head tilted back toward the truck. "Seems like there's a lot of that going around."

"You wouldn't believe how these kinds of domestic situations make normally sane people go crazy. Strong people, too. You'd be surprised. Just like I'm surprised at you. Of all people. Tammy No."

Hearing her own old high school nickname tightened a lump in her throat. She'd been such a good church-going girl, admired by adults but a "Goody Two Shoes" among her peers.

"I don't know what rode over me, Dozer. I really don't."

"So, how is Kenny's truck? Drivable? Stoppable?"

"It's straight-from-the-dealer perfect. Hardly any mud in the wheel wells even."

"I'd like to take your word for it, but time and experience stole my trust. When something happens to a couple going through what y'all are going through, we always suspect the ex. Mechanics can tell when a brake line's been cut. I'd hate to have to send a deputy to get permission from Kenny to take a look at his truck." He cocked his head as if to say, you know what that means.

Tammy Jo's mind went there. Her stomach hardened. Kenny and Homewrecker would crow and jeer about her lapse in judgment all over town, let alone at every horse show all summer.

"I saw Kaylee—before anything happened." She had to prove she hadn't damaged the truck, yet keep her sabotage attempt from Kenny for as long as possible. An idea sparked. Something she could do that maybe Dozer couldn't.

"Hypothetically speaking," she made up her plan as she went, "what if a person ran out to the poles out on the street, ripped down some signs advertising the game, flipped them over, and slid them under the truck to leave until the final moments of the game, before people started leaving for their cars."

Her mouth went dry but she kept on going. "Anything leaking would show up on the white paper." Afraid to check for Dozer's reaction, she wrapped things up for a big finish, like they did on "Law & Order" on TV. "Especially if the wife of said truck owner who's not quite an ex-wife so she still co-owns just about everything he owns puts down said cardboard."

She sucked in a huge breath of hope. "What do you think?"

Her knees shook enough to shift the hair tufts sticking out of the bottom of the black knit cap. Half-time was coming up. They wouldn't be alone for long. She had to sell this fast. "If there are any spots under the car by the fourth quarter, no one will be more surprised than me. What do you say?"

"The first time a good citizen loses control and screws up like this," he waved his left hand as if he were painting her rumpled dirty ninja suit, "we try to cut them some slack, especially if we catch them before anything bad happens. We're not so accommodating after that."

The horse was out of the barn and grazing on the azaleas, but she had to ask. "Even if the truck's fine, do I need a lawyer?"

"Unless something happens to Kenny and his girlfriend on the way home, all you need is a divorce lawyer. A good one."

Happier tears burbled in Tammy Jo's eyes. She sniffled and wiped her nose on her black leather gloves.

Dozer shook his pointer finger at her. "Now, you need to work fast. Make sure you pick up all that junk you brought. Every speck. Set it aside, and then do your hypothetical experiment. Let that lawyer wreak your vengeance. Stay 'good people.' Don't let anything bad happen to those two 'cuz they're not worth your downfall. Protect them like you protected that little girl."

The notion of protecting Kenny and Ashley made her skin itch, but she saw the logic in it. Logic could be used for good or ill.

Relief washed over her like a warm rain on a parched field. No arrest. No prison. Not tonight. "Thank you, Dozer."

"Get a move on. It's almost halftime."

She already had bagged her tools. She hurried out to the street where she'd seen posters for the game. In a half-whisper, she added, "And thank you, Lord, for sending a child to lead me out of darkness."

Because Tammy No was *back* and back on her game.

CRIME ON HOLD

by Claire Ortalda

Since I'm unemployed now and also have learned a few things, I think I should write a casebook for would-be criminals. I have the title for Chapter Three: Victim Selection. Certain types of people are not good candidates for victimization. In fact, I would counsel, abject poverty or prison time may seem preferable to any contact whatsoever with this sort of hardened victim.

My experience in this area began in 1981, in the early days of Silicon Valley when tech firms were sprouting like mushrooms in newly-razed orchards. Luckily for me, or so I thought at the time, my temp job for a venture capitalist morphed into a full-time position in the office of one of the biggest developers in the Valley.

My immediate supervisor was named Jackie, a pretty woman, maybe thirty, about my age, something of the lioness about her, with her long tawny straight hair, high forehead and green eyes. She informed me that, though there were a stack of invoices to be paid and a pile of papers to be filed, my first priority was to answer and direct phone calls.

"Don't ever interrupt Les when he's in a meeting or on the phone unless it's important. But if it's important, you absolutely *must* put the call through."

This was pre-cell phone, when calls were screened not by the receiver with a glance at the incoming number, but by griffin-like receptionists.

"Uh … how do I know if it's important?"

Some expression I couldn't identify flitted across her tanned face. Glee? Pity? Bitterness?

It could have been any of those. I knew that Jackie, long-time assistant to Les Tarnow, the wealthy developer who was now my employer, made less per hour than the rather humble figure I had demanded. Rightfully, she could have been miffed by that but Jackie had much, much bigger fish to fry. She was angling for a percentage of one of the many office buildings Les owned in Silicon Valley, including the campus that housed Bilberry Computers. I knew all this because of that temp position for the venture capitalist occupying the office in the back.

"Um," I repeated. "How will I know?"

This time there was no mistaking the gleam. "Oh, you'll figure it out."

She returned to her desk and picked up the phone, shaking her shiny hair sideways to accommodate the receiver. The office was a long, rather narrow one with storefront type windows at the front emblazoned with a sign, Tarnow & Tarnow, Developers. On the left, as you entered, was Carl's office and next to that, his brother Hugh's. Hugh was the other Tarnow and his contribution seemed to consist of checking in every day in garish plaid pants and yellow sweaters before hitting the golf course. On the right were my desk and Jackie's. Behind us was a small lunch room dominated by a fountain soft drink machine such as one sees in fast-food restaurants. Les was a serious diet cola addict, though his waistline had not benefited from his abstinence from sugar. Les was big and fat. He less walked then rolled across the cheap carpet at regular intervals, setting the pens in my pen cup atinkle, carrying an enormous plastic cup, on his way to the break room for another refill of his necessary chemical nectar.

He always smiled but in a very perfunctory way on these journeys and he always wore the same sort of clothes, giant cream-colored chinos and short-sleeved plaid shirts. Les may have been a multi-millionaire but he didn't waste money on fancy duds or office. He drove a grandly-finned antique white Cadillac with the foot well of the passenger side full of sticky, empty ice cream containers.

My phone rang.

"Tarnow & Tarnow Developers," I answered.

"Let me talk to Les," a male voice said.

"Who's calling, please?"

A pause, then a chuckle. "Mmmm. You're new, aren't you? What's your name?"

"Susan."

"Well, Susan. This is Doug Jensen over at Wells Fargo. Put me through to Les, will you? We're in the middle of a deal and he told me to call him right away with the numbers."

If anything sounded important, this was it. "Just a moment, Mr. Jensen."

I put Mr. Jensen on hold and hesitated with my finger over the lighted button that was Les's line. I pressed down and was on the line, plunged into the middle of a conversation between Les and another man.

Though I believed my action had created a noticeable click on the line, Les didn't stop talking. I became privy to the financing of a new development east of Bailey in Sunnyvale.

When the other man said something, I jumped in. "Les—"

"Hell, no!" Les bellowed. "Not over four point five."

"Now, Les, be reasonable—"

"Les," I ventured again.

"Who is it?" Les barked. "Who's on the line?"

"This is Susan. A Mister—"

"Who the hell is Susan?"

"Out front? Jackie's assistant? The new secretary?"

"What do you want?"

"Um, Mr. Jensen of Wells Fargo is on the—"

"I don't want to talk to him. Get off the line!"

I did.

I pushed the hold button. "Um. Mister Jensen. I'm sorry. Les is in a meeting right now and can't be disturbed."

"Oh, yeah, right. Tell him to give me a call, wouldya, babe?" He hung up without leaving a number.

Les's door banged open and he rumbled across the open space to my desk. "Don't *ever* ..." His fat sausage of a finger was waggling very close to my nose. "... interrupt me to tell me Wells is on the phone when I'm already on the phone to BofA!"

"But how would I know—"

But he was already charging back to his office. He slammed the door then opened it again immediately. "Get me a diet cola!"

I scurried into the break room but not before I caught a glimpse of Jackie, staring straight ahead, the phone still at her ear as if she were on hold and the faintest traces of a smile uplifting the ends of her lips.

It was not long before the phone rang again.

"Tarnow & Tarnow Developers," I said.

"Get me Les," a female voice said.

"May I ask who's calling, please?"

"Who's this?"

"I'm Susan, the new secretary—"

"Well, I'm Les's wife. Put me through."

"Just one minute, Mrs. Tarnow—"

"I don't have a minute—" but I put her on hold anyway.

It was the same scenario when I clicked into Les's line. Numbers and percentages barked back and forth between Les and some other male. I heard the words "carrying costs."

"Les," I jumped in.

"What do you want?"

"Your wife is on the—"

"I don't wanna talk to her!"

"But—"

"Get off the line!"

I did. I hit the hold button. "Mrs. Tarnow, I'm sorry but Mr. Tarnow is tied up in a meeting—"

"Tied up in a meeting!" she scoffed. "Give me a break. He's always in a meeting. Tell him it's about Lindy. That's our daughter, in case you don't know and he forgot."

Oh, no. She would not make me beard the lion in his den again. I put her on hold and poised my finger over Les's button. Then ... I withdrew it. I drummed my fingers on the desk for a few minutes then hit the hold button again.

"I'm sorry, Mrs. Tarnow, but he says he absolutely cannot get away at this time. He'll call you as soon as he can."

"Bullshit!" Mrs. Tarnow said and hung up.

Jackie's lips twitched. "You're learning."

* * * *

And so it went. I was nearly eviscerated once when I put through John Parnell. I had seen the logo Parnell-Tarnow on some stationery so, as I explained to Jackie, I assumed he was Les's partner. Little did I know that Parnell was suing Les. It was at this juncture that Jackie acquainted me with that old saw that evidently everybody knew but me: "ASSUME means making an ASS out of U and ME." So sorry.

Anyway, I got pretty good at fielding calls and engaging in the kind of wink-wink conversations in which I pretended to be the model secretary and the caller pretended to believe what I said. I learned to recognize the voices and names of officers from every major bank in the area and principals in most of the development and venture capital firms in the Valley, as well as a host of contractors. I went through a whole pad of pink phone slips in short order.

My employer's wife, Dorothy, had taken to stopping by, their ten-year-old daughter in tow, and physically barging into Les's office, so I had fewer phone encounters with her. She was a blond woman you might have been tempted to call overweight unless you happened to see her standing next to her husband. She had a permanently enraged expression on her face. Their daughter, Lindy, had adopted a habit of pulling at what appeared to be a gold rabbit's-foot charm on a chain around her neck while staring at the corner where the wall intersected with the ceiling.

This obviated the need to look her parents in the face or even pretend to be listening. I didn't think it was a bad technique.

* * * *

One day, after I had gotten pretty used to jumping in on Les's phone calls and pretty impervious to his bluster, someone called who was not on my mental list of bankers, developers, tenants, money men, or people who wanted to sue Les. This man had a slightly foreign accent.

"It is necessary to speak to Mr. Lester Tarnow," the voice said.

"May I ask who's calling, please?"

"I will identify myself to Mr. Lester Tarnow only."

Well, that ain't gonna work.

"I'm sorry," I said. "Mr. Tarnow is in a meeting. May I take a message?"

"I have to speak to Mr. Tarnow."

"I'm sorry. He is not accepting calls at this time."

A pause and a sound like he was sucking his teeth. Then: "He will take this one."

"No, he won't," I intoned breezily. Jackie gave me a thumbs-up on the way out the door for lunch. We were almost friends by now, a united front against Les, except she was still using me as the crowbar that would get her a percentage ownership of a building.

"Then he will never see his wife and daughter again."

"What?"

"We have them. And the little girl's gold foot of rabbit, too. They are safe. For now. But we must have two million dollars by tomorrow morning. Ten a.m. sharp."

This was real, then. My throat constricted. "I will get Mr. Tarnow for you," I burbled. My finger stabbed the hold button.

I punched Les's button. "… that goddamn racketeer of a paving contractor …" came his voice.

"Les!" I screamed. "It's Dorothy!"

"I don't want to talk to her! Get off the line!"

"No, no! She and Lindy have been kidnapped—"

"Oh, bullshit!" The line clicked off.

I sat at my desk, stunned.

Les slammed out of his office, jabbing his finger my way. "You tell that SOB from Chalmers Construction that he either pours today or I will see him in court." He pushed out the glass front doors.

I stood up. "Les! Dorothy is kidnapped!"

The door swished closed. I rolled back my chair and ran. At the door, I saw Les maneuvering his white elephant of a Cadillac backward out of his parking space.

"Les!" I screamed. But he was gone, charging to the accompaniment of honking horns into the traffic on Wolfe Road.

I was alone in the office.

I rushed back to my desk. The hold light no longer glowed red. The kidnapper must have hung up. I punched 911.

"9-1-1. What is your emergency?"

"My boss's wife and child have been kidnapped!"

The operator must have just gone through the soothing-voice refresher course because she wasted time asking me to please calm down and even to take a deep breath, which I did, preparatory to delivering a blast of hysterical bleats along the line of "You've got to do something!" When she finally got the whole story out of me, though she expressed surprise that the husband had refused the call and then left the office, she asked me to hold.

That was my line and my response was the same as many of my own victims: "I don't want to hold! I want—" Click.

I waited some minutes, standing behind my desk and fidgeting with the coil of my phone. Finally, a Sergeant Nichols came on the phone. She asked the same questions the 9-1-1 operator had.

"What are you going to do?" I asked when the sergeant fell silent.

"Well, miss, normally, it would be the husband and father that would make this call. The fact that he is not concerned leads me to believe that perhaps you, well … I'm sure you mean well."

"You don't believe me, either!"

"You have, of course," Sergeant Nichols said in her careful voice, "called the residence?"

Uh, no, I hadn't done that.

"Why don't you do that, and I'll have a car drive by the residence as well. If you do happen to get another phone call, why don't you have Mr. Tarnow call us, and we'll go from there."

"There is a ten-year-old girl involved here," I said.

"Yes. I noted her age. Can you give us the address of the residence?"

I could feel heat rising in my face. "Uh. I …. Hang on a minute."

I leaped to Jackie's desk and scrabbled around. I knew Jackie paid all of the Tarnows' personal bills as part of her duties so I assumed the bills or the checks or something would have the address. I tugged on the drawer where I'd seen her withdraw the large checkbook. Locked. Damn.

I punched the open line on Jackie's phone. "I'm getting it. Give me a minute."

"I pulled it up here," said the unflappable Sergeant Nichols. "I'll contact the local police department and suggest they send a car by. Please have Mr. Tarnow call them if he gets any additional information." She hung up.

She was good. She should work in Les's office. I slammed the phone down and rattled the locked desk drawer. I jerked the flat middle drawer open. Perfect organization in little dividers of sticky notes, pens, paper clips, stamps. No key. Slam. I checked all her other drawers. No key.

I drew Jackie's rolodex close to me, flipped to "T." No Dorothy. I flipped to "D." Yes, here it was: Dorothy and the number. I dialed. The phone rang hollowly ten, twenty times. Damn. As Sergeant Nichols no doubt would say, that could mean anything. Dorothy could be out shopping or she could be bound and gagged somewhere.

I wondered what the name of Lindy's school was. If she were in class as usual, then that would tend to put the lie to the sinister voice's assertion. Or at least half of it. If I had the Tarnows' address, I could perhaps figure out what local school she attended. Hell, I didn't even have the city since obviously they didn't live here in Sunnyvale, according to Sergeant Nichols. And, come to think of it, Lindy was a rich girl. She probably went to a private school, one of dozens nearby. I gave the locked drawer another vicious yank.

Maybe I had something in my drawer I could use for a pick. I dashed over to it and scrabbled around in my middle drawer, which was a mess of pink message pads, gum, uncorralled paper clips and … a key. Hmm … I dashed back to Jackie's desk and inserted it into the locked drawer. It clicked over immediately and slid open. Wow. High security. But at last I had access to the large desk-set check binder which, hopefully, would have the address Sergeant Nichols had not seen fit to make me privy to. I flipped the cover open. No. A P.O. box. But behind the desk set was a neat file of bills. I found their power bill and that, at least, had the Tarnows' home address: 2612 Gelfen Place, Atherton. Figured. City of the elite.

I flipped through the pile of bills. Here was one: Peninsula Preparatory School. I dialed the number, identified myself as Les Tarnow's personal assistant (slight exaggeration, there) and asked if Lindy Tarnow was in school today. Not surprisingly, I was told that they could not give out that information. I explained the situation and was kicked upstairs to the principal.

"This is very serious," she said.

"Yes, it is," I answered. "No one is in the office except me, and the kidnapper called and I … don't know what to do."

"You should call the police."

"I did. They said Mr. Tarnow should call but I can't get a hold of him. If you could confirm that Lindy was there, well, then maybe the whole thing is a hoax."

"Please hold on a minute," the principal said.

The minute stretched to three. I used the time to flip through more bills. Ah, a country club bill.

"Miss?" came the principal's voice.

"Yes."

"I think we may see our way clear to telling you that Lindy is *not* in school today. And that no one has called in with an excuse."

"Oh, God," I said.

I hung up and called the Magdalena Golf and Tennis Club. Maybe Hugh would be in the bar and not on the links. He was, though I had to wait a while before he lumbered to the phone.

"Hugh. This is Susan in the office."

"Who?"

"Susan. You know. My desk is next to Jackie's." I'd been there two months by now, for pete's sake.

Some slow machinery in Hugh's brain was activated. "By the front door?" he finally said.

"Yes. Hugh. Listen. No one's in the office and this man called who said he'd kidnapped Dorothy and Lindy!"

Hugh, unbelievably, laughed. "Some kind of joke. Or maybe Les paid someone to do it." He guffawed and I even heard what sounded like a slap of palm on plaid.

"Hugh. This is serious. I was hoping you could help."

"Me?"

My molars ground against one another. "Can you at least tell me what kind of car Dorothy drives?'

"Well, she's got two but she usually drives a big black Mercedes. Yeah!" he hollered in my ear. "My tee time's up. Don't worry about it. Les plays these jokes, you know. " He hung up. I practically threw the receiver back onto its plastic cradle. Worthless hunk of plaid.

I remembered there was an area map in a back filing cabinet and ferreted that out and spread it on my desk. I found the Tarnows' street, crumpled the map clumsily and with address in hand, dashed out to my car.

* * * *

Les and Dorothy's house looked like several architects had had a food fight. White painted brick here, Corinthian columns there, a Frank Lloyd Wright-ish swooping roof line slashing across the left hand side. The three-car garage was set back from the street. Luckily, it had small decorative windows on each garage door. I peeked in. There was a red Honda in one slot, but the other two were empty. And the Honda appeared to be up on blocks. That meant Dorothy was in her Mercedes. I hoped she wasn't in the trunk of her Mercedes.

I rang the bell. No answer. Again, again, again.

Back in my car, I tapped the steering wheel. I really didn't know what to do. The best thing, then, was to return to the office. Les may have returned. Or the supremely competent Jackie. Or the kidnapper could call back.

None of the above. I availed myself of a diet cola and chewed ice cubes. The phone rang. I grabbed. "Yes? I mean. Tarnow & Tarnow, Developers."

"Les there?" came a voice that did not sound like the kidnapper's.

"No!" It was close to a scream.

"Jed Chalmers here. You tell Les we've got a hold-up here—"

"No, I won't!" My frustration overflowing, I channeled Les, word for word. "You either pour today or Les will see you in court!"

Silence. In the background I could hear the canister of a cement truck rolling. It seemed to have a slight hitch to it. Roll, roll, a grainy grinding sound. Roll, roll, grind. Then, "*What* did you say?"

"You heard me."

Roll, roll, grating grainy grind. Then a laugh. "You must be the new girl. Don't let it get to you, babe." And he hung up.

I slumped at my desk. Just how long a lunch break was Jackie going to take today? Oh, wait a minute. Hadn't she said something this morning about the dentist? I leaped to her desk and consulted her desk calendar. Yes. Dr. Lew. 1:30. After a leisurely lunch, no doubt. I returned to my desk, aching at the thought of poor Lindy, the honey-haired little girl with the permanently beleaguered look. What was she suffering this very second?

The phone rang again and I snatched it. The same slightly foreign accent, the same request for Mr. Tarnow. Some perverse impulse made me tell him that Mr. Tarnow was in a meeting and could not be interrupted. Would he leave a message?

A pause. In the background, I heard the beep-beep-beep of an automatic back-up alarm on a truck. Then a dull rumble.

"You know who I am," he finally said. "You have heard our demands. What kind of man refuses to save his family?"

"He's assembling the money right now. He asked me to get assurance that his wife and daughter are well."

"He will have that assurance when he hands over the money," said the voice.

"Where?" I demanded. "Where is he to deliver the money?"

"I will call back," the voice said. "And this time he will answer me." He hung up.

I scrabbled through the thin pages of the phone book for the Atherton police number. Surely they could not be as phlegmatic as Sergeant Nichols.

I'd dialed three digits when I paused. That sound. In the background when the kidnapper called. That rumbling sound. Roll, roll, grainy scratch. Could it be?

I tore through Jackie's rolodex. Chalmers Construction. I dialed with shaking fingers and got through to Jeb. "Mr. Chalmers! This is Les Tarnow's assistant. His wife and daughter have been kidnapped, and I need to know if you can see a black Mercedes anywhere on or near your construction site?"

"What?" he said.

"Just look!" I screamed and having had prior congress with my hysteria, he agreed and put me on hold. He was back in moments. "There is one, actually, at the far end of the pour. It's almost hidden behind a construction trailer."

"Does that trailer have a phone in it?"

"Well, sure."

"Then this is what you have to do."

It took a few tries but I finally got him to agree to send two of his cement trucks over to the Mercedes and block its exit. He was not to go in the trailer—too dangerous—but wait for the police whom I was calling right now.

The rest was on the six o'clock news, with great visuals. The churning cement trucks flanking the elegant car like two gray elephants, the police surrounding the trailer. The culprits, two of them, actually Chalmers' security guards hired to protect the equipment, flat down in the graded dirt. A miserable-looking Lindy and an irate Dorothy being helped from the trunk, whereupon it could be witnessed Dorothy haranguing the erstwhile hero, Jeb Chalmers, the cops, even the reporters. The best shot was when she went over and kicked the prone and handcuffed perpetrators.

Was I thanked and feted? No. Les berated me for talking to a valued contractor in that manner and made my life even more miserable until I quit in largely-ignored high dudgeon. I heard later that Jackie got her 1%

of the new Bilberry building, and Lindy became only the second child in U.S. history to sue her parents to undo her adoption.

Les bought a sports franchise with his millions and was seen on the news happily slurping a gigantic cup of cola. Go, team.

SIGHT UNSEEN

by KM Rockwood

"Heart attack, my ass." My cousin Reginald spit on the slushy mud next to the grave and headed toward his battered pickup truck.

Right behind him, Mother and I climbed into my Escalade.

As we left the cemetery, I peered at the lowering sky. "Looks like snow."

"Probably."

"Maybe we should just head back to DC. Skip going back to the home place." I'd had to juggle my work load at the law firm to take the day on such short notice for my great grandfather's funeral. I couldn't afford to get stuck in a blizzard.

Mother frowned. "That would be rude. The aunts have been cooking for days. We don't have to stay long."

Sighing, I followed Reginald's pickup as it joined the ragged line of decrepit vehicles snaking uphill on the gravel road.

"Somehow I didn't think he would ever die." Mother lifted a tissue to her eyes, careful not to smear her makeup.

"Was it a heart attack?" Great Pawpaw, as everyone called him, had been in his nineties, so his death hadn't surprised me, but Reginald's vehement comment threw a doubt into my mind.

Mother shook her head. "That's what the death certificate says. And hypothermia. But he had such a strong heart. I wouldn't be surprised if he hadn't had a little help with dying. With that crew, things aren't always what they seem."

We rode along in silence. Mother had left these hills long ago, moving to Washington just before she gave birth to me. From early childhood, I knew better than to ask about my father.

She'd worked hard, but money was tight. In the school summer breaks, I'd be sent to the big family home back in the Appalachian Mountains where I tried to keep up with my cousins. Seemed like I was always trying to prove myself. Without much success.

Until I was old enough to get a job myself. Then came college, and law school. I hadn't been back in years. Neither had Mother.

But the funeral of her grandfather—Great Pawpaw, everybody called him—was something Mother didn't want to miss. I suppose I didn't want to miss it, either. He was one of those larger-than-life figures to me.

When we got to the home place, a sprawling structure with innumerable entrances and porches, I left the Escalade down the driveway so it wouldn't get parked in. As we walked up the front steps, the aromas of roasting meat and baking bread reached us.

Inside, sturdy women wore flowered aprons over their funeral dresses. They bustled around, laying out an elaborate feast. Next to them, my slender mother, despite wearing a sleek gray suit and modest jewelry, looked like a delicate songbird among crows.

An aunt shoved plates in our hands. "Enjoy."

"Watch what you eat," Mother hissed under her breath. "Everything's fried in lard. Even the vegetables."

I stood near a window, holding the half-filled plate and looking anxiously out at the dark sky. My cousin Seth sidled up next to me, a jelly glass filled with dark liquid in his hand.

"That all you gonna eat?" he asked. "Or are you waiting for dessert to be set out?"

Seth was a couple of years older than I was. In those long summers, he'd been delegated with the task of minding me. He'd egged me on to numerous questionable stunts, and we'd gotten into our share of scrapes. To this day, the scar on my right thigh twinged whenever I thought about him.

"Good to see you, Seth," I said, not entirely sincerely.

"Been a while." He raised the glass and said, "Want some? Plenty in the jugs on the back porch."

Moonshine. "No thanks. It's a long drive back. I don't want to be drinking."

He shrugged and took a swig.

"Were you there when Great Pawpaw died?" I asked.

"Nah." Seth grinned through his scraggly beard. "Nobody was there. He was up at his still."

He picked at his teeth with his thumb nail and explained. When Great Pawpaw hadn't come home for a few days, everybody figured he'd been sampling his wares a bit too much. They went looking. There he was, facedown in the creek.

His body had to be hauled down on a mule, no easy task since rigor mortis had set in and his limbs wouldn't bend. He smelled pretty ripe, and the mule, latest in a long succession named Blue, wasn't happy about it.

Great Pawpaw'd already dodged a few appointments with his maker. He died where he was happiest. They'd miss him, but it wasn't a tragedy.

I asked, "Did he drown?"

"Old Doc Richards, he put heart attack on the papers. Said it was about time for the old coot to pass, and putting down heart attack prevented problems. What's it matter? Dead is dead."

"What do you think?"

Seth scratched his chin through his beard. "He prob'ly drank hisself to death. Or just got drunk and maybe fell and drowned. Or froze. The nights are pretty cold."

Mindful of Mother's earlier comment, I asked, "Could somebody have helped him along?"

"Why would anybody do that?"

"Well, he owned a lot of property. Who inherited it?"

Seth looked at me strangely. "You haven't heard?"

"Heard what?"

Staring into the depths of his glass, Seth said, "Uncle Sebastian's gonna go over the will after we all have supper. You gonna stay for that?"

Great Pawpaw had a real will? I swallowed my amazement and said, "Not unless Mother wants to stay. She's not expecting to inherit anything."

"Can't imagine he had much womenfolk might want. If there is, they'll work it out theyselves. Uncle Sebastian gets title to the home place and all. But ..." He took a chug of the dark liquid and glanced around. Leaning close to me, he said, "Unless I'm mistaken, he left you the family deer camp."

That was a surprise.

I remembered the deer camp. It was a rambling log structure they called "the cabin" on about 120 wooded acres.

With all the other men in the family, why would he leave it to *me*? I didn't even hunt.

"You're the new owner," Seth said, "but I hope you don't mind. The boys already done made this year's plans." As if cleaning guns and trading tall tales about past misadventures could be considered plans. "First two weeks in December. We was figuring we'd go ahead, if'n you don't mind. Great Pawpaw would've wanted that. Maybe you can come this year."

"Certainly." I grew up with stories about the deer camp. Of course I was always back in the city for school by the time everyone went, but when I was a kid, I'd nurtured a hope that someday they'd ask me to come up with the men and older boys. A shadow of the old longing stirred gratefully, although if I really was the new owner, maybe they felt they had no choice. I cast my mind over the workload waiting back at the office. Even with careful planning, I couldn't take two weeks off. "I won't be able to make it until the second week, though."

Seth shrugged. "I suppose that's what happens when you work for wages." He peered into his now-empty glass. "Might be hard to find a decent buck. They all blend in pretty well anyhow, and by then they'll be wary critters."

I didn't really want to kill a deer. Or even shoot a rifle. "Mostly I'll just take pictures. And I'm looking forward to a good male bonding experience." Aside from this bunch, I hadn't really known any men when I was growing up.

"Well, now." Seth paused. "I don't know about that. 'Course, every-body does their own thing. But if you're into male bonding, you prob'ly ought to bring along your own male."

I felt myself blush. "Not like that."

"Okay." He sounded doubtful. "I'll let the boys know, just in case. Never know who might be interested."

The snow held off, so Mother and I stayed while Uncle Sebastian went over the provisions of the will. I was the new owner of the deer camp.

On the way home, I said to Mother, "Maybe this is Great Pawpaw's way of making sure I'm included in the family traditions."

She snorted. "They're a bunch of crooks. I don't know what they're up to, but they wouldn't just *give* you the deer camp. There's something we're not seeing."

Mother had a lifetime of reservations and resentments about her family. But they were still our kin.

As the sun went down, an icy snow began falling, making the unlit roads treacherous. I was glad I had four-wheel drive.

* * * *

The second Friday of December, I left my office early. I'd stocked up on warm clothing and a new sleeping bag. The back of the Escalade was packed with cases of beer—I figured a fresh supply would make me more welcome—and groceries.

Uncle Sebastian's directions were useless. They referred to Granny Duncan's pumpkin patch and the pasture with goats. GPS devices don't work where roads are nameless and houses have no numbers.

"Just drive straight to the water tower outside town," Mother told me. "Turn left and keep going past the old coal breaker to the end of the road." She wasn't happy I was going, but she didn't try to stop me.

Dusk was falling when I came around the final turn and saw the cabin. The rain had stopped. Several pickups and farm trucks in varying stages of disrepair were parked haphazardly in front. I pulled in behind a gray flatbed truck, making sure to stay well away from an alarmingly deep ditch next to the road. The scent of wood smoke hung in the air. I gathered my new sleeping bag and the knapsack and headed up to the cabin.

Rapidly approaching headlights rounded the bend, heading straight for me. I dropped what I was carrying and leapt back against a huge tree, expecting to be crushed into it. At the last second, the headlights swerved. With a resounding crash, the vehicle attached to the headlights slammed into the rear quarter panel of my Escalade, which skidded away from the impact. Right toward that deep ditch. I watched as it teetered on the edge for a few seconds before gently sliding over the edge.

Reginald climbed out of the now-stopped truck and peered down into the ditch. "Damn," he said. "Leastways, it didn't turn belly up."

The crash brought a tangle of bearded men in flannel shirts stumbling out onto the porch and into the road.

Uncle Sebastian stood stroking his beard, peering at Reginald. "What's the hurry, boy?"

"I got me a buck," Reginald said. "First one this trip."

Uncle Sebastian shook his head. "Didn't shoot from the road, did you, boy?" he asked. "That ain't legal."

"No, sir. Didn't shoot'm at all. Hit'm with the truck."

Uncle Sebastian nodded. "Messed up bad?"

"Nah. Neck broke. I throwed'm in the back of the truck. Figured we could dress'm out here."

"You and Billy take'm out back and see what meat you can save. Trophy buck?"

"Used to be. Damn antlers all busted up. Hit'm in the head."

As Reginald and Billy unloaded the deer carcass, Uncle Sebastian and I joined the crowd looking down at my Escalade.

"Need to get a tractor. With a winch," someone said.

Uncle Sebastian spit tobacco juice into the ditch. "Might have to wait 'til the end of the week, when we get back home. Come back up and haul it out then."

I stared dismally down the steep slope. I'd planned to stay the whole week, but I wasn't thrilled with not being able to change my mind. Assuming the Escalade was drivable when it got back upon the road. I said, "Maybe I should just call for Triple-A to come get it out now."

"Ain't no phone here," one of the young cousins noted.

I reached into my pocket. "I've got my smart phone."

Several of them looked on with interest. "He got one of them there smart phones," one said. "No wires or nothing."

"Do it work up here?"

I tried it. Sure enough, the screen flashed "No signal." I put the phone back into my pocket and glanced down at the Escalade. "Too bad. I got some groceries in the back there," I said.

Uncle Sebastian looked interested. "Groceries," he said.

"Yeah. And a few cases of beer."

Uncle Sebastian raised a bushy grey eyebrow. "Beer," he said.

"Yes, sir," I said.

He looked around. "Why don't you go on in and get settled? Seth here'll show you where Great Pawpaw's room is. We figured it was yours now."

I gathered my things from the slushy road where I'd dropped them. Someone was tying a rope to a tree and uncoiling it as he prepared to climb down the embankment toward my Escalade.

Inside the cabin was darker and colder than outside. A fire burned in a huge stone fireplace, but all the heat seemed to be going up the chimney. Seth stopped to light a lantern. "No electric." He adjusted the flame. "You prob'ly want to keep a lantern with you."

I hadn't expected electricity. Or indoor plumbing. "Thanks, I brought a few flashlights." And toilet paper.

We went down a long hallway to the last door. He gave it a shove. It didn't budge. "Latch stuck." He put his shoulder to it and heaved. The door fell in, collapsing flat on the floor beyond.

Seth stepped inside and lifted the door, leaning it up against the wall.

A raw wind sliced through the room. Seth held up the lantern. "Looks like Great Pawpaw left the window open. Air it out, I guess." He went over to the casement window and reached for the latch. It came off in his hand. He grabbed for the free-swinging window and tugged. The window slammed into the frame and smashed, scattering bits of glass and wood on the floor.

Seth stood back and scratched under his beard. He kicked most of the debris out of the way with his scuffed boot and reached out the opening once more. "Shutter," he said, pulling a solid wood panel toward the opening and securing it. "Won't let much light in, but ought to keep the wind out, at least. It's gonna get real cold tonight."

I dumped my knapsack and sleeping bag on the unsteady bed shoved up against a wall. A musty smell filled the air as dust and feathers rose from it.

"Feather bed," Seth observed. "Don't care for the chicken stink myself, but Great Pawpaw always said ain't nothing warmer than a good feather bed."

I dug out my largest flashlight and followed Seth back down the hallway. We went into the kitchen. A wood stove stood in the middle of one wall. The air here was much warmer and smelled of wet wool clothes. And men who hadn't washed up in while.

"Fetch yourself a drink," Uncle Sebastian said, nodding toward a row of jugs on a bench against the wall. "We got your truck, or whatever that thing is, back up on the road. Boys're bringing in the beer and groceries."

I was thoroughly chilled and figured a drink of the family specialty might do me good. I looked around. "Where are the glasses?" I asked.

Uncle Sebastian chuckled. "Men don't need no glasses. Just grab a jug."

He stuck a thumb through the handle on the neck of one of the jugs and swung it up to rest on his shoulder. Wrapping his lips around the opening and raising his arm, he tilted it forward and took a swig.

He smacked his lips and handed me the jug. "Good stuff. Some of Great Pawpaw's last batch."

I started to say something about germs, but I'd sound like a wuss. Besides, no germ could survive contact with the contents of those jugs.

Swinging it up and resting it on my shoulder, like I'd seen Uncle Sebastian do, I tilted it up to take a drink. A huge glug poured into my mouth and down my throat. I couldn't breathe, but I managed to cough and choke back the vomit that rose in my throat.

I've never drunk kerosene so I couldn't be sure, but it tasted like kerosene smells. I felt a burn all the way down my esophagus to my stomach. My ears flamed. Tears came to my eyes.

"A man's drink, huh?" Uncle Sebastian thumped me on the back.

I glanced behind him and saw half a dozen bearded smirking faces. I didn't trust my voice, so I just nodded and raised the jug again. This time I managed to take only a little sip. It still burned.

The rest of the evening was a bit of a blur. I did remember suspicious questions about the groceries. "That white stuff, sliced real thin. What was it?"

"Turkey loaf. For sandwiches."

"Didn't have no taste at all. Nothing like turkey usually tastes."

"Domesticated turkey, not wild. Did you try a sandwich?"

"Sandwich? No. Put it in the stew. We're short on meat 'til that buck Reginald got's ready. Them slices just kind of dissolved."

I switched over to drinking beer, but I was too far gone to know to skip the stew. What was in it besides dissolved turkey loaf? My digestive system rebelled. I struggled to my feet. "Where's the outhouse?"

Seth grabbed a lantern. I got my flashlight, but didn't have time to go for my toilet paper. Did they still have a Sears catalog hung on a nail out there? Hadn't Sears stopped sending the catalogs?

We headed into a full-blown mountain blizzard.

Seth waited outside the outhouse as I struggled with lowering my pants in the limited space. The seat was shockingly frigid against my bare behind.

"Best be careful," Seth hollered through the door. "Seat's metal. Your butt can freeze right to it."

I left pieces of skin on that seat.

When I finally ripped myself up and got my pants almost fastened, I said, "I think I'll just turn in now." Seth took me through a side door.

My head was spinning. When I tried to unfasten the knapsack to look for PJs, I dropped it upside down on the floor and the contents scattered. I just unrolled the sleeping bag, kicked off my boots and crawled in. During the night, I dreamed that I was the centerpiece at an ice-carving contest, and someone was whittling away at my nose and ears.

The next morning, weak sunlight shone around the cracks of the shutter. The sleeping bag felt very heavy. Cautiously, I lifted my head. Three inches of snow had accumulated on top of me. I looked across the room. My possessions were strewn out on the floor, covered with snow. I could see daylight around the shingles in the roof.

I struggled out of the sleeping bag. My clean underwear was frozen to the floor. I would have to wear the same clothes I had worn yesterday. And slept in. I supposed I wouldn't smell any worse than anyone else. I had to empty snow out of my boots before I could put them on.

Coffee was boiling on the stove. It tasted dreadful, but caffeine and warmth were welcome. I felt my headache fading, but I wasn't going to try to eat anything.

"Sleep all right?" Uncle Sebastian asked.

"A bit chilly."

He nodded. "When it gets real cold, most of us just bunk here in the kitchen near the stove." He gestured toward a few prone forms lined up against the wall. "What with that male bonding thing, though, we figured you'd be better off in Great Pawpaw's room. Sometimes a man needs his privacy."

I needed to use the outhouse. I opened the door and stepped onto the back porch.

My eyes were dazzled by sunlight glinting off brilliant white. Everything was covered with glittering ice, and that was dusted with snow. Stunningly beautiful. With the sun, it wouldn't last long.

Camera in hand, I walked around the house, filling the memory card with one incredible winter wonderland scene after another.

A growling motor sound approached. Curious, I stepped around a corner of the house, just as a speeding snowmobile rounded from the other direction.

The snowmobile flung me back against a tree.

I ached all over. My limbs didn't seem to move, but my head felt like it was floating. The last thing I remember was Reginald's startled face as he sat open-mouthed on the snowmobile. And Uncle Sebastian pulling a satellite phone from his pocket, extending its antenna.

* * * *

When I woke up, I tried to make sense of my surroundings before I opened my eyes. Hospital smells and sounds.

I looked up, my eyes taking their own sweet time to focus. Uncle Sebastian hovered over me.

"Broke your shoulder good, boy. So soon after you got here. Shame, really. Didn't get a chance to hunt at all."

I tried to sit up, but pain overwhelmed me and I lay back down. "Wasn't there a snowmobile?"

Uncle Sebastian nodded. "Good thing Reginald has a snowmobile. Had to meet the amb'lance at the highway. Couldn't have got through with a truck. Not 'til we put a plow on a tractor and clear the road a bit."

I wasn't sure I wanted to know the details. "Now what?"

"Your mother's gonna come up and take you back to DC. Says you'll mend better there."

"How about my stuff?"

"Seth brought some of your clothes and your camera and the flashlight. Rest of it we'll bring down to the home place when we come."

"How about my Escalade?"

Uncle Sebastian looked away. "That truck thing? Bit of a problem there."

"Snowed in?"

"There's that, too."

"What do you mean, 'that, too'?"

"Afraid we didn't move it far enough away from that hole when we got it out."

"Back into the ditch? Reginald hit it again?"

He stroked his beard. "Not exactly."

"What exactly?"

"There's lots of old mine tunnels running underground. Sometimes they collapse. 'Specially if they get some weight on top. Like a truck. Then with the weight of the snow …"

I closed my eyes again. "So it's in an old mine tunnel?"

"Not *in* the tunnel. The top just caves in. So the ground sinks about five or ten feet."

"So it's in a hole five or ten feet deep?"

Uncle Sebastian beamed. "You're one smart boy. No wonder you make out so good in the city."

"Can you haul it out again for me?"

"Yep. Soon as we can get a tractor up there."

"When'll that be?"

"Spring thaw. Right now it's froze in mud, up to the axles."

"You all knew about the mine tunnels in the area. Is that why Great Pawpaw left the hunting camp to me?"

Uncle Sebastian turned away to peer out the window. "Prob'ly. He figured you was the only one got the money to fix what needed to be fixed. Tunnels run under the cabin, too. And pay them back taxes."

"Back taxes?"

"Yeah. Great Pawpaw, he ain't had the money to pay them the last few years. Didn't want the land to move out of the family."

I took a deep breath. It hurt my lungs. "He figured I'd pay them?"

"He hoped. Our men folk set real store by that deer camp. Only way he saw to keep it in the family."

My mother's comments about Great Pawpaw's death nagged at my foggy brain. "How do you think he died?"

Uncle Sebastian shrugged. "He was feeling poorly. Chest hurt. Said he wanted to be up in the hills, at his still. Alone. Seemed only decent to let him go."

"So you don't think anybody did anything to him?"

"Nope. He went the way he wanted to."

I sighed. "I didn't even see any deer."

He chuckled. "Oh, they're there. Got to look careful."

"Did anybody get any?"

"Reginald got the one with the truck."

"That's all?"

"Not a problem. We farm 500 acres in the lowland. Get crop damage permits to take deer. Got enough venison to last the winter before we got to camp."

* * * *

Mother took me back to her apartment. I manage to get to work, but I need a lot of help with things like bathing and dressing. I can't drive yet, so the Escalade being in a mine tunnel is a moot issue. For now.

I wanted to see if any of the pictures came out. Mother loaded them into her computer and pulled them up. The scenes were as breathtaking as I'd remembered.

And there, right in the middle of the first one, was a ten point buck staring back at me.

THE THUMP AND TAG

by Melinda B. Pierce

My boss, Aiden Raine, parked his four-door truck two blocks away from O'Keefe's Pub. When I didn't move, he tapped his fingers on the steering wheel. "This is the part where you get out."

"I can't do this."

"Do I need to go over the plan again?" he asked.

"Yes. In detail." I used my index fingers to draw an imaginary square. "A PowerPoint presentation would be nice, too. Let's go back to the office."

"Listen, Jessica." Aiden shifted in his seat and leaned toward me. "If this wasn't a millionaire client with million dollar files on the line, I'd simply wait for Ben or Reese to quit hugging the toilet. But we need to move fast on this."

I scrunched my face at the passive-aggressive reminder of why his usual agents couldn't do the job. After temping for three months at A.R. Investigations as a receptionist/secretary, it had been my turn to bring in Friday breakfast for the team. I'd wanted to impress everyone so I made my mom's special Dulce de Leche recipe to go over pastries. Being lactose intolerant, I'd never tried the stuff, but my family always praised the caramel flavored sauce. The milk had smelled a little strong when I made it, but the expiration date was fine, so I'd assumed it couldn't be spoiled.

I was wrong.

Six hours later, the entire team began fighting for bathroom stalls. Aiden had been saved by coming in late from a client meeting. By the time he'd arrived, the sauce bowl had been licked clean. I was pretty sure Ben had done the licking.

"Show me the transmitter again, and you repeat the plan from the beginning," Aiden said.

I unzipped my purse and pulled out the little white card with the almost transparent transmitter stuck in the middle. I repeated the plan back to him in a monotone voice. "It's a simple thump-and-tag. I sit near the target. You call the target. The target pulls out his phone. You bump into the target very hard and cause him to drop his phone. I pick up the phone and apply the transmitter to the back while you apologize. Then I hand the phone to him and beat feet."

"It's a simple thump-and-tag," he repeated. "In and out."

"What if he doesn't have the phone on him?"

"Everyone has their phone on them."

"What if he notices I'm sitting too close to him?"

"I doubt he'll even nod his head at you. You're unrecognizable, in a good way."

My mouth popped open. "Is there a good way to be invisible?"

The corner of Aiden's mouth lifted into a half smile. "I didn't say you were invisible. And your ability to stall should've been listed on your resume." He rested his hand on my shoulder and gave it a gentle squeeze. "This jerk downloaded a ton of sensitive files today. He's going to act normal and sit at his favorite Friday night hangout for a few beers and then he's going to disappear. We need to know where he's going, who he's selling to, and I need *you* to plant that transmitter."

"Okay. Fine." After all, I owed it to the team. If I got this right, they'd possibly forgive the food poisoning. It'd be nice to make this temp position a permanent one.

I exited the truck and stepped onto the sidewalk. Friday night patrons crowded the sidewalks in Tampa's Hyde Park Village. Couples and groups of adults headed across the street to the movie theater. The new Bond movie had released and everyone who got their vicarious kicks about living the life of a spy parted with their money in the ticket line. I preferred RomComs where the final scene ended on a sweet kiss and not with explosions and death.

A car horn honked, and I realized Aiden had prompted me to start walking the two blocks to the pub. I passed a large storefront glass and checked my reflection. Unrecognizable brown hair on top of an unrecognizable face on top of an unrecognizable yet somewhat curvy body. At least I'd worn my favorite flowery dress to work. I straightened my spine. There was something to be said for the confidence a favorite dress could give a girl.

I marched the remainder of the way to the pub without a backward glance. At some point, Aiden would enter the pub behind me. After his "unrecognizable" comment, I decided ignoring him could be easily accomplished.

Some of the after-work crowd pushed past me as I entered O'Keefe's. The horseshoe shaped bar was crowded, and I jumped on the first empty stool I saw. I'd play musical chairs until I could get close enough to the target. I checked my phone again for the photo of the guy so I'd know who to get closer to.

Jon Hickory had one of those faces you were sure you'd met somewhere before but couldn't quite place. His looks fell somewhere between handsome and a face only a mother could love. I glanced around the bar twice before I located Jon directly across from where I sat. The stools beside him were occupied but I could tell he was alone. He had his phone in his hand and was thumbing the screen.

The bartender blocked my view and placed a coaster in front of me. "What can I get you?"

I opted for a local tap brew. When the bartender moved, I glanced at Jon's now-empty seat. I swiveled my head in every direction searching for him. What I was supposed to do if he left the pub before the thump-and-tag? I groaned and put my head down on the bar. I just wanted to answer phones and file things.

A guy pushed in between me and the lady on the stool next to me. "Bad day?" he asked.

"You have no idea." I lifted my head and came inches away from our target's face.

He smiled big and creepy. "You don't remember me, do you?"

My *oh crap* meter rang bells loud in my ears. "Should I?"

"Four years of high school together at Armwood. We were in at least six classes together throughout the years."

I curled my lips in and bit them together hard. My peripheral vision caught a glimpse of Aiden. I shifted my gaze to him, and he shot daggers back at me. I grabbed my beer and took a long sip to stall for time. It was possible Jon and I had attended high school together, but I didn't remember him.

Jon put his phone in the inside breast pocket of his suit jacket. The thump-and-tag could still work. I pushed forward.

"Wait, I think I do remember you." I over-smiled and prayed I didn't resemble a psycho gopher. "You're Jon, right?"

"Yeah, yeah." He leaned back and his gaze drifted down and back up my legs. "You haven't changed a bit. Well, except you've put on a few pounds."

I drank heavily from my mug to stop any retort. Few pounds, huh? I put my hand on the side of my face and did a little finger wave to signal Aiden. There was no reason to drag this mission out. He needed to thump this jerk now.

Jon called the bartender over and asked for another beer. He returned his attention to me as his phone chirped a ringtone. With his creepy smile still in place, he leaned in closer. "So, what are you doing now?"

The phone continued chirping from his breast pocket.

Go time. I slid the card from my purse slowly as I answered his question. "Um, just some temp work here and there. Administration mostly."

The chirping stopped. I glanced toward Aiden, whose face tightened.

"What about you?" I slipped the transmitter off the card with my index finger.

His phone chirped again. He didn't make a move to answer it.

The muscles in my back tensed.

"I work for Bluddle Tech over on Kennedy." He wiggled his bushy eyebrows at me. "I'm doing pretty well, I might add."

The phone started its third round of chirps. I pointed to his pocket with my free hand. "Aren't you going to answer that?"

Aiden wasn't more than three steps away from us now. I could feel the irritation radiating from his body.

Jon shrugged his shoulders. "I can get that later. I'd rather catch up with you."

Aiden turned and headed to the back hallway leading to the restrooms. I slid off the edge of my seat which almost put me groin to groin with Jon. "Why don't you hold my seat for me while I run to the ladies room?"

"You're not ditching me, are you?" Jon asked. He gave me another eyebrow wiggle, as if he knew on some cosmic level I couldn't leave.

I patted his chest. "No. No. Of course not."

I pushed past the ever-growing crowd toward the back hallway. Aiden waited for me beside the door to the ladies room.

"What happened?" Aiden asked.

"This isn't my fault. He says he knows me from high school."

"Does he?"

"I don't know. High school was eight years ago. Would you remember everyone from your high school?"

"Yes."

"Of course you would. What do you want me to do now?" I waved my finger with the transmitter still stuck to it in front of his face.

"Change of tactic. Now we'll have to use the flirt, thump, and tag maneuver. You've got to give him your number."

"I'm not giving that creep my number."

"Give him a fake one, Jessica. Just find a way to get him to pull out his phone."

"I want a permanent position at your firm."

"What?" He pushed away from the wall to his full height.

I refused to be intimidated. "Office manager. Take me off temp and hire me as the office manager with full benefits, and I'll flirt this guy into a mushy puddle."

"Fine. Deal. Only if you promise to never, ever bring Friday breakfast again."

"Okay. Fine." I swirled away from him and tried not to squeal with excitement.

As I came around the corner I noticed Jon leaning close to the woman who'd been sitting on the stool next to me. He'd lost interest fast. I'd be damned if I lost his attention now. Benefits were on the line.

I smoothed my dress and pushed in between him and the woman wearing too much perfume. "Miss me?"

Jon's smile dimmed. I guess he'd thought he'd found a better fish in the sea of women hanging out at the bar. Too bad. Aiden had better be ready to thump.

I yawned, wide-mouthed. "Whew. It's been a pretty long day. I've really enjoyed catching up. Why don't I give you my number, and we can catch up another time."

His smile dimmed further and he held out his hand. "Why don't I give you my number? I'll put it in your phone."

I tapped my fingers on the bar and held the finger with the transmitter very still beside my leg. Jon was going to fake number me. My promotion to office manager was dead if I didn't get him to take out his stupid phone.

Aiden moved behind Jon and leaned through to order from the bartender. Out of options I used my free hand to lock onto the back of Jon's neck. I pulled his face to mine and landed the slobberiest, most awkward kiss I could muster on his lips. To my amazement, he didn't struggle, and while he twisted his head back and forth I put my hand inside his pocket and smoothed the transmitter onto his phone.

Mission accomplished. I un-sucked his face from mine and slapped the crap out of him. A few pounds my round rump. He'd be wondering about that kiss for years to come. Hopefully, in jail somewhere.

I stalked out of the pub and back to Aiden's truck where I waited on the tailgate.

Aiden finally walked around the corner wearing the goofiest grin I'd ever seen. "What the heck was that?"

I pulled out my lip gloss and applied it to my shameful lips. I smacked them together twice before answering. "That is the kiss-and-tag maneuver."

STEP AWAY FROM THE COW

by C.C. Guthrie

I'm not an animal person, but even I could tell there was something different about Spike, and it wasn't size. Everything at the Texas Stock Show, the multimillion-dollar farm animal extravaganza, was big. The tractors for sale, the mangos on a stick, and the animals in the Show were all over-sized. A twenty-five pound rabbit? No surprise.

Spike might have been one of those good luck bunnies. He certainly drew Show spectators to his cage like magic. If some of his luck happened to rub off on me, I wouldn't turn it down. But out of an abundance of caution, I kept my distance, just like I did with all the other Stock Show animals.

The Show barn was busy as spectators walked by. I could tell from the conversations I overheard I still didn't have the animal lingo down, especially when it came to cows. Even though I could tell the difference between a cow and a bull, it was just easier to call everything a cow. But what a heifer, steer and yearling were, I didn't care. I was there to do a job, not take a vocabulary test.

For some crazy reason, the Show put rabbits in the barn with the cows, or bulls or whatever they were. The Show barns were big warehouse-sized cinder block structures with concrete floors. Nothing like those wood buildings on the TV shows with Hoss or the kids on the prairie.

The cow barn had a weird bump out on the front so the rabbit cages went there, off the long passageway where spectators strolled. On the south side were giant rolling doors. That's how the kids got the cows to and from the competitions. Think animal beauty pageant with red carpet photo ops. Coiffed animals paraded around an arena while judges scrutinized the contestants with the intensity of frat boys at a strip club. Middle and high school kids with the highest scoring animals won big-money prizes and scholarships.

Between the rabbits and the passageway at the front and the big doors at the back were stalls where the cows were parked between competitions. I leaned against the metal rail that separated the spectator side of the barn from the cow side and waited. And there it was, the comment I heard at least three times an hour. Despite Spike's rump forward position, people always stopped.

"Oh, my god, Harvey. Look at that one." The woman's voice trailed off as she bent to read the label on Spike's cage.

Rabbits were the smallest animals in the barn and the smallest money-wise in the Show. A Grand Champion cow could go for a quarter of a million at auction. The prize for the winning bunny probably wouldn't cover a year's worth of carrots.

The woman turned back to her companion. "It's a rabbit."

Engrossed in his smart phone, Harvey didn't look up. "Well, of course it's a rabbit." His left hand swept vaguely in the direction of the cages. "They're all rabbits. It's the rabbit section."

"But look at it. It's the size of a cocker spaniel. And it's gray."

Harvey looked up. "Marge, don't be ridiculous."

That's what I had to put up with. Working the Show was one of those karma things people always talked about. I didn't dislike animals. I just didn't know anything about them. Three weeks at the Show was cosmic payback for something.

I had tried to get assigned to the midway, but the Captain thought women would blend in better in the barns with all the kids and what he called Show Moms. Since I wasn't old enough to have a kid there, I wasn't sure how well that was working.

Back when I was in the Patrol Division, I didn't worry about a Show assignment. Those were for detectives and uniforms on bicycles and horses. A police officer on a horse at the Stock Show? PR sprinkles on the city's cupcake.

But allowing bicycle and horse patrols inside the barns was a whole other thing. A lawsuit waiting to happen. There was barely enough room for spectators to walk by and gawk. The public paid for the privilege—in case you missed it, I'm using the word ironically—to sidestep piles of hay and well, you know, other stuff, to look at the animals.

Because the Show's a cash cow, pardon the expression, the Department put low seniority plain clothes detectives like moi in the barns to handle criminals that always show up when there's a crowd. Event Security was for fights and lost kids. Nothing was going to turn off the tap that poured big bucks into the city's coffers. If you don't believe me, talk to the mayor.

So there I was, cheek to jowl with animals, big animals, big animals that weren't litter box trained. Cows let fly with whatever, whenever. First thing I learned, when the tail goes up, step away from the cow. The second thing, always yield to the cow. One wrong step and hello crushed foot. I made a point to stay behind the rail that separated the lookers from the animals.

A woman with a stroller replaced Marge and Harvey in front of Spike's cage. I was happy to see she showed some sense and kept her hands on the stroller, not giving anyone a chance to slip her purse off the handles. I did not want a chase.

Spike had his backside to the woman, so I turned around to watch the stalls where the cows stood, oblivious to the attention focused on them. The kids clipped, spritzed, dried, combed and sprayed like glamour pit crews grooming a herd of Hollywood stars.

A dead ringer for Julia Roberts in her teen years pushed a cart up the center aisle between the stalls. The whole contraption looked unsteady, but she maneuvered it expertly, dodging humans and animals. Mounted on the thing was a mega-sized canister-shaped hair dryer the kids used after the cow wash. In another stall, a tall teenage boy wearing dusty jeans and a tee shirt with a questionable brown stain sprayed something on his cow. Bovine mousse, who knew?

"Hey, it bit me."

I looked back at the rabbits. A guy sporting Nineties gangsta style stood in front of Spike's cage. His left hand held onto jeans hovering at thigh level. He looked at his right index finger as if he'd never seen it before. A poor excuse for a soul patch quivered on his chin.

"It bit me. That thing bit me."

I strolled over. Spike still faced the back of his cage.

"It's a rabbit. That happens when you stick your finger in its face. I've heard they're color blind. It probably thought your finger was a carrot."

Spike turned his head and looked right at me.

"They oughta warn people animals are dangerous," the guy said. "I could be injured for life. Probably impact my earning potential. I'm gonna, like, have to, like, maybe sue."

I grabbed his finger and gave it a once over. Not a scratch. "Yeah, sounds like a plan." I pointed to my left. "There's a first aid station just beyond the concession stand. Ask them to take a picture so you can file a claim. You'll need documentation when you talk to your lawyer." I promised myself a visit to the station later to see what they thought of my advice. It was sure to perk up their morning.

"Documentation for a claim, I'm gonna need that." The guy looked like he'd discovered a winning Powerball ticket and confidently headed off in the wrong direction.

I patted myself on the back and decided to take a taco break when a loud voice bellowed through the building and stopped me cold. "Hey, that guy, he took my purse."

I looked to see who yelled and swiveled my head so many times I expected it to turn all the way around like a cartoon character. Sound echoed through the huge building, bounced off the walls, making it impossible to identify who raised the alarm. Spectators stopped moving. Being mid-week, they were mostly older couples and mothers with rug rats. Oh, great, a barn chase.

Activity in the animal stalls came to a halt. The kids realized something was happening on the spectator side of the rail and switched off dryers, hair clippers and blaring radios. Attention shifted from the animals to the front of the building. Everyone listened to voices narrate the pursuit over the security guard radio frequency.

I tried to sound like a concerned civilian and not blow my cover. "Hey, everyone stay back." I gestured at the rabbit cages and caught Spike's eye. "Let the security team take care of this."

The mothers and toddlers followed my suggestion and retreated. Everyone else lined up like cheerleaders waiting for the football team to run by. I squeezed in next to an old geezer in a VFW hat as a short, wiry guy chased by two guards sprinted into view.

When the runner was about ten feet away, I stepped out and planted myself in front of him. The suspect looked right, then left. The hamster wheel in his head turned as he considered the options. Blast through me and get knocked down. Barrel into the crowd and get tangled up with the old people. He picked door number three.

The suspect took a sharp left, darted past the rail, down the center aisle between the stalls. Ah, jeez. If I followed I'd be within cow kicking range. The guy passed the first stall before I'd even cleared the rail. He'd be home free if he made it out the back doors. I ran down the aisle, yelling at the kids to move.

Suddenly, women began to swarm. I didn't know where they came from, but there were three of them for every kid and cow. Like bees, they responded to a silent signal and moved in front of the stalls. With that arm-out action they use when a car stops suddenly, the Show Moms formed a defensive line as effective as a squad of riot police. In the stalls, the kids held tight to their animals.

Ahead of me, the suspect hit a slippery skid on the concrete floor and his arms began to windmill. He flailed. I gained on him. Something splattered my face. Ah jeez, barn floor blowback. He was down, sliding on his knees, then he was up.

While he tried to regain his balance, I eyed the distance to the rear doors. The Julia-look-a-like and the gangly kid who had been styling his cow stood between the last stall and the doors. She held one of those long sticks the kids used to urge their cows along and the boy had a can of cow hair-product.

With freedom in sight, the suspect put on a burst of speed. When he was even with the last stall, the girl swung like the Babe at bat. The stick smacked him mid-shin and his legs flew up. Brown stuff rained down on my faux polo. Ah, jeez.

The suspect hit the concrete with a thud, and the boy stepped forward. He mashed the nozzle on his can and a stream of pungent goo spewed out. The suspect yowled and clawed at his face. I slid up, barely missing assault by aerosol.

By the time I called off the kids, got the suspect up and handcuffed, I hardly noticed the smelly smears on me. When I perp-walked the guy out of the barn, I'm sure Spike winked as I passed his cage. The animal thing was starting to grow on me.

OF ROOSTERS AND MEN

by LD Masterson

I swear, one of these days I'm going to kill that rooster.

I pulled my pillow over my head to muffle the relentless crowing. *Give it a rest, Duncan. It's not even dawn.*

It wasn't that I minded getting up early. At home, I jogged five miles every morning before work. But at home, my phone alarm woke me when I decided, to music I liked, with a nice background of traffic noise and sirens … songs of the city.

Oh Lord, there he goes again. It was no use. I pushed the pillow aside and stretched, my hands hitting the old familiar headboard that I'd painted purple with white daisies when I was twelve. Mom had kept my room ready for me, even after I moved to New York, just in case I ever wanted to "come home." But after she died—was it seven years already?—Dad had turned it into an office for himself, leaving my bed against one wall, my daisies hemmed in by his massive roll top desk and a short bank of file cabinets.

I guess it's Cassie's office now.

My big sister Cassie. The banging of pots and pans told me she was already up and making breakfast. I rolled out of bed, shrugged into my robe and slippers, and headed for the kitchen.

"Good morning, Ella. You're just in time. Coffee's hot and the oatmeal's ready."

Oh, yum. I poured myself a mug of coffee and watched her plop a ladleful of gray oatmeal into a bowl and add a splash of milk. My soul yearned for a mocha latte and a fresh bagel, but there was no corner deli out here in the boonies.

"Thanks, Cass." I carried mug and bowl to the heavy oak table.

Sometimes it was hard to remember I grew up here. Mom, Dad, Cassie, and me on our small family farm, a couple miles from Middle of Nowhere, Ohio. They loved this life. I couldn't wait to leave. I knew I belonged in the city, and that's where I've been the past twelve years. That's my world.

Cassie sat in her usual place, across from me. Someone once told me we were a study in opposites. I guess that was true. I was short, thinner than I wanted to be, and I liked my dark hair long over my shoulders. Cassie was the classic image of a mid-west farm girl—tall, curvy frame, fair skin dotted with freckles, light sandy hair cut in a short no-fuss style. This morning she was wearing jeans and a plaid shirt I recognized as Dad's.

"I appreciate you coming back," she told me. "I know it's hard for you to get away."

The twinge of guilt was strong enough to make me shift in my chair. "Well, you know … it's a small gallery. Not a lot of staff to cover for someone when they're gone." My standard excuse, to avoid visiting. I'd been faithful the first few years—back when Mom was alive—coming home for holidays and such, but after she passed, I barely made it once a year. When Dad died last winter, I hadn't seen him in eight months and his sudden heart attack had given no time for good-byes.

"I should have been here sooner." I flew home for the funeral but only stayed a couple days. "It wasn't right to leave you with all this."

"No, I really needed the time to go through everything. It was easier alone."

Almost in unison, we dipped our spoons into the oatmeal.

"Mmm. Good," I lied. For a farm girl, Cass wasn't much of a cook, although I'd never tell her so.

Cassie set her spoon back into the bowl, untouched. "I just don't know what to do. I don't want to give up the farm."

And there we were, back in our conversation from the night before. The reason for my visit. The settling of Dad's estate.

"I don't want you to. Really, I don't." I didn't. Cassie loved the farm. She belonged on the farm. But Dad's will left everything to both of us, fifty-fifty. What could I do with half a farm?

"Then don't make me."

"Cassie—"

"I'm not trying to cheat you. Half the farm is yours, and I'll pay you for it. Like a mortgage, in monthly payments."

"I know you're not trying to cheat me. And I'm not trying to hurt you. But we've been all over this. I want to use my inheritance to expand the gallery and to buy that great loft I told you about. I can't do that with monthly payments."

Cassie shoved her chair back and carried her uneaten oatmeal back to the counter. I heard her whisper something about "not fair." I followed and put my hand on her shoulder, felt her slump.

"Look, we'll talk to the bank people this afternoon. I'm sure they'll give you the loan. I'll get the money I need, you'll keep the farm, and you'll make those monthly payments to the bank instead of me. It's all going to work out."

She turned and gave me a weak smile. "I guess."

An awkward silence was broken by Duncan, calling our attention to the emerging pre-dawn light.

Cassie straightened and seemed to give herself a mental shake. "I need to feed the goats."

"I'll get dressed and help you."

The morning was one long reminder of why I belonged in the city. The July air was hot and sticky, and thick dust clung to my legs as I walked. The stupid goats were uncooperative and ungrateful. One young buck slammed me against the side of his pen and stomped on my foot. I preferred feeding the chickens … or would have, except for Duncan.

He strutted around the yard, showing off for his ladies. A young Rhode Island Red, very handsome and downright mean. Before I left home, we'd had old George. He was a pussycat. But this guy was all bad attitude with razor sharp spurs. I gave him a wide berth.

For some reason, being in the yard brought back more fond memories than the house. Cassie and I chasing runaway piglets. Splashing in puddles after a hard rain. Taking turns on the ice cream churn till our arms were limp. I stared at the field beyond the barn—a sea of short green corn. Knee high by the Fourth of July. Wasn't that the old saying? When I'd been here for the funeral, there were only dead broken stalks sticking out of the snow. How had Cassie managed the spring planting? I never thought to ask.

My pail of feed empty, I wandered past the chicken coop, a handful of ever-hopeful hens following along. Their desertion seemed to annoy Duncan. He stalked a few feet in my direction then turned, fluffed his feathers and hopped onto a fence post, his back to me and the flock. It tickled me. I never knew a rooster to sulk.

I watched Cassie cross from the barn to the house, moving with her usual purposeful stride. Damn. She deserved to stay on the farm. She was the one who took care of Mom at the end. And Dad, after Mom was gone. This place was her home. It was her life.

Maybe I didn't need my full share right now. I'd already put down the deposit on the loft but I could hold off on the gallery investment. A smaller loan would be easier to get and the payments—

"Ella! Help! Help me!"

I whirled around, sending chickens flapping out of my way, and ran toward the house, but when I saw her through the kitchen window, I pulled up short. She was struggling with someone. A man. A big man. Her shirt was torn and I stood there frozen as he struck her. The smack of his hand against her cheek rang through the air.

Help. I needed to get help. I pulled my cell phone out of my pocket and punched in 9-1-1. Do they even have 911 out here? What would I do if—

"Logan County 911. What's your emergency?"

"Oh, thank God. I need help. A man broke into our house. He's attacking my sister!"

"Where are you, ma'am? Are you in the house?"

"No, I'm outside but I can see them. He's hurting her." I took a step toward the house then backed away, afraid he'd see me. "We need help. Now!"

"Give me your address."

I rattled off the address and threw in the nearest state route and cross street. "Tell them to hurry."

"We have a unit in route now. He should be there in twenty minutes."

Twenty minutes? In the city, they'd be here in five. There'd be people around. And I'd have my pepper spray or, even better, the .38 I kept hidden in my closet. Out here I got ….

"Ma'am. Ma'am. Please stay on the line. I need—"

"No! No! … Ella!"

Screw this.

I shoved my phone into my pocket and ran along the fence toward the side door. As I raced by, I grabbed Duncan by his legs, swinging him off the fence. He squawked in surprise and flapped his wings, twisting in my grasp, trying to reach me with his sharp beak. I held tight to his legs, swinging him as I ran.

Even in sneakers, my footsteps thundered my arrival on the wooden porch. *Hang on, Cassie. I'm coming.*

I yanked the screen door open and charged into the parlor. The intruder was already there, filling the doorway to the kitchen. There was no sign of Cassie. Either she had gone silent or the angry shrieks coming from Duncan were drowning her out. I hoped it was Duncan.

The guy was big. Bigger than he looked through the window. But not scary big. Not "been working out at the gym" big. More like "too many beers in front of the TV" big. Short hair and dark rimmed glasses. And he was wearing dark slacks and a white dress shirt. Who breaks into a house wearing— Oh! And a very big gun in his hand.

He lifted his arm, grabbing the gun in both hands, turning the barrel toward me. I swung my arm as hard as I could and hurled Duncan.

Big or not. Armed or not. This guy was no match for a pissed off Rhode Island Red. I stood there as blood sprayed and feathers flew and cries of man and bird filled the room. The man staggered, one hand grasping wildly but only finding a few of Duncan's tail feathers. I couldn't see the hand with the gun. The two fell together, shattering the antique table that had been my mother's. Splintering wood and crashing glass added to the din. For a moment everything went still, and Duncan started to pull away. I thought he was done, ready to return to his hens, but the idiot on the floor grabbed the rooster's neck and received a fresh slashing of spurs for his effort. I took a step forward with some half-formed thought of entering the fray.

The gunshot was an explosion, drowning out all other sound. I dropped into a half-crouch, eyes squeezed shut, hands over my ears, as if that would protect me.

When I dared look, the bloodied intruder was sprawled on his back across a bed of broken glass and wood, the still form of a rooster lying beside him. The world had gone silent, except for the ringing in my ears.

I eased closer. Slash marks criss-crossed the intruder's face and his white shirt was drenched in red. I guessed the parts of him lying on the broken table hadn't fared much better. He groaned but didn't move. Neither did Duncan.

The gun was on the floor next to the man's outstretched hand. Had he managed to fire or had it just gone off in the struggle? Did it matter? I grabbed it then backed away.

Cassie appeared in the kitchen door. The sleeve of her shirt was torn at the shoulder and blood trickled from the corner of her mouth. I tried to smile to show her everything was fine. It was all over.

"Wayne!" The panic in her voice matched the shrill cries I'd heard from the window.

Wayne?

She raced across the room and dropped to his side, cradling his head in her lap.

"What have you done?"

The accusation was definitely aimed at me. What *had* I done? Had I made a mistake? But she had yelled for my help. Hadn't she?

"Wayne, darling. Can you hear me?"

Darling?

"Cassie, who is that? What's going on?"

She turned to face me, the anger in her eyes at odds with the streaming tears. "It's all your fault. I would have sent you the money. Every month, just like I said, even though you don't deserve it. The farm should have been mine. All mine. You left. You left and I stayed. The farm should have been mine."

I opened my mouth to answer her but no words came.

"But nooo. You had to have your money now. For your stupid loft and your stupid gallery. You *knew* I couldn't come up with that much money without selling."

What was she saying? "But we were going to the bank. You were going to get a loan."

"I've already been to the bank." Her words exploded like another gunshot. "They turned me down."

The man stirred slightly and she turned her attention to him, dabbing at the blood on his face with her shirttail.

"I take it this man wasn't attacking you?" My voice sounded strange, stiff and formal, while my heart and mind were locked in battle. This was Cassie. My big sister. This couldn't be happening.

"No. This is Wayne." Her voice was smaller now. "My boyfriend."

Not an intruder. But he had a gun. I put the pieces together in my mind, still trying not to see how they fit.

"He was here to kill me."

"Score one for the city girl." The snark gave way to a resigned sigh. "You called 911?"

The police. I instinctively reached for my phone then stopped. "Yes. They're on the way."

She nodded. "Well … you were supposed to. We needed you on record, telling them we had an intruder."

I tried to process her words but my brain felt as thick as that morning's oatmeal. "And they'd arrive and find me dead."

She turned to face me now. "Yes. And me all bloodied and battered crying over your body. Poor, brave, Ella who died saving my life."

"And Wayne?"

"Wayne was never here. He's out making sales calls today. And my description of the killer wouldn't sound anything like him." She glanced down at him with a rueful smile. "He just needed to bury the gun."

The gun.

I looked down at my hand and the gun that had been brought there to kill me and slowly turned it toward my sister. I half-expected her to argue or plead with me to let them go, tell the police it was all a mistake.

"Cass …."

She gave me an unreadable look and shook her head. There was nothing else to say.

Cassie returned to dabbing at her boyfriend's wounds. I lowered myself into a chair, keeping the gun steady, and listened for the sound of approaching sirens.

* * * *

I've been back in the city almost two weeks now. This evening I'm enjoying a scrumptious pastrami-on-rye in my tiny apartment. I love my corner deli.

Cassie and Wayne confessed to the police. The County Prosecutor—who wasn't the country bumpkin I'd expected—cut them a pretty generous plea deal, but I was okay with it. I guess people do crazy things when they're desperate and once I got past the whole "my sister tried to kill me" thing, I almost felt sorry for her.

I'm selling the farm, of course. I don't feel *that* sorry for her. Cassie had been getting offers on the place since Dad died so I told the realtor to just take the best one. The lawyers will take care of her half for now. And I'm moving into my dream loft next week. As soon as I make new—outside the city—living arrangements for my current roommate.

One almost-recovered, still pissed off, Rhode Island Red.

THE NEW SCORE

by Alison McMahan

The elderly gentleman's not heavy. But he's tall. Gangly. Hard to grip. He squirms and flexes like a puppy that just smelled the vet's office. Fortunately, his skin is dry so he doesn't slip through my gloved fingers.

I shove him into the maw of carpeted darkness that is the trunk of the limo, gently as I can. He stares up at my masked face, his jaw working. I touch a finger to the duct tape over his mouth. "Shh. Shh. You won't be in here long. I'll send someone for you."

His tuxedo pants are too short, the shoes too big, the shirt too tight. His jacket pinches my shoulders. But it will do. And in the pockets? An ID card and a VIP invitation to the green room. I hang the ID around my neck.

The old gentleman's eyes are closed. I think he's praying.

I tap the card to get his attention. He opens his eyes. "Thanks for this, man. It'll really help."

I put the pass in the jacket pocket and my hand finds the old gent's wallet. I toss it into the trunk and it lands on his stomach.

He looks down, sees the wallet, and looks back up at me, eyes wide.

"That's yours. I would never take anything of yours." I pull on the jacket lapels. "I'll make sure this goes back to the place where you rented it."

He struggles and shrieks through the tape as I slam the lid shut.

I take the mask off, hook the stun gun onto my belt and slide the mini-tablet into my pocket.

Something rattles in the jacket liner pocket. A pill vial. Coumadin. Old gent has heart trouble. Good thing I didn't drug him; I'm not here to kill anybody.

At least, not yet.

I leave the hotel garage and walk the few blocks to the Dolby Theatre. The cloudy day bathes everything in a flat, unglamorous light. The rain has left the surface streets glassy. Up ahead, the plexiglass tunnel over the red carpet doesn't look like much, especially with all the people in ponchos and raincoats huddled around it.

The way they're all jammed in makes it easier for me to slip through. People make way for a tuxedo on a red carpet.

At the first layer of gate-checkers, I pick the youngest, prettiest female and hold up my pass, making sure my hand covers most of the picture.

She glances at my face and immediately looks away, like everybody does. She scans the old gent's ID without asking me to take my hand off my picture.

"Welcome to the Academy Awards," she mumbles, already looking at the person in line behind me.

It can't be that easy.

Now the shimmering length of the red carpet lies ahead of me, the press boxes are jam-packed, the entertainment mannequins on their altars, the microphone scepters in their hands, waiting for the sacrifices to be led to them. How many times did I dream of being one of them? My work nominated like them, a pass to the VIP room like them, walking the red carpet like them.

And here I am.

Focus.

Robert. Just ahead.

Proof that the gods are with me.

That short, suave, shiny, smooth, bastard. As glittery as any Hollywood glitterati.

He vamps for the paparazzi. If I didn't know better, I'd think he was Tom Cruise.

We're in the line that's supposed to shuffle along, hoping to get glimpsed by the cameras, not stopping. But as soon as an A-lister moves away from the curvy interviewer chick with the E! Logo mic, Robert slips into his spot.

The ease with which he fits in astounds me. The only reason I haven't been thrown out yet is because I'm invisible to people, or rather, I become invisible to them after that first glance at my ruined face.

I inch forward and sideways until I'm in earshot.

The interviewer looks at Robert, squints, checks her cue cards, then checks the ID card hanging around his neck. She doesn't recognize him.

He slides his eyes along her body with a come-hither smile.

She knows the camera is on her. "Hey! You're that actor—you were in—remind me."

No one can resist Robert's grin. "I know, I look like Russell Crowe, right? And just think, I look this good without having had any ribs removed."

He guides her hand inside his jacket. She feels. She pulls her hand away with a smile.

"But actually, I'm a composer."

His smile morphs into his best hangdog expression. Will she melt or smelt?

She melts. "What are you up for?"

"Best Song, for *Lena, Spy Warrior*."

He hums a few bars. Waves his hand for her to join in. He's so transparent, trying to create an Oscar moment, something the TV editor will use to break up a tedious stretch of divas in designer dresses.

Just as I think she's going to sing along with him, she pounces.

"Oh, right. You're the one who sued—"

Robert's smile gets sucked into the thin-line pursed-mouth expression I know so well. "*I* was *sued*. Baselessly. And I won. Now I'm scoring the reboot."

His glower intimidates the interviewer. She turns to the camera. For a moment I glimpse the tendons in her neck. She's not as young as she seems.

"And there you have it, everyone. Robert Cattrell, composer of the theme song for *Lena, Spy Warrior*."

She clicks the microphone off, looks over her shoulder.

"Ooh, look, the youngest Tanning sister is coming up!"

This is clearly Robert's cue to keep moving down the carpet, but instead he leans in to her ear. I inch forward, close as I dare.

"Such a pity about the little Tanning sister. All that plastic surgery. Such a young girl. Should be illegal. Don't you think?"

He air-kisses her. She does a double take, reaches out as if she wants to say more, but he's already slipped into the crowd.

I shuffle after him, making sure to keep Robert two people ahead of me.

We reach the security enclosure for the Dolby Theatre. This is the moment where my plan makes or breaks.

The security guards here are the real deal. I aim for the rookie, but that's a mistake. He points at my badge, which I've turned backward.

"Turn your badge around, sir."

Overzealous little prick.

I turn the badge around, my fingers over the old gent's face. The guard studies my face. He's too new at this to hide his reaction. His lip curls, his nose wrinkles, his head shakes. He slides his eyes down the picture on my badge.

"That is certainly not you, sir." Rookie's all business now.

I look at my badge. "What? What do you—"

With my other hand I shove the stun gun into his side and zap him.

He shudders. Collapses into my arms.

"Hey! Hey!" It takes two beats for the other guards to look at me. "Help! This man is sick!"

I stumble, as if he were too heavy for me, and drop the unconscious rookie on the ground. The guards leap to my assistance.

"What's the matter with him?"

"I don't know. Heat stroke, maybe?"

The rookie's body is now blocking the entrance. A crowd piles up. I slip away, hoping no one will notice how tight my jacket is or how short my pants are.

I have to hurry now. I only have a few minutes before that guard comes to.

The CW interviewer is talking to J.J. Abrams.

And there's Robert, edging his way toward J.J.'s spot, as if some of that A-lister glitter might rub off on him.

A young assistant, so sizzling hot he should be at a casting call, blocks his way. Robert leans in to whisper to him, but I can hear his *sotto-voce* clearly from where I am. "Do you think Fox would still want his show if they knew he was gay?"

Hot assistant goes pale. "But he's married—he has three kids."

"You want your moment on TV? Ask him. See how he reacts."

The supermodel-wannabe tries to question Robert further, but Robert has moved on, humming the theme song from *Lena, Spy Warrior*.

This is my moment. I grab his shoulder with one hand and press the stun gun to his ribs.

"Go that way."

I can't see his face, but hear him gasp, and then his breathing speeds up.

"Trent?"

He's hyperventilating.

I jab him in the ribs with the stun gun. "Don't make me use this. Millions of volts, hurts like hell, and you'll shit yourself right here on the red carpet."

Robert straightens up. I stay just behind him and slightly to the side, like I'm his plus-one, like we're the best of friends, like we're really partners.

The way we should have been.

We stop. Pose for a gaggle of photographers.

I press my cheek to his. A few lower their cameras when they see my face, others snap away, unheeding.

I know none of those pictures will make it to the blogs or the glossies.

"How did you get in here, anyway? Weren't you driving a limo?"

The cameras still flash, so Robert doesn't move his lips or shift out of his snow-queen smile.

"One of my clients helped me out." I push him away from the paparazzi and we start down the aisle again.

"Someone with a talent like yours shouldn't be driving a limo."

"Just figured that out, did you?" I steer him out of the line and toward the green room. Robert hesitates at first, but I jab the stun gun into his ribs again, and we move forward.

"I couldn't talk to you while you were suing me, Trent. Let's sit down and work things out now."

He makes it all sound reasonable, his voice soothing, seductive, shattering.

I do my best to keep control of the situation, to not get sucked into the quicksands of his manipulative mind. "Sure. How about here?"

I show my green room pass to the assistant guarding the door. She avoids making eye contact with me but preens under the wattage of Robert's smile. She waves us in.

"VIP pass for the green room. Wow."

I keep my voice cheerful and jab him in the ribs with the stun gun. "Let's have a drink before the show starts."

We step aside to let Tom Hanks and Rita Wilson leave. Robert jumps forward, his hand out, which means I have to move forward with him or the stun gun will be revealed. Hanks shakes hands with Robert but makes no move toward me.

"Wonderful to see you again."

I know Hanks has no idea who Robert is. A-listers are really good at this red-carpet playacting.

Rita includes both of us in her pasted-on grin. "The shrimp cocktail is divine!"

A shudder starts in her shoulders and runs down the length of her lovely body. Yup. She saw my face.

Her shudder, more than anything, reminds me why I'm here. Robert befriended me, in spite of my face. He brought out the beauty I was capable of, for anyone to hear without having to look at my face. And when it all paid off, he promised the income would go to fixing my face.

He gave me all that, and then he took it all away.

I push Robert into the green room. There's a screen in the corner that shows the crowds pouring into the Dolby Theatre. A message flashes, urging people to take their seats.

There are still a few people in the room, but when the lights flash red and yellow, everyone files out.

We are alone.

For the first time since I realized I was betrayed.

There's a nice, plush sofa, but I push him into the wooden chair with chrome arms. "Whiskey?"

Robert looks up at me, that artificial smile still glued to his face. "You know it."

He looks around at the room. I wonder if he's looking for a phone or an intercom or something he can use as a weapon. Let him try.

I step up to the counter, set down the stun gun, select a whiskey bottle, and pour. I can see my face in the smoky mirror behind the bar. *Really, with enough money, everything is fixable.*

Robert's promises still echo in my head.

Just wait until we make it big, then we'll fix it.

I drop some ice cubes into two glasses and stir them both vigorously with a spoon. I know this will irritate him, and sure enough, it does.

"You don't need to stir it. Didn't you learn anything from me?"

He jumps up, reaches out. He pretends to reach for the glass, but what he really wants is the stun gun on the bar top.

I step forward, and he instantly takes a step back. His fear brings a tickle of pleasure to my middle.

I take a step toward him again. He takes another step back. Hits the chair, sinks into it. I push the heavy crystal cocktail glass into his hand.

I hold my glass up. "Did you really get the contract for the reboot of *Lena, Spy Warrior*?"

Robert smiles, although his cheeks still glow hot. "Sure did."

I clink glasses with him, then take a sip of my whiskey. Robert does the same.

I cough. Robert's eyes crinkle, his mouth bunches up in a patronizing smile. "Not used to the good stuff, eh?"

I shake my head, ball up my fist and pound my chest.

To remind me how much better he is than I am, he downs his drink.

"Oh look, they're playing our song."

Sure enough, the TV now shows a woman dressed in the steampunk getup that *Lena* made famous, singing her heart out.

"It's *my* song," I remind him.

"Let me turn the sound up." Robert starts for the remote, which is also on the bar.

Next to the stun gun.

I grab it. "Allow me."

I turn up the volume, but not too much. Robert's eyes are now glued to the screen.

"Louder. I've waited my whole life for this!"

The fake smile, the patronizing grin, all gone. He's not lying. This really matters to him.

I push the button that says *mute*. It's so much fun, to watch him cringe, to make him realize that this is *my* moment.

I refill both our glasses, as if nothing had happened, add more ice, and stir vigorously, to the beat of the song I can still hear in my head.

"I said. You don't. Need. To do that!"

"Sorry. Got carried away, with my song and all."

I hand him his drink.

"So, how'd you do it?"

"Do what?" Robert takes a big swig. He knows we're getting down to business now.

"How'd you get the contract to score the reboot? You can't write music to save your life."

Although his cheeks are red with anxiety and whiskey, Robert beams at me, proud. "Did what I always do. Played your tunes over their footage. Put on my act. Works like a charm, every time."

Yeah, I remember.

I try to look soft, like the way he's playing me is working. "Your silent-movie-accompanist shtick. I used to love watching you do it."

Robert doesn't fall for my act. His eyes flicker over to the stun gun, still on the bar, then back to me. Now he looks at me with steady eye contact, his lips slightly parted, and leans forward. As if I was still his friend and partner, his boy toy and whipping boy.

"I need you, Trent. I can't do this alone."

My traitorous heart believes him. A drumming in my chest radiates warmth through my body. Everything goes super-sharp. The smell of the shrimp cocktail sauce on the coffee table, the taste of whiskey on my lips, the whirr of the air-conditioner.

"Please, Trent. Let's work together again. It'll be just like old times."

"As your partner?" I try not to let any hope leak into my voice.

Robert looks at me, as if his answer is obvious. "You're the one who writes the music. I just sell it. I need your music. And you need me to sell you."

I almost believe him.

"So you want to be partners again."

Robert's face lights up. He's hopeful now, I can see it.

I've got him.

But there's hope inside of me, too, like a hungry baby that sees his parent hold up the bottle, *almost ready*. He'll agree to my conditions, we'll smile, he'll lead me into the theater, we'll accept the golden statuette together, at the after-parties he'll introduce me to everyone as the real composer, I'll play my ideas for the reboot for him—

"We are going to be so rich, Trent."

I pull the tablet out of my pocket. "Prove it. Sign this."

It's not so much that his expression changes. It doesn't. It just freezes on as his relief evaporates.

I show him the signature page. "You agree that I get equal credit, my name first, and we split the money 60/40."

Robert holds up his finger.

There's applause coming from the theater.

For me.

For my song.

The song Robert stole.

"And if we win tonight, you take me up on stage with you and introduce me as the real composer."

Robert *tsk-tsks*. Like a teacher scolding a child. "I can't do that. You know I can't. I've already sold it as my work. I can't just show up with a partner now."

"Sure you can." I point to my twisted, scarred, face. "You could say it was me who didn't want to come forward. But you couldn't let me miss my moment of glory. So you made me come up with you."

Robert shakes his head.

"I can sell your talent, Trent. But I can't sell your face. Don't you understand? This is Hollywood. Just take the money. Think. Of all. That. Money. Trent."

I take a step back and hold up my glass.

"Another one?"

Robert studies me. I look back with his same frozen grin. The one I've learned from him.

"Sure."

I take his glass, take it to the sink, rinse it out. I rinse my own out too, carefully, with soap, and dry them both with a paper towel, taking care not to let my fingers come into contact with the glass again.

"Hey, I thought we were having one more."

"I'm not sure you have time." I put the glasses back where they were, then put the paper towel and the stun gun in my pocket.

"They're about to announce best song."

I gesture at the screen, where Machete, the MC, wears a baseball cap backwards over his long black hair, a blue "We're #1" foam finger in one hand and a yellow plastic bat in the other, and mouths his jokes silently.

Robert stands up. Straightens his coat. Runs a hand through his hair. He really thinks he's out of here.

Robert wobbles. His hand clutches at his stomach.

"Shh, shh, you better sit down."

His eyes go wide.

"You said I was your partner." Now it was my turn to play the scolding teacher. I listen to the timbre and melody in my voice. Perfect pitch, right on key. Really, I've learned a lot from Robert.

"You didn't tell me I was your ghost-composer. You did wrong, Robert. You were a bad boy, very bad."

"What … have you done to me?"

"Just a little broken glass. In your first drink. Tiny, shimmering stars of broken glass. So small. They won't work too fast."

Robert is pale and sweating now. I hold the tablet out to him.

"But you might want to sign this before it's too late. Before you bleed too much, inside. It will take a while, but then, it will take a long time for someone to find you in here, and even longer for them to figure out what's wrong. And you have that rare blood type, Robert, you were always so proud of it. How long will it take them to find the blood you need? Do you think all that can happen before it's too late?"

Robert's mouth opens and closes. He takes a deep breath.

"How much time?"

"Well, I'm not sure, old man. I happened on this bottle of Coumadin—" I hold up the old gent's pills and shake them for him "—brilliant find, so I put that in your second drink. That'll make you bleed more. Unless someone gets you to the hospital soon, you'll bleed out internally."

"You didn't. You're lying. You couldn't."

"I could. I did. You're feeling it a little now, aren't you?"

He doesn't answer, but he's white around the eyes and green around the lips. It's not pretty. He points at the cameras in the ceiling. "You won't get away with this."

I nod. "Yep. While you were slandering celebs, I pulled out some cables. Good thing I know my electronics. And it got the guards running around, trying to figure out the source of the problem."

I hand him the tablet. "Better sign while you still can."

Robert takes the tablet, but his hand is shaking, so he sets it back down on his lap. He holds the tablet steady with one hand and signs with the index finger of the other.

As soon as he's done I pick up the tablet, check the signature, save it.

I give him back the tablet. "Email it to me and to our lawyers."

Robert looks up to say something, but I shake my head and remind him of what he already knows: "It has to come from your account or it's worthless."

I watch him go to his email, address the document to me, and cc our lawyers.

He hits send.

A surge of adrenalin goes through me. It's done. I've succeeded.

I take the tablet and put it in my pocket. If Robert lives, I'll get half the proceeds from the song.

If Robert dies, I'll get it all.

"Oh, look." I point to the screen. "It's the littlest Tanning sister. Aw, isn't she cute?"

"Trent." Robert's voice is desperate, his breathing jagged.

"Ooh, and Russell Crowe is her co-presenter. She'd make a great Lena, don't you think? When they do the young Lena episodes? And he can be the warrior father that teaches her all her martial arts skills."

"Trent. Call an ambulance."

I turn to him, smiling the smile I learned from him. As if we were back to how we were, back in the old days, when I thought we were really partners. "Sure, Robert. Sure."

"Trent, you need me."

"Not anymore." I'm talking to him, but watching the screen. "Once you're gone, they'll have to start another search. And I'll be ready. New face, new suit, new score."

I tap the tablet in my pocket.

"Trent!"

"Shh. I don't want you to miss this."

I turn up the volume just as Robert screams for help. It doesn't take much to drown him out.

"And the Oscar for best song goes to …" Russell Crowe hands the open envelope to the littlest Tanning sister.

Robert staggers to his feet then collapses onto the rug.

I nudge him with my foot.

"Oh my god, Robert, Robert, here it comes!"

"Robert Cattrell, for the theme song to *Lena, Spy Warrior*."

The Academy orchestra plays our song.

My song.

I nudge Robert with my foot again. He doesn't move.

Onscreen, Russell Crowe and the littlest Tanning sister look around expectantly, but no winner appears, as he is on the floor, at my feet. Where he belongs.

"Thank you for this, Robert. Really." I address him as if I was addressing the Academy audience. "I couldn't have done it without you."

As I speak I wipe down everything again. I check Robert one more time. He won't wake up.

They replay the opening measures as I make my way out of the green room. I stroll down the now empty red carpet.

As soon as I'm outside the Oscars enclosure I stop at a payphone and call 911. I hold the paper towel over my mouth and tell them about a limo parked where it shouldn't be, and it sounds like someone might be in the trunk.

FAIRY TALES CAN COME TRUE

by Teresa Leigh Judd

Jenny gazed around the large banquet room and wondered: How the heck did she get here? Her white apron and black uniform temporarily discarded, she wore a clingy gold cocktail dress and sported diamonds in her ears. She had swept her auburn hair up in what she hoped was a sophisticated chignon and had even sprung for a manicure.

Tonight she was a guest at a Country Club soiree, when normally she would be carrying a tray and offering canapés to the glittering company who surrounded her. Cinderella at the ball couldn't have felt more out of place. She shifted uneasily on her uncomfortable high heel sandals and looked around for someone to rescue her.

A voice at her elbow asked, "A glass of wine, Miss?"

Jenny turned to see one of her fellow workers holding out a tray of sparkling wine glasses.

"Zach, thanks," she said, picking up a drink.

"Whoa, Jenny," Zach said. "You sure clean up well, but what are you doing here? Aren't you supposed to be working this party?"

"I wish I knew."

"What do you mean?"

"Yesterday, I got a big box delivered to me at home. Inside were these clothes, an invitation to this party and a note that said 'Jenny, don't disappoint me. Please come.' I checked the name and address and it was definitely meant for me. As you can see, the clothes are my size. I was curious so I took the night off and came. Now I'm here, and I don't have the least idea what I'm supposed to do or who I'm supposed to meet."

"Well, good luck with that. I have to keep moving." Zach turned away.

Jenny scanned the room again, hoping to catch the eye of the mysterious person who had sent the invitation, but no one seemed the least bit interested in approaching her. In fact, most of the guests were studiously ignoring her. Apparently, elegant clothes and expensive jewelry weren't all it took to crash high society.

Enough of this, she thought, draining her glass and setting it down on a nearby table. She eyed her expensive manicure as she did so and sighed. One day at work and that would be the end of her beautiful nails. A big waste of money. Still, she did have a whole new outfit, and it looked like she was going to get to keep it since no one had approached her since she had entered the room. The diamond earrings could probably pay her rent. Slowly, she made her way through the laughing, chattering people and out into the hall.

"Where do you think you're going?" A gruff voice spoke behind her as she turned toward the cloak room.

At the same time, a large hand grasped her arm and turned her around. She was confronted by a rough looking man stuffed into an ill-fitting tuxedo.

"I … I was just getting my coat," Jenny stammered.

"Hey, you're not going to cut out on us after we gave you those great duds, are you?"

"Who's us?" Jenny asked.

"Follow me," the man said, nodding toward the back rooms of the club. "There's someone waiting to meet you."

"Why can't he come out here?" This did not bode well, Jenny thought. Not at all the kind of encounter she had hoped for. This guy was really scary.

"He's what you call shy." The big man grabbed her arm again and pulled her down the hall.

"Let go of me." Jenny tried to wriggle her arm free from his grasp. "You're hurting me."

"Hey, lower your voice. You'll disturb the other guests. No one is going to hurt you. Don't you want to meet your Prince Charming?"

Jenny reluctantly followed him down the hall to a small meeting room at the back of the building. As she entered, a tall distinguished man rose from one of the chairs. The room was dimly lit and she didn't recognize him at first. Then he stepped into the light.

"Dad?" Jenny gasped. "I thought … I thought you were still in prison."

"Out early for good behavior," he said with a wink. "I've been out for a month. I told them I'd gotten religion."

Jenny grasped the chair in front of her. "You always were a con man. That's how you ended up there in the first place, right? So, what is this all about? The mysterious invitation, the new clothes? Speaking of which, how did you know my size?"

"You had a few things in your locker, which gave me the size."

"You were in my locker? How did you get in?"

"It was easy. I found out your work schedule and showed up here when you were off. Then hung around 'til I could get in there." He smiled. "One golfer looks pretty much the same as another in a club like this. No one looks twice if you're dragging a bag of clubs."

"If you wanted to see me, why didn't you just contact me?"

"Would you have seen me? Or slammed the door in my face? Hung up on me?"

She hesitated a moment, then said, "You have a point."

"This way, I figured you'd be curious enough to show up, and I could talk to you before you ran away from me."

"Well, you figured wrong. I'm out of here. I don't want anything to do with you." Jenny turned to the door but found it blocked by the huge man who had accompanied her into the room. "Let me out!" she demanded.

"I will, after you've heard me out," her father said. "You might as well have a seat."

Jenny plopped down in a chair in front of him.

Her father said, "I am appalled at the way you're living. A single mom, menial job, barely paying the bills."

"I'm taking classes at the junior college," she said defensively.

"That's all well and good, but I've decided to help you get out of your rut."

"*Now*, you want to help me?" She had to hold back from yelling. "Where were you when I was growing up? Oh, that's right. In and out of prison."

He shrugged. "So I wasn't the best father. I know that and want to make amends. I've come up with a scheme that will make us both rich."

"Oh no, none of your schemes. I may just be getting by, but I don't fancy following in my father's footsteps right into a jail."

"That's the beauty of the plan. It's practically risk free."

"Practically?"

Ignoring her sarcasm, her father pulled a picture out of his pocket and pushed it toward her. "Take a look at this."

Jenny picked it up and then shrugged. "So you have a picture of me from the newspaper?" She started to slide the paper back to him and then paused. "Wait, my picture has never been in the paper as far as I know." She looked up to see her father smiling.

"Read the caption."

Jenny read aloud, "Marcia VanDevere, daughter of oil tycoon, Willard VanDevere, appointed chairwoman of this year's charity fundraiser." She looked at the picture again, staring at the woman's face. "I can't believe how much she looks like me. We could be twins."

"You've probably heard that everyone has a lookalike or two, but they never meet. If they do meet, everyone marvels at the resemblance, and it makes a good human interest story. Well, apparently you are her lookalike."

"Weird. But it's no surprise nobody ever noticed the resemblance. We don't exactly move in the same circles. Some of the members here might know her, but no one really looks at servers that closely, and the VanDeveres belong to the country club up in the Heights. Unless we were standing side by side, it's doubtful anyone would see the resemblance."

"Exactly. I only noticed it because the black and white photograph emphasized her features."

"So, because I look like this girl, you suddenly appear in my life and become fatherly? You surely can't expect me to pretend to be her. Her family would see through me immediately."

"I wasn't thinking of her family. Only strangers. People who had never met her, who wouldn't know her mannerisms and all."

"And who would these strangers be? And why would I be with them?" And what's in it for you, she wondered.

"She is in charge of fund raising for some foundation. I thought we might hit up a few smaller corporations for donations. We set up a bogus bank account. Once the checks have been deposited, no one will know the money didn't really go to the charity. There is almost no way to track it."

"So, your idea of 'practically risk free' is for me to impersonate someone in order to defraud a charity?"

"You won't have to do anything but rent a post office box and open a bank account. I'll print up some official looking paperwork that says I'm working for the charity. Since the money is being sent directly to the bank, there should be no question."

"Oh, and how am I supposed open these accounts?"

"As it happens, Dan here has recently come into possession of her wallet." Her father gestured towards the big man and pushed a stack of small cards across the table towards her. "Here's her driver's license, health insurance card with her social security number, and a few other forms of ID."

"Okay. Enough of this. I absolutely refuse." Jenny stood and turned towards the door. "Let me out of here."

"Oh, you can leave, but if I were you, I wouldn't."

"What do you mean?"

"I mean, if you value your job, you'd better listen to me. You've already made yourself conspicuous by turning up at this party where don't belong. And wearing diamonds, at that. People will wonder if you might have been involved in some of the small jewelry disappearances occurring at the club lately. Oh, and an anonymous phone call, letting them know you come from a criminal family, might cause them to check your locker. Perhaps they'd find a 'missing' ring shoved in the back behind the aprons." He leaned back in his chair and winked at her. "I'm thinking they won't take a chance on keeping an employee who is so suspect, nor will they be willing to give you references."

"You'd do that to your own daughter?" Jenny was astonished.

"It's for your own good, little girl," her father said. "You'll end up with your job and a nest egg to help out with little Bobby's college fund. That is his name, isn't it? Bobby?"

"I'm not your little girl and you stay away from my son," Jenny shouted at him. Then she sat back down and buried her head in her hands.

"Now," he continued, "in the next few days, you will receive a wig and a new outfit more suited to Marcia VanDevere. After that, you get the post office box and open a bank account. We want to use that big branch downtown. More impersonal."

* * * *

As promised, Jenny received several deliveries of expensive clothes and accessories in the next few days. Also included was a wig, styled and colored to match Marcia's hair. Each time one arrived, she shuddered and pushed the boxes out of sight. She kept hoping that her father and his friend would give up the idea, and she would be set free. She jumped whenever the phone rang. She felt as though she was carrying a huge weight on her shoulders, and it was all she could do to drag herself to work each day.

After a week had gone by, she began to relax. Maybe it would be all right after all. She could just flat out refuse to do it. But there was her son, Bobby. No, she couldn't risk it. She knew her father would have no compunction about carrying out his threats.

Then the dreaded phone call did come. "We have everything set up," her father said. "I need you to rent the post office box and open the bank account using the post office box as the address."

"I don't know if I can do it," Jenny protested. "Isn't renting a post office box under an assumed name a federal offense?"

"Actually, you're just renting one under her name. It technically belongs to her."

"Really, Dad, that's your rationale?"

"You'll be fine. Call me on my cell phone when you've got it all set up. After that, it's all up to me." The phone clicked off.

The next day Jenny pulled out the outfit she had been sent. Once dressed, she felt a little better since at least she looked the part she was to play. Then she drove across town to a post office where no one would recognize her. She walked up to the counter, presented her ID and rented a box under Marcia VanDevere's name, indicating that it would be used for business associated with the charity she was chairing. She asked for two keys and left.

Next, she went to the bank her father had designated. Walking up to the bank, her knees were wobbly and her hand shaking. *I'm a rich socialite*, she repeated over and over to herself. Then, taking a deep breath, she pushed the heavy door open and went in. It was a large branch with multiple tellers and a cold, impersonal feel. Bank employees and customers bustled across the lobby.

Jenny approached the nearest desk. Luckily, she didn't have to stand in line because if she had, she would probably have cut and run. Sitting down in a chair in front of the bank officer, she said, "I'd like to open a checking account."

"Certainly. Do you have ID with you?"

"Yes." Jenny handed over the driver's license and the other cards her father had given her. She held her breath and waited for the banker to challenge her identity, but he just began typing information into the computer. She glanced around to make sure no one was approaching her. What if someone who knew Marcia came in and started talking to her? Her stomach knotted up.

"Could you please add the name of the charity to the account and use this post office box as a mailing address?" she asked. "I'm trying to keep all the charity business in one place."

"No problem."

After what seemed an interminable wait, he looked up and handed her some paperwork. "Here you go, Miss VanDevere. Your debit card should arrive in two or three days. Bank statements are sent on the fifteenth of each month. We appreciate your business."

"Thank you for your help." Jenny turned and hurried out of the bank, glancing back over her shoulder to make sure no one was following her. Wiping a light film of sweat from her face, she jumped into her car and headed home to change clothes.

* * * *

The next day, the muscle-bound Dan showed up at her apartment to collect the post office box key. She gave him one of the keys and the paperwork.

"Thanks, doll," he said and left.

"Doll? Humph!" She slammed the door behind him.

With a great deal of relief, she realized her part of the scam was over. She packed away the new clothes for possible future use and went back to her job.

But she couldn't put it behind her. Curious as to how much her father had been able to raise, she started checking the P.O. box for a bank statement in the middle of the month. She figured her father wouldn't bother once he could use the debit card to look at the balance. When the statement arrived, she tore it open and was appalled at the amount. Her father was indeed a slick conman. Too bad he hadn't taken up fundraising as a legitimate career.

Jenny felt sick. All those donations ending up in her father's pocket instead of doing the good work it was intended for. She had to find some way to make it right. She couldn't go to the authorities. After all, she was an accessory and even if they didn't arrest her, there would be publicity and she would surely lose her job.

Eventually, she came up with a plan that would allow the money to go to its intended destination but let her remain anonymous. She addressed an envelope to Marcia, put the bank statement inside, and marked the outside "Very Important. Open Immediately."

* * * *

The following morning, she spotted a small article in the newspaper: "Anonymous Benefactor Raises Money for Charity."

The article went on to say that Marcia VanDevere wanted to publicly thank the individual who had solicited donations from some of the smaller businesses in town and that the considerable amount of money raised was very much appreciated. She respected the fact that the person wished to remain anonymous, and she wanted to reassure him that the money would be put to the good use this person intended.

Jenny snorted. Anonymous benefactor, indeed.

Her phone rang and, as expected, it was her father.

"What did you do?" he yelled.

"What do you mean?"

"The account's been closed. The money's gone."

"Really? I can assure you, I didn't take it. When did this happen?"

"Sometime yesterday afternoon, I think," he said. "It was all there in the morning when I used the ATM and now there's nothing left."

"I was at work all day yesterday. We had a big luncheon, and I had to stay overtime. You can check." Jenny tried not to laugh. "I did see an article in the paper announcing that an account full of donations had been found. Didn't you see it?"

"No. The paper today?"

"Yes. Check it out. Something about an anonymous benefactor. Maybe one of the donors told her. Or the bank contacted her for some reason. After all, her name was on the account." She paused, choosing her words carefully so she would not give herself away. "She probably transferred the money to the main fund. She might not have alerted the police since an investigation could tie up the funds. This way, she has the money, the account is closed, and there are no more complications."

She held her breath until her father said, "That makes sense."

"What are you going to do now?"

"I don't know." There was silence. Then he said, "I guess I'll be okay if there is no investigation."

"Maybe you should think about leaving the area for a while," Jenny said in a concerned tone. "Just to be safe."

"You're right. I think I'll head out west for a bit." His voice was different, as if he was already thinking ahead. New place, new scheme. "Take care of yourself, little girl. Sorry you didn't get a nest egg for Bobby's college, but at least you have nothing to worry about now. I'll drop you a card now and then."

"Do that," she said, with a grimace.

* * * *

Back at work, she found herself lightheaded with relief, but she also realized the whole incident had increased her self-confidence. If she could fool a bank manager that she was a woman as well-to-do as Marcia VanDevere, maybe she presented herself better than she realized. Maybe she would apply for the managerial position at the club. She'd heard it would be opening up soon. In the meantime, she was just happy to have the whole ordeal over with.

Zach smiled to hear her singing under her breath. "Looks like the old Jenny is back."

"What do you mean?"

"Well, you've been awfully depressed and quiet lately. I thought it might have had something to do with your date for the party last month. Wasn't he the Prince Charming you were expecting?"

"Nope. Wrong fairy tale," Jenny said. She picked up a tray of drinks. "I think he was more like someone from the Brothers Grimm."

BIOGRAPHIES

Cori Lynn Arnold, author of the novel *Thin Luck*, has worked as a hotel housekeeper, handy woman, laundry attendant, radio disc jockey, library clerk, historical photographic archivist, mathematics tutor, teaching assistant, photo lab junky, portrait and wedding photographer, high school algebra teacher, internet security researcher, security analyst, computer programmer and ethical hacker. She currently resides in Connecticut and works as a part-time mother and full-time author. Find her on Twitter: @ corilynarnold and Facebook: CoriLynnArnold

Susan Alice Bickford was born in Boston, Massachusetts, and grew up in Central New York. Her passion for technology pulled her to Silicon Valley, where she became an executive at a leading technology company. She now works as an independent consultant and author. She splits her time between Silicon Valley and Vermont. Her first book, *A Short Time to Die*, was released in February 2017. Contact Susan at www.susanalicebickford.com, www.facebook.com/susanalicebickford, and @bixxib on Twitter.

In her dewy youth, **Susan Daly** wanted to be Trixie Belden, the thinking girl's Nancy Drew. Even more, she wanted to *write* about such feisty heroines. Life intervened, but now, a refugee from the mind-numbing corporate world, she's found peace and happiness killing off deserving victims. Her stories have appeared in *The Whole She-Bang* anthologies 2 and 3. She lives in Toronto, a short commute from her superlative grandkids. You can find her at www.susandaly.com

Anita DeVito writes fast-paced smart thrillers and mysteries designed to entertain, satisfy and delight. Find her on Amazon, iTunes, Barnes & Noble and Kobo. Sign up for Anita's free entertainment quarterly—Equinoxious—and start each season with a fun filled collection of short stories, puzzles and games. Join through her website www.AnitaDeVito.com or go to www.Facebook.com/AnitaDeVitoWrites and click "Join My List."

P.A. De Voe is an anthropologist and Asian specialist who writes historical mysteries and crime stories immersed in the life and times of Ancient China. She's published short stories, *From Judge Lu's Ming Dynasty Case Files*, in anthologies and online. *Warned*, second in her Chinese YA trilogy (*Hidden*, *Warned*, and *Trapped*) received a 2016 Silver Falchion award in the Best International category. For more information and to get a *free* short story go to padevoe.com.

Kate Fellowes is the author of five romantic mysteries, including *Thunder in the Night*, for Crimson Romance. Her work has appeared in several anthologies, as well as *Woman's World*, *Victoria*, *Brides*, and other magazines. Her working life has revolved around words—editor of the student newspaper, reporter for the local press, cataloger in her hometown library. She shares her home with a variety of companion animals and blogs about work and life at katefellowes.wordpress.com.

Beth Green grew up on a sailboat but these days is most often found ashore—currently Prague, Czech Republic. Beth is a former reporter, English teacher and travel blogger; she is now a full-time freelance writer. When not writing for clients or plotting international crimes to take place in her fiction, Beth enjoys reading, scuba diving, and the art of slow travel. Connect with her on Twitter: @bethverde.

C.C. Guthrie was not a Show Kid and has never owned a cow. She was born in Oklahoma where her family has farmed and ranched since Indian and Oklahoma Territory days. "Step Away From The Cow" is inspired by four generations of wise Show Moms, Dads and Kids that have enriched her life. She lives near Fort Worth, Texas. No animals were harmed in the writing of her story.

Teresa Leigh Judd was born in Washington State, Teresa graduated from the University of Washington and headed east to work in the "other" Washington for several years. Back in California, she lived in the northern California foothills with her husband, Ken and worked as a manufacturer's sales rep, selling gifts to small retail stores. She was a member of the Sacramento chapter of Sisters in Crime. Sadly, on August 17, 2016, Teresa unexpectedly passed away.

Obsessed with books, dogs, and creepy old houses, **Su Kopil** writes short fiction about peculiar characters. Her stories have appeared in magazines and anthologies including: *Woman's World*, *Murder Most Conventional*, *Flash and Bang*, *Destination Mystery*, and *Fish or Cut Bait*. She is the owner and founder of EarthlyCharms.com, a graphic design company that has been working with authors since 2000. Pop in at sukopil.com or follow @INKspillers.

Rhonda Lane covered "cops & courts" for a Connecticut daily newspaper. She created The Horsey Set Net, a horse blog with an international readership, and writes crime fiction set on the fringe of Kentucky horse country. A Connecticut resident, she's a member of Sisters in Crime, Mystery Writers of America, and Romance Writers of America. "On Like Donkey Kong" is her fiction debut. Find out more at rhondalane. com.

Chelle Martin is an award-winning short story author and the creator of Dog Mom Mysteries. She is a member of Mystery Writers of America, Romance Writers of America, and Sisters in Crime, including the Guppies and Central Jersey chapter of which she is President. For more information, please visit www.ChelleMartin.com or like "Dog Mom Mysteries" on Facebook.

LD Masterson lived on both coasts before becoming landlocked in Ohio. After twenty years managing computers for the American Red Cross, she now divides her time between writing and enjoying her grandchildren. Her short stories have been published in several anthologies and magazines, and she's currently working on her second novel. LD is a member of Mystery Writers of America, Sisters in Crime, and the Western Ohio Writers' Association. Catch her at: ldmasterson-author.blogspot.com or ldmasterson.com.

Alison McMahan is an award-winning screenwriter, author and filmmaker. Her books: *The Films of Tim Burton: Animating Live Action in Hollywood* (Bloomsbury 2005); the award-winning *Alice Guy Blaché, Lost Visionary of the Cinema* (Bloomsbury 2002), translated into Spanish, film rights sold; a historical mystery novel, *The Saffron Crocus* (Black Opal Books, 2014), which won the Rosemary Award for Best YA Historical in 2014 and the Florida Writers Association's Royal Palm Literary Award in 2015. www.AlisonMcMahan.com

Liz Milliron has been making up stories, and creating her own endings for other people's stories, for as long as she can remember. After fifteen years in the corporate world, she finds making things up more satisfying than software manuals. Her stories have been published in online magazines, *Lucky Charms: 12 Crime Tales*, *Blood on the Bayou*, and will appear in *Mystery Most Historical*. Visit her at lizmilliron.com.

Bern Sy Moss is a writer of short mystery stories living somewhere in the Midwest. Her stories have appeared in the Darkhouse Books' anthology, *Destination: Mystery*, *Woman's World* magazine and the Akashic Books Noir Series, *Mondays are Murders*. She is a member of Mystery Writers of America, Sisters in Crime and Short Mystery Fiction Society.

Claire Ortalda, winner of Georgia State University, *Fugue* and Hackney Fiction Prizes and co-editor of *Fightin' Words* (2014, Heyday Books), has been published in numerous magazines and anthologies. Inspired by a beautiful disabled cat to write her children's novel, *The Stair in the Wall* (Kindle), she is now returning to her first love, mysteries, with a series set in Anchorage starring a female reporter-sleuth who is beginning to fear she somehow personally incites murder. www.claireortalda.com

Melinda B. Pierce grew up in a small-town in Georgia, but her southern heart now belongs to Florida. Her childhood adventures began with a variety of books borrowed from the one-room public library. Her grown-up adventures have included serving as a Military Police Office in the United States Army, working intake for a social services office, and becoming a certified paralegal. All her adventures have led to a love of reading and writing.

Rita A. Popp has worked as a newspaper reporter, public relations specialist, university writer and editor, community college instructor, and volunteer literacy tutor. Her mystery stories have appeared in *Mysterical-E*, *Postcard Shorts*, and *Every Day Fiction*. Three of her flash fiction pieces have won honorable mentions in *Alfred Hitchcock's Mystery Magazine's* "Mysterious Photograph" contest. She has drafted her first mystery novel and is plotting a second.

KM Rockwood writes stories that give voice to people living on the fringes of society. A varied background, including working in industrial settings, supervising an inmate work crew in a prison, and teaching in alternative schools and county jails, forms the background for short stories and novels. The Jesse Damon Crime Novel Series (Wildside Press) features the difficulties faced by a man paroled from prison as he tries to reenter society. Visit kmrockwood.com.

Steve Shrott's mystery short stories have been published in numerous print magazines and ezines. His work has appeared in twelve anthologies—several from Sisters-in-Crime. Two of his humorous mystery novels were published, (*Audition For Death* and *Dead Men Don't Get Married*) as well as a book on how to write humor. Steve's comedy material has been used by well-known performers of stage and screen, and some of his jokes are in The Smithsonian Institution. steveshrottwriter. weebly.com

Mo Walsh has also published crime stories in *Mary Higgins Clark Mystery Magazine*, *Woman's World*, *Spinetingler*, *Flash Bang*, and five editions of *Best New England Crime Stories*. Winner of the 1998 Mary Higgins Clark Short Story Contest and a Derringer finalist, Mo coauthored the "killer trivia" book *A Miscellany of Murder*. A member of Sisters in Crime and Mystery Writers of America, Mo is president of MWA-New England. She lives south of Boston. www.mowalshwriter.com

www.ingramcontent.com/pod-product-compliance
Lightning Source LLC
Chambersburg PA
CBHW031419250626
47155CB00004B/1550